MW00810663

BAND TOGETHER

TEACHERS' LOUNGE
BOOK 2

PIPER SHELDON

WWW.SMARTYPANTSROMANCE.COM

COPYRIGHT

This book is a work of fiction. Names, characters, places, rants, facts, contrivances, and incidents are either the product of the author's questionable imagination or are used factitiously. Any resemblance to actual persons, living or dead or undead, events, locales is entirely coincidental if not somewhat disturbing/concerning.

Copyright © 2024 by Smartypants Romance; All rights reserved.

No part of this book may be reproduced, scanned, photographed, instagrammed, tweeted, twittered, twatted, tumbled, or distributed in any printed or electronic form without explicit written permission from the author.

NO AI TRAINING: Without in any way limiting the author's and publisher's exclusive rights under copyright, any use of this publication to "train" generative artificial intelligence (AI) technologies to generate text is expressly prohibited. The author reserves all rights to license uses of this work for generative AI training and development of machine learning language models.

Made in the United States of America

Print Edition

ISBN: 978-1-959097-75-4

CONTENT WARNING

Reader be advised this novel has one instance of deadnaming a trans character.

CHAPTER 1
MARI

The catchy earworm that was the early aughts smash hit by Vanessa Carlton played in my head as I was makin' my way to downtown Green Valley, Tennessee. The sun shone brilliantly as it peeked over the tall pines of the Great Smoky Mountains; the air was fresh with late-summer sweetness, and I was on my way to the downtown location of Donner Bakery to pick up a delicious order of cakes and pies. Though the school year had just begun, I had the weekend off and plans that weren't centered around my band students for once.

Curious glances flew my way as I passed Big Bob's and Big Ben's, skipped around Black's Southern Staples, shimmied past Viking MMA and Stripped, and headed toward Donner Bakery. I wasn't always this relaxed, but this morning, good mood and positivity vibrated off me.

The only thing that could make this day better was knowing that by the end of it, my parents and brothers with their families would all be back in town. For the first time in years, we'd all be together, and this visit would knock their socks off. Maybe they'd all even consider moving back to Green Valley. Maybe by next Christmas we'd be living near each other once again, like all the other close families in town.

The idea thrilled me.

"Where's the fire, Mariam Mitchell?" A woman's voice cut through my reverie as Maxine Barton blocked my path forward. She narrowed her eyes at me. The older woman was the picture of a Southern lady but wielded her thoughts and opinions like weapons.

Flanking her were Becky Lee Monroe, Julianne McIntyre, and Janice Cooper. Individually, Becky Lee, with her blessed gene pool, was the mother of the Monroe brothers, Julianne was the retired head librarian, and Ms. Cooper was the former band director whose position I took over at Green Valley High School. Collectively, they were an incomplete sampling of the local group self-dubbed as the Bunco Broads: a group of retired women who met every Thursday for fierce competitive play of the game bunco. Or at least so much as Clara Hill had told me. It was rare to get an invite to that club.

I would have been a little intimidated by all these women if not for the soothing presence of Ms. Cooper. My former band instructor was always a pleasure to see.

"Good morning," I said and fixed my features into a smile. "How are y'all this morning?" I waved to each woman in turn.

I was usually willing to shoot the breeze with the fine folks of Green Valley, but today I was in a rush, and this group of women could chat my life story out of me if I wasn't on guard. My apartment still needed cleaning, I had to confirm reservations at the Lodge, and then I still had to head over to Knoxville to pick everybody up from the airport. Thankfully, their flights would all land at similar times, and I wouldn't—

"Are you listening?" Maxine snapped her fingers in front of my face.

"Yes, ma'am."

"It's a little early to be collecting donations, isn't it?" Mrs. McIntyre asked not unkindly.

"Remember, you'll catch more flies with honey than vinegar," Maxine added. "She's lucky she's blond and pretty."

Internally, I flinched. Not at the sort of *complisult* about my looks, but because it was true that most of my time around town, when not spent directing band performances, was spent walking door-to-door to get donations from the shop owners. When compared to sports, music programs were about as high priority as a mosquito farm in the summer. And I had, more than once, been accused of being aggressive, maybe even pushy, though I preferred to think of myself as highly motivated. If I didn't care about the various band programs, nobody would.

"No fundraising today," I explained. "I'm headed to Donner Bakery. My family is back in town for the weekend."

Ms. Cooper beamed at me. "How lovely. You send everyone our love."

"Is that why you're walking like there are ants in your pants?" Maxine asked.

Maybe I had been rushing a little bit. "Uh, I—"

2

"It's been a while since they've been back, hasn't it?" Ms. Cooper asked, shooting Maxine a look.

I glanced up the street where the line from the bakery was now stretching to the door. A fission of tension gripped me as I calculated my time. "Yes, Ms. Cooper."

"Call me Janice. Ms. Cooper is my former stepmother," she said with a wink. She placed a hand on my shoulder, her wooden bangles clanking. "Plus, we're peers now that you direct the band."

"Right. Janice." I struggled with the casual name. Ms. Cooper had always been my favorite teacher. She had that inspiration for music and life that I hoped to infuse in my own students. She helped get me into college and vouched for me when I applied for her position after she announced her plans for retirement. I owed her everything. "Mom and Dad come home every other Christmas, but Jonas and Noah and their families haven't ever been here all at once since my niece was born."

Even saying it out loud, I worried about jinxing this visit. I'd been trying for years to get all our schedules matched up. Or rather, their schedules. This weekend was a chance for us all to be together again and remind them of how important family was.

"You are practically glowing with excitement," Becky Lee said, her large blond bob shining.

"I'm very excited," I admitted with a smile.

"This is a big day. We won't keep you," Becky Lee said.

The group of women started to move on. "Have a nice day, y'all," I said.

I had been just about to wog (walk/jog) at a respectable pace when I noticed Janice lingering. She glanced at the retreating women and held out a hand to stop me. "Just one more thing, Mari," she said. "If you have a minute."

"Of course." My phone in my pocket vibrated, and the line outside grew. If I didn't hurry up, they'd run out of the best pies and banana cakes. But this was Ms. Cooper. She changed the trajectory of my life. I smoothed my features into a smile. "What can I do for you?"

"As you know, as everybody knows I'm sure, my son is back in town." She patted her short, tight, graying curls.

I nodded. Everybody did know of her son. Leo Cooper was one of the most successful Green Valley alum. Since he was a few grades younger than me, I only saw him as my favorite teacher's weird little son named Leonard. I had vague memories of a scrawny, wannabe emo kid. All I knew of him now came from clickbait headlines.

He'd been touring with his band, The Burnouts, as their drummer until recently, when he suddenly announced his early retirement and moved back to Green Valley. He'd been notoriously reclusive in the six months he'd been back. If I was being entirely truthful with myself, and though I would never say this to Janice, he struck me as another egotistical drummer who thought the sun shined out of their—

"But I thought it might be good for him to get out more. See how the town has changed and grown. He's been a little cooped up," she explained.

"Oh, ah, okay."

My brain raced to connect the dots of this conversation. I was the only band teacher for three band classes and the before- and after-school electives. Every weekend for the foreseeable future was booked. Even getting this weekend with my family required heavy lifting to my schedule and a few IOUs to Clara Hill. I had no time to be Janice's celebrity son's hometown tour guide.

I'd seen the videos of him online—not just the thirst traps uploaded by the Burnnies, but the ones where he stomped off stage or remained stonily silent in press interviews. He might have been from Green Valley, but he never thanked the town for his success or brought any of that fame back to help the town that formed him.

"I've heard about your star student, Cath Beckett," Janice said, switching gears.

"Yes. Cath is incredible. She's applying for the Berklee College of Music." Pride filled me whenever I got to sing Cath's praises. I couldn't take credit for her raw talent, but I certainly had been trying to give her every opportunity to succeed, just as Janice had done for me. If ever there was a person going places, it was Cath, and you bet she appreciated her roots.

"Someone mentioned that she needs a percussion tutor for her college audition?" A sinking suspicion started to tingle the back of my neck, worse than my previous assumptions.

"I'm waiting to hear back from a friend of mine, Devlin. He's the conductor for the Symphonic Orchestra of Knoxville. Even though he's too busy, he knows a lot of people," I said. Connecting back with him was one of a hundred items on my to-do list for the day.

"I had an idea that might help Cath and my son." She flipped her hands out in hopeful excitement. "What if you asked Leo to tutor Cath?"

My knee-jerk reaction was to laugh or maybe weep, but Janice's look was so sincere and pleading that I genuinely considered it.

The facts were that Leo had shown no interest in Green Valley since his return. He'd purposely avoided being seen and interacting. He hid at his mom's house and did whatever guys in their late twenties without a job and with no bills to pay did. I shuddered to think. I highly doubted that even though Janice's intentions were good, he would go along with it. The fact that she was asking me rather than him spoke volumes.

More than that, I needed to do what was best for Cath and her future career as a drummer. Was this really the best fit? The excitement in Cath's voice as she spoke of Leo's return was telling, but she needed to be consulted first. And didn't they say to never meet your idols? Whoever *they* were.

I must have hesitated too long because she stepped closer and lowered her voice. "Don't be fooled by what the gossips have said. He's a good man; he just needs a little push. Somebody with your . . . tenacity."

Not even nine in the morning, and already I'd had my pushiness referenced twice.

"Have you asked him?" I asked.

"I first wanted to check with you." She flicked a look at her waiting friends. "And truthfully, I think it would be better coming from someone else. Coming from me, it would seem like—well, he might take it the wrong way. I wouldn't want him to know it was my idea in case I accidentally hurt his feelings."

I looked back to the bakery line, now ten people deep out the door. My heart sank. I couldn't disappoint Janice.

"Okay. If Devlin doesn't work out and Cath is on board, I'll talk to your son."

Janice's face lit up. "Thank you. That's all I ask. And remember that he's very comfortable at home and might need a healthy shove out the door. I give you permission to do what's needed. That's why I know you're the best for the job."

"Why me?" But I knew the answer.

"You're a motivated individual. A strong-willed woman."

Oof.

Unfortunately, for most of my life, for most women like me, that rarely felt like a positive. In Janice's case, it was meant as a compliment.

"He needs someone to shake up his routine and get him out of his shell. Only a major shake-up can motivate him. He used to be so excited about the future. I want to see that spark back. I think *you* will really help. Music and Cath."

Chances were another solution would present itself, and I could forget all about this request. This was a future bridge to cross. For now, I needed to focus on my upcoming visitors and getting those pies.

"I'll keep you posted," I said.

"Great. Mari, thank you. This town is better for having you in it. I appreciate you."

I beamed at her words.

With another quick goodbye, I made my way to the back of the line at Donner Bakery, my buoyant mood back in place. I had so much on my mind that Leo was quickly pushed aside.

I barely made it in time to grab the last banana cake of the day and a couple of pies. Returning to my apartment, I had my arms loaded with groceries and various goodies for the visit. I'd put everything away and sprinted around my apartment, cleaning as fast as I could. I blasted music as I went and sang along to a good vibes playlist. When a song from The Burnouts came up, I skipped it and pushed away thoughts of Janice and her request. I'd almost forgotten that my phone had been ringing until I went to call the Lodge. In the past few hours, I'd missed several calls from my parents and brothers.

I stared at the notifications, and it felt like someone made me swallow a bunch of rocks.

"Don't assume the worst," I chastised myself.

I was about to call my mom back when my phone vibrated again. It was Noah, my eldest brother.

"Hey, Noah. I was just about to call you back."

"Hi, Mariam. Yeah, it's Noah."

"I know. I just said—"

"Listen, I'm here at LaGuardia." He sighed with gusto. "It's been a shit show today. I don't know where you've been, but we've all been trying to reach you."

"I'm sorry. I was just—"

"Here's the deal. Mom and Dad's flight was canceled, so I booked them tickets here instead. Got them a straight shot, first class." The anxiety in my chest plummeted to my stomach.

"What? But I—" Heat burned my cheeks as he interrupted me again.

"Don't worry, Asim and I will cover it. Maybe you can do the Christmas gifts this year? Anyway, when Jonas heard, they just decided to stay in North Carolina. I guess Alice didn't want to drive all day with the kids. She's not feeling good."

I felt an anger burn up inside me. It was the same feeling of being at the dinner table and having everybody talk over me. I wanted to scream out just to be heard. I took a steadying breath.

"But I've made all these plans," I said, impressed by how calm I sounded.

"I know, kid, sorry. But it's not a great time at our firm anyway. Just a lot going on. We'll try to make Christmas work this year."

I fell back against the counter. I felt so *stupid*. I had been so excited and made so many plans. All this food. All the people in town I told. Oh God, I got my students to volunteer to perform for them. I rubbed at my burning eyes.

"Mariam? Hang on, Mom wants to say something."

"They're already there?" I almost yelled. I gripped the phone.

"No need to yell," he chastised. "Like I said, direct flights. We just picked them up. Hang on."

I scrubbed at my chest. Those swallowed rocks now felt like burning coals.

"Mariam, it's your mother."

"Yeah, I know—"

"I'm sorry things worked out this way, but don't take it out on Noah. The boys and their families are just so busy. You'll understand when you have a family of your own. It's not easy for everyone to pick up their whole lives to travel to the middle of nowhere."

I squeezed my eyes shut. "I know. I just—"

"Calm down. I don't know how many times I've told you that temper of yours isn't very ladylike."

I ground my jaw.

"I was going to suggest you fly out," she said.

Straightening up, I'm hopeful. "Yeah? They'd fly me out too?"

I pause at shuffling and Noah's muffled voice in the background. "They just bought our flights, honey. They can't foot your bills too." More talking. "Also, they only have the one spare room, but he said there are a bunch of Arby's nearby?"

"What?" I winced.

"Oh. Airbnbs."

"I can't afford a last-minute flight and stay in New York. I'm a teacher in Green Valley," I said softly.

"Those were your choices."

"Mom," I gasped. "I love being a teacher. You know what my students mean to me. That's not fair."

"Calm down," she repeated, and my blood pressure spiked. "We support you, but can you think about it from our point of view? We have three children pulling us in all different directions. I have to go. Sorry it didn't work out. When you have a family of your own, you'll understand. Love you," she said.

"Love you too." The words sounded hollow.

She ended the call, and I blinked back the pain with slow and even breaths.

Don't cry. Don't get angry. Be rational.

I might have been shocked if it had been the first time, but this was the pattern. If anything, I was the fool for thinking this time would be different. Maybe it was selfish to expect everybody to fly out here when I was the only one single and without a "real" career or family.

I looked around the small apartment. Cold and empty. Four pies and a banana cake stared back at me, and a long, unscheduled weekend stretched ahead.

CHAPTER 2
LEO

A shadow moved over me as I bent to tug out a sneaky weed that invaded my row of brightly colored perennials. I held my sun hat as I lifted my gaze to the newcomer. I noticed the giggling baby first, chubby cheeks and gurgling mouth gnawing on a clear plastic ring. My focus moved up to the massive form blocking the sun. A grumpy man attached to the baby looked down at me behind dark sunglasses.

Nerves set me on edge until I recognized my guest. I didn't get a lot of visitors, and that was the way I preferred it.

Setting down the pruning shears, I dusted off my gloved hands on my very masculine gardening apron, then stood to greet the brooding man. I tugged my gloves off before tapping my earbuds to pause Neil Peart and the rest of Rush in my ears. The sounds of my peaceful garden *rushed* in, pun intended, as I did. Birds chirped, and bees buzzed in the gentle sanctuary. I only had a few more weeks of this perfect summer weather before fall swept through Green Valley, but, based on the big man's scowl, there would be no wasting his time.

I dropped my gloves onto the shears and greeted my unexpected guest, extending my hand. A bead of sweat rolled down my back in the humid summer air.

"Devlin. Good to see you," I said.

He released one of the hands wrapped protectively around a chubby baby foot to shake my hand. His fist was massive, but I'd seen him play piano with unfathomable gentleness. At least my tall frame and lengthy arms made my profession as a drummer easier. *Former* profession.

9

"Leo. The yard looks very . . . colorful."

"Thanks. My chrysanthemums took a bit to flourish this year. But you know, you just have to give them a little love and attention, and they'll open up. There was a pretty intense bout of critters, but I managed them."

I bit my tongue to avoid blabbering about the dangers of infectious local garden pests. I rarely said the right thing at the right time and even less often realized my faux pas until it was too late.

My former music camp counselor and local musical prodigy blinked at me. He'd had his hands full since the birth of his child and taking over the Symphonic Orchestra of Knoxville, aka the SOOK, as a full-time conductor. Not to mention the occasional shows he and his cellist wife, Kim, put on.

He was big and scary when I was a preteen, and not much had changed in the past fifteen years, even though I'd sprouted to over six wiry feet. I was that sort of tall that people didn't notice as much because I was always the quiet kid, the odd kid. After I left this town and had success, several people from my class were asked about me and said they just thought I was "weird and quiet." Not much had changed since I'd returned. I'd been avoided like the plague and was still an outcast in my hometown.

I was fine with being left alone. I had Janice and my garden. I didn't need anything else.

"Anyway. How are you? You have a baby," I hedged—another pun definitely intended.

Devlin made a sound like a growl in affirmation.

"Cute girl."

"Boy," he corrected.

"I thought you had a girl?" I asked as I reached out to wave. The baby reached for me, gurgling happily before Devlin grabbed my hand with two fingers and pushed it away slowly but with determination.

Message received. I guessed my digging through manure didn't make him keen to let me poke his child.

"I did. Then a boy," he said.

"Oh wow. Good work."

"It was mostly Kim." He glared up at the sun and back toward the baby, tugging the baby's hat more securely on his head.

"Here, we can sit on the porch in the shade," I offered and led him to the wraparound porch of the updated craftsman-style house. It was the best gift I ever bought for my mom, and incidentally myself, after moving back. That and the gift of her retirement she was several years overdue for.

Devlin followed me and sat in the wicker chair across from me. "Nice apron, by the way," he said as he sat.

My threadbare Foo Fighters tee and jeans were partly covered by the army-green canvas gardening apron. "Thanks. It was a gift from my mom."

"The hat really completes the look."

"Real men care about skin cancer." I tapped the large brim of my sun hat. "So. I'm assuming you didn't come here to catch up about my garden. What brings you down to Clearview Lane?"

Devlin was one of the few people who had reached out to me since my return to Green Valley. Small towns were cesspools of gossip, and my "sudden exit" from The Burnouts was already theorized about enough. We had all signed NDAs, and thankfully, Devlin, a man who had a past of his own, wasn't about to dig into it. He wasn't chatty, and we had that in common.

"I came here on behalf of a friend," he said, jumping right into it.

A nervous tug just below my collarbone had me glancing away. "Are you thirsty?"

"No, thank you."

"Have you seen my mom in a while? I'm sure Janice would love to see you. She always talks about how you were one of her most prized pupils. I don't remind her that I was also her pupil for most of my life."

"Tell her I said hi, but no. I have to be quick. The baby has to be down for a nap in thirty minutes."

"Gotcha." I didn't have kids but knew enough to never mess with a naptime.

I cleared my throat, grasping for another distraction. Devlin didn't give me the opportunity.

"My friend, the band director at Green Valley High School, needs a favor. We were counselors at camp together," he said. I didn't want to act surprised at his mention of friends, but the man had worn a bandanna to cover his face for most of his adult life. He didn't exactly scream "talk to me" before that, yet even he had more friends than me. "They have a student who plays drums."

The tugging sensation at my chest grew, as did a tingling sensation under my fingernails. "Oh yeah?" I glanced out at the garden. After he left, I would have to finish pulling weeds and then check on the roses. There had been an aphid infestation earlier in the year, but the ladybugs and neem-oil had helped. I'd need to keep a close eye on it.

Devlin cleared his throat loudly, and I brought my attention back to him. He looked pointedly at where I was aggressively tapping my thumb against my knee. I sat up straighter, trying to keep my nerves under control.

"This kid is incredibly talented. They have an audition for Berklee College of Music in February."

"Fantastic," I said.

"But they need a tutor. The talent is there, but they need someone to help prepare them for the audition."

The dread building up inside my chest poured out, and my thumb tapped wildly again. "Yep," I said. "Good thing *the* Erik Devlin lives right here in Green Valley. With a new and improved, fancy recording studio in his home, from what I hear."

"And a new baby. A toddler. I work full time and so does Kim. Along with my responsibilities with the SOOK, I also work closely with my other friend's charity, Triple F."

Another friend? Damn. The Devil of the Symphony had me beat twice over now—unless you count my mom, which I totally did. Janice was rad and fun to hang out with.

"That's quite the résumé."

"I don't have time," he said with finality.

"The band director friend?"

"No time either. One person to teach all the music classes at the high school. Regardless. Neither of us . . ." He hesitated and cleared his throat. "Have the talent required to help. I'm proficient at percussion, but it's not my forte."

Failure. Loser. Loner.

The pent-up energy was officially bursting out of me. I couldn't sit still, so I stood to pace.

A fat bumblebee swerved drunkenly toward my guests. Devlin's whole body tensed, and his massive muscled arms wrapped around to cocoon the baby. I gently shooed the bee back in the direction of my honeysuckles. "Bee free," I whispered, amused at my joke.

Inside my head, I was chanting, *Please don't ask me. Please don't ask me.*

"Will you tutor the kid?" Devlin asked.

Well, shit.

"Look, man . . ." I tugged my hand through my sweating hair. "I didn't go to college. I can't even read sheet music. What the hell do I know about that stuff? I shot out of this town and on tour the second I was eighteen."

Vander and I, windows down, flipping the bird to Main Street as we drove our falling-apart tour van out of this small town once and for all, never to return.

At least that had been the plan.

"You and I know it's more than about reading music," he said.

"You can't teach passion."

"You can uncover it."

You have greatly overestimated me. "Just take him up to Knoxville," I said instead. "The city probably offers a lot better options."

"Her," he said.

"What?"

"The student. Pronouns are she/her."

"Oh. Okay. Well, same point."

"Not enough money. No car."

"Isn't that where your other friend's charity could come in?" I asked, feeling desperate.

"It's a charity, not a bank. All fueled by donations and volunteers," he said pointedly.

"I don't think I'm the right person for this." I rubbed my chest at the thought of leaving the house, being in town, at the high school, being *seen*. All the looks of judgment and hatred rolling off the citizens of Green Valley. My own mother didn't know why I had left The Burnouts, and I wanted to keep it that way. "I have a lot going on," I said, avoiding his gaze.

Devlin glanced around my idyllic yard.

"Plus, I retired," I said, dusting off the porch railing. That was what everybody thought, at least. I left the band, took my money, and bought my mom a house in my childhood town. They weren't entirely wrong. I thought of the drum kit in the basement, covered and untouched since I got back. A cold sensation prickled up the back of my neck as I thought of it in the dark, by itself, after years of rocking out venues filled to the brink with screaming fans.

"Just watch her play," Devlin said. "You'll see what I'm talking about."

"There's no point." I sighed, finally meeting his gaze. This kid was auditioning for the big leagues. I was a washed-up rock star with no band. If she wanted a snowball's chance in hell, she would be better with literally anybody else. "I-I can't." *I'm not playing, I'm not good enough.* "I'm busy."

"With the Bunco Broads?" he asked.

"Those women take their game very seriously. Janice had to vouch for me to get in, and I'm hanging on by a thread. Plus, I have plans to look into beekeeping and maybe start incorporating local fruit trees. I just don't have time."

His dark gaze scrutinized me. I looked away. I remembered this from camp, the way he scared the shit out of us with just one long stare, like he was reading out all our biggest insecurities.

"That's disappointing," he said after a beat.

I clenched my jaw. Devlin was the closest thing I had to an older brother figure, so his words cut me. I was trying to protect the girl. I wasn't the right person for this.

Devlin's phone chirped, and he stood.

"Tell your friend the band director I'm sorry, but I can't help him," I said.

"Her."

"Oh for three," I said softly. "Tell *her* I wished it were different, but I'm not the guy for the job."

Devlin stood. "She's not going to like this."

I shrugged. If I were a different person on a different path, maybe I would be the right fit to help. But I wasn't. And anyway, I was happy here. Or at least getting closer toward whatever that meant. Things were fine. Why would I want to introduce any complications into my sublime retired life?

"She can be . . . tenacious," he added, scratching the back of his neck.

"She'll find someone."

"Don't say I didn't warn you." And with that not at all ominous goodbye, baby and scary man walked down the porch and to his car.

"Devlin—" I wanted to shout after him that I once single-handedly stopped a fight at a show by diving into the crowd. I could handle a local band teacher, but the words got tangled on my tongue. I didn't want to disappoint Devlin, but the time wasn't right. "I'm sorry," I said.

Devlin shook his head. "Okay," he said with a wave. He didn't glance back, his large frame having to duck under my archway covered in creeping trumpet vines.

I wiped my forehead, feeling a chill despite the intense heat.

"Pfft," I said to myself. "What is the worst she could do?"

CHAPTER 3
MARI

The silence in my apartment was deafening. The uneaten food and presents for my niece and nephew sat mocking me.

At first, I was filled with the numbness at being let down once again. Then, the self-pity that maybe it had been my fault for having any expectations. Then, the guilt of expecting busy people to bend to my will. Finally, came the pain in my chest that felt like a growing chasm that would swallow me alive. I did not care for that feeling. Nope, *nope*. The best thing was to focus on something else.

Like pie.

I grabbed a fork and a whole pie and wandered to my bedroom. I huddled into my blankets, prepared to wallow away the hours with calories and bad TV. The long, eventless weekend stretched ahead of me. I couldn't even leave the house and risk running into somebody and deal with the questions about my lack of company.

I forked the pie into my mouth.

"Oh no," I said around a mouthful of banana cream pie. Cath and the rest of the seniors in the marching band who had volunteered to put on a show needed to be notified of the change of plans. Humiliation burned my cheeks. Had I really thought my family would be excited about a marching band performance from the local high school? That version of Mari was delusional. That Mari bought pies and had high hopes. This Mari needed to just focus on where she was needed. Cath and the students were my focus. They needed me, and I could help them.

My phone vibrated as it rang on my vanity. I shuffled out of bed and raced to answer. A brief shimmer of hope that maybe Jonas and Alice might still come flooded me like a bolt of adrenaline until I saw the name on the screen.

"Hello?" I answered.

"Hey, Mari."

"Hey, Devlin. How are you?" My voice came out sort of tight and shaky. When I looked in the vanity mirror, I was surprised to find that I was pale and a little queasy looking. My eyes glistened. I pulled myself together. These pesky emotions would have to be compartmentalized and dealt with later.

"Are you okay? Is this a bad time?" he asked.

"I'm fine." I kept my tone businesslike.

I shook my head, remembering why Devlin was calling. Cath. This was about her. Her whole unmarred future still sat in front of her. No wasted plans, no forgotten family members, just hope and . . . jumping catfish. I was being morose.

"Were you able to find somebody to help?" I asked excitedly.

"Sort of. Have you heard of Leo Cooper?" Devlin asked.

I dropped my fork into the pie tin. "More so lately," I muttered.

"Don't let the gossip fool you. He's a good guy."

"Hmm."

"And very talented. He's the best drummer for the job."

"Okay." This was now two trusted people who vouched for Leo. Maybe I could give him a chance. This was about Cath. "Cath is very eager to start preparing. I just need to check with her."

"Except he can't do it." Devlin finished. Maybe he could have led with that . . .

I stared at the wall, unable to find my words for once.

"I'm sorry. I really wanted this to work for you and Cath."

"He said no?" I asked. Weirdly enough, and maybe this was a side effect of my renowned forceful nature, but Leo's denial to help made me want to *refuse* his refusal. He should want to help. He should want to give back and nurture the next generation. Janice was such a caring and giving person, how had the apple fallen so far, gotten so rotten?

"He said he's got too much going on," Devlin said. He was silent a moment, then added, "He said he was busy and something about wasting time in a small town and with a stupid music program."

"Excuse me?" I said through clenched teeth. "He said that? Are you kidding me?"

Anger started to bubble in me. This was a nice change of pace from the chasm of pain. The anger felt good. It felt like focus. It felt like taking charge of a situation.

"Something like that," Devlin mumbled. "I didn't want to say that, in case it upset you."

Raging, raucous red overtook my emotions. Of course. Wouldn't want me to ever get upset. I heard my mother's voice telling me to calm down and be ladylike. The words spilled out of me.

"He's got a lot going on? No, Devlin. You and I have a lot going on. He's a spoiled rock star who doesn't want to help the community that raised him."

The only reason I even considered this far-fetched plan was because of Janice. That and Leo's talent, of course. I had wrongfully assumed that any decent person would want to help.

There was a pause. I heard the happy gurgle of a baby in the background. Devlin made a sound I couldn't identify. "I guess he can't be bothered. If I couldn't convince him, I can't imagine anybody can." The challenge hung in the air.

"Ohhh, haha oh." My reflection cackled manically. "No. No. That's . . ." I couldn't even get words out; my tongue was too tied. "I'm going to go talk to him. I got Ben Huntsford of Big Ben's Dulcimer shop to donate to the jazz band, and we know he still uses one-ply toilet paper to save money. I can sure as hell win this goob over. Where does he live?"

This was the cherry on top of this day. My body burst with unfocused anger. It blasted all around like a pinball. The anger was a welcome distraction that I thoroughly latched on to. More importantly, I thought of Cath and her talent being wasted. Not on my watch.

"I really shouldn't say . . ."

"You know what? Never mind," I said, trying to sound light.

Clara had mentioned him before. Shared about his weird daytime activities and the never-ending parade of older women coming and going from his house. How he never went anywhere or did anything. I could figure out where he lived in less time than it would take to write it down.

"I really should tell you to leave it be," Devlin said, but if I wasn't mistaken, he wasn't all that convinced.

"Okay," I said, my voice high and tight.

"Okay?" His skepticism rang clear.

"You can say that you told me to leave it be."

"I tried, you know. I just . . . maybe I could help Cath, if I move around—"

"Don't you dare. You have enough going on. Thank you, though," I said.

"You're okay then?"

"Fine and dandy. Right as rain. Happier than a toad in a downpour."

"Convincing." The baby started crying. "I gotta go. Keep me posted."

The call ended, and the anger merged into a plan. This guy thought he was too good for this town, huh? Too badass a rock star to help the children of his own community in need?

Well, I wouldn't be the hot-headed cliché people made me out to be. I was going to be smart. Rational. Make a plan. No more of this reactive, intense Mari stuff.

But I sure as hell wasn't about to give up.

"If he's too good to leave his house, then . . ." I muttered out loud, now fully distracted from the remaining ache in my heart, a plan formulating. I paced my short hallway.

Maybe it was the disappointment of another long, lonely weekend stretching ahead of me. Or the knowledge that another person was abandoning this town. It wasn't ladylike, I should keep a lid on the frustration. I could use honey rather than vinegar, but the tendrils of an idea were forming and spreading through my brain like the sticky tentacles of an octopus.

No more moping. No more wallowing. So what if everybody else in town had family, and I was totally alone. I gripped the counter and took a deep breath in.

I wasn't alone. I had the bands, my students, and Cath's future to focus on. I would narrow my focus on my students and forget anything else. I could make that happen.

Janice had said Leo just needed a good push. Might as well be me who pushes. And really, maybe he just needed a proper welcome to Green Valley.

Turned out, I did have plans for the weekend.

CHAPTER 4
LEO

I shot out of bed, heart racing and confusion coursing through me.

"What's that? Who's there?" I slurred.

Bright, early morning, pink light filtered through the cracks in the blackout curtains.

In my hand was a lamp I didn't remember grabbing as another shout of commands were called from outside, followed by a crash of cymbals. I set a hand to my racing heart and blinked the rest of my sleep away with a shake of my head.

Seconds later, horns blared a loud, quick tempo as snare drums and another cacophony of cymbals.

"What the hell?" I put down my illuminating weapon, stumbled to pull apart the panels of curtains, and was blasted with a ray of sunshine straight to the face. I hissed like a vampire. I hadn't witnessed a sunrise since I was on tour and that was only because I never went to sleep. As it wasn't the Stone Age, there was no evolutionary advantage to seeing the sunrise when your job didn't require it.

From my second-story window, the neighbor's massive pine took up most of the view. The residents of Clearview Lane had all complained about it needing to be trimmed for months. Those dry branches at the top were asking for trouble, but this wasn't the time to let that transgression be my focal point. I had plenty else on my plate as a group of maybe fifteen *hooligans* stomped in somewhat coordination to the jaunty tune they tutted and trilled. Other neighbors appeared on their porches, coffees in hand, confusion on their faces, or they peeked out their windows.

I see you, Clara Hill.

The band of no-good ruffians had spread out and were headed dangerously close to the shrubs and creeping vines.

"Not the dahlias!" I yelled, sprinting out of the room and hammering down the stairs as fast as my feet would carry me.

Janice sipped coffee serenely at the table, head bobbing slightly to the melody. Her gray curls were shorter than mine, and her signature tortoiseshell glasses sat low on her nose as she looked at her phone. The woman already had her bright red lipstick on. Where did she have to be so early?

She glanced up with a sweet smile. "Good morning, darling."

I scrubbed my hand through my hair, a loose curl flopping into my eyes. "Are you aware there is a marching band in the front yard?" I asked.

The horns and woodwinds continued to blast so loud that the patrons of Daisy's Nuthouse had to be wondering what the hell was going on.

"Oh, I don't think that's the whole marching band. Are you aware that you forgot a shirt?" She gestured to me, her bracelets clinking like wind chimes.

I stood akimbo. There hadn't been time to get dressed, but I probably couldn't go out in only my boxers to a bunch of youths. I glanced around the kitchen. My choices were a raincoat I would likely rip at the seams or a flowered apron hanging on a hook on the back of the kitchen door. "Can I borrow your wrap?"

My mother sighed. "Darling, it's a caftan. And it's silk. Careful hands." She shrugged out of it, leaving her in all-black shirt and pants.

I carefully wrapped the red-and-gold paisley *caftan* around myself. Most of my legs were on display, along with a large slice of my chest and abdomen. "Am I crazy, or am I pulling this off?"

My mother looked at me over her glasses and nodded.

"That's all you have to say about the band on your lawn?" I asked.

"They sound tight, considering how early in the year it is," she answered serenely.

"You are in on this." I slid into my sandals as I studied her.

"I had a chat with the band director, yes."

Band director? The pieces slid into place.

"Is this because I wouldn't tutor that kid?" I had to raise my voice because the music got louder with every passing minute.

She shrugged and picked her phone back up to play her bubble game with her coffee.

20

I shook my head. "If they crush my echinacea, I will never forgive you!" I called over my shoulder as I went into the front yard.

They were in full swing now, scurrying around like clenched ants.

"Hey!" I yelled but wasn't heard. Or, more likely, was ignored. The eyes of the neighbors were on me, and I wrapped myself up tighter, knowing this would be the talk of the town today.

My sudden nerves at the spotlight made my throat tight, but I tried to get the attention of the person leading the performance.

The classic marching band performance of "Sing, Sing, Sing" morphed into another song—one I knew all too well—at the direction of the woman up front who swung her arms wildly as she shouted a command I didn't understand.

I squinted as sun glared through the trees, hiding her from view.

"You're kidding me." I rolled my eyes skyward as "Small Town Escape" by The Burnouts filled the air. Perhaps our biggest hit, before my departure. It was a hack job, but recognizable. I had to give them some credit. They managed to sound this good considering I only turned Devlin down a few days ago.

"Very clever," I mumbled, feeling the weight of all the onlookers. I just wanted this to stop.

The band split to reveal a tall kid in a white tank top, with athletic arms and long black hair, holding a marching quad set. The rest of the band quieted down as the girl with the quads looked up at the woman directing and then at me. I saw a nervous twitch of her cheek before she seemed to swallow her fear and glare with determination.

I recognized that look. That "screw this small town, screw this person who doesn't think I'm good enough" look. I felt a shiver pass down my neck as she began her solo. A similar solo I had played a hundred times on this very song but not on marching quads.

I grumbled.

She really was good, insanely good for a high school kid, but not as good as I was. *When I still played.* She was stiff and a little tentative.

When she finished, I clapped, hoping the madness was over. Janice popped up at my side, clapping and whooping loudly, drawing even more attention.

"That child is going places," my mother said. "Hopefully," she added pointedly.

"Thank you for that, Janice," I grumbled.

Just then, the woman who'd been conducting turned and headed toward us.

All coherent thought left my mind. The sun shone on her blond ponytail, a faint smile on her lips. Her dark eyes seemed to be full of secrets and knowledge. She came to the porch to greet us as the rest of the band gathered around the drummer. As she approached, I could see the director had a large smile and perfectly aligned white teeth. Her frame was tall and slender, and she wore jeans and a striped sweater.

I couldn't speak. I couldn't manage a full breath in.

"Lovely to see you again. The kids sound really great, Mari," my mother gushed.

"Thank you, Janice. I learned from the best," the woman, Mari, said.

Mari. This was the friend of Devlin? This was the woman who needed my help? Why did she have to be so beautiful? She had an air about her that I always envied in people, like she was already unimpressed and indifferent to the opinions of everyone around her. *She* had the rock star energy I always tried to emanate.

"You make this retired old gal feel good." Mari smiled as Janice spoke. Was she blinking in slow motion? Did the sun shine brighter as it reflected off her? She was incredible. "Mariam, this is my son, Leonard. I don't know if y'all have officially met yet."

"I haven't had the pleasure." She smiled wider yet and extended a hand. When our hands met, I had that slowing down of time feeling again. I had to stop looking at her so much.

"Leo," I corrected quietly, not sure if she even heard.

Look away. Don't make it any weirder. Release her hand. The brief touch of her soft skin went too fast, and I debated who even decided how long a handshake should be.

She looked me up and down, and I once again remembered that I wore my mother's floral caftan. "Hi, Leo. I'm Mariam. Mari, rhymes with Atari, to most. I'm the band director at Green Valley High."

I opened my mouth to speak, but all that tumbled out was the mumbled worries about the marching band being dangerously close to my azaleas. My mother quietly clicked her tongue at my behavior.

"How was your family's visit?" Janice asked. Mari flicked another look my way. Maybe I should have gone with the raincoat. Or said something more than a mumble about my garden.

Mari tucked her hands in the back pocket of her jeans and leaned back. Mari's smile twitched and widened. "You know, it didn't work out. We are all so busy."

"Oh no," Janice said and patted Mari's arm in sympathy. "I know you were looking forward to it."

22

"You know how it goes." Her smile widened but felt forced and unnatural to me, and I'd only just met her. "Actually, I'd love to chat more, but I don't want to take any more of your time. I gotta get these kids to school before the first bell."

My mother *winked*. In all my years, I'd never seen my mother wink. But I got it, there was a presence to Mari that I had not expected. Was that what Devlin had meant about being a force? She certainly was a force. I almost couldn't stay standing. But not because she was scary, as he implied. Was that what he had implied? Now I couldn't recall his ominous and ambiguous warning. When I looked at her, I couldn't get the sound of heavenly harps and birds chirping out of my brain long enough to focus.

"I'll let you kids chat," Janice said. "See you at the big game."

"Can't wait," Mariam said.

"Coffee's ready when you're done." My mother squeezed my shoulder as she went back into the house.

I had been about to apologize with a prepared explanation of why I couldn't help the obviously talented student. I assumed that was what this had all been about. A last-ditch effort to prove the drummer's skills.

The second the screen door smacked closed, Mari's demeanor changed. The smile fell off her face, her features morphed into sharp lines, and her eyes narrowed, fox-like and calculating. "Welcome back to Green Valley," she said, hands clasped, the warmth gone from her face.

"Is this a six o'clock welcome committee?"

"This is just a few volunteer members of my marching band."

"Okay, I—" I tugged at my curls, ready to confess.

"We just wanted to welcome you back. And insist that you come to our first show at the homecoming game. The whole town will be there. I'm sure you wouldn't want to miss it."

"Listen—" I tried again, humiliation burned me up. The watchful eyes of the town made everything in me feel my most insecure.

"Aye, pup pup pup." She pinched my lips together with her fingers. This was the second time she touched me, and my brain made a special note of that. "No excuses. No more talking. Just be there tomorrow night."

This close, looking into her brown eyes, feeling the full force of them, she reminded me of Peggy Lipton from her *Mod Squad* years combined with Gwen Stefani in No Doubt. Both incredibly cool and breathtaking women. I was outmatched by her. She was a force. This was what Devlin had meant. I was in awe.

And she thought I was a self-centered, washed-up rock star. Fantastic.

Nothing I could say would change her first impression of me. It matched what the rest of the town thought anyway.

I gently grabbed her wrist and removed her hand from my mouth, stretching my lips, wondering how long until her touch would fade away.

"I wouldn't have even gone to a football game when I was in high school." It was the worst thing to have said. Why was that the excuse I came up with?

Her features sharpened. It was true that I barely went to band, and that was only because my mom was the teacher, but I didn't do marching or jazz or any extracurricular. I practiced with Vander. Day or night. Weekday or weekend. Every spare moment filled with practice, writing, playing covers of our favorite bands, and daydreaming about The Burnouts' big break. And I wasn't ever beloved around town. I was the weird, shy kid with painted black nails and a freakish growth spurt.

"The choice is yours," she said, ignoring my pathetic protest. "You go to that game and see Cath play, or you experience this lovely welcome committee every morning until you go insane."

"Whoa." I stepped back, palms raising. I glanced up, but her students were too far away to hear. Or help.

"I don't care if you think you're too good for this town to 'lower' yourself to help my student."

"I never—"

"But Cath is the rare sort of musician that comes along once a generation, and I will be *damned* if I let some spoiled, washed-up rock star—"

"Hey, now."

"—ruin her chances to get into a good school. I don't care if you're busy. You will make time. You will help this kid out of the goodness of whatever is left of your little, shriveled, dark heart, or so help me God."

By the time she finished her rant, her cheeks were flushed, and her chest heaved. A flush of red spread from just below her collar to behind her ears. She came to my chin, yet I had never felt smaller. I tried to speak, but having her mad at me took me by complete surprise. I knew this town hated me, but I had thought maybe because she'd taken over for my mom, she was one of the few who would not assume the worst about me.

I had been wrong. Just like everyone else in this town, she thought I was the weird kid or the grown-up, spoiled rock star who thought he was too good for this town. I needed to make her understand, but how?

"I'm not—it's just that—" Her eyebrows raised expectantly, ready to combat whatever flimsy excuse I could muster. And that was all it'd be— flimsy—because she was right. Not about me being self-entitled and all that (*ouch*), but because I didn't want to do it. There was no way I could help a virtuoso drummer get into college. I was an uneducated, unmoored former drummer. Why did this woman even *want* my help?

But I waited too long to finish the sentence, and she'd made up her mind. Everything she'd suspected had been confirmed in my silence. If only I could ever say what I wanted in the moment, ask for what I wanted.

"That's what I thought. Welcome home. I looked forward to seeing you again."

Loser.

I would help if I could, but I was not the person for this job. Not even my own mother knew my reasons for being back in Green Valley. I opened my mouth to argue. The screen door swung open again, and Mari's demeanor melted into the sugary sweet Southern style from earlier.

I shuddered. She was terrifying, after all.

Janice came back out with a tray of the blondies I made last night.

"I have goodies!" Janice was swarmed by students after her pronouncement. To me, she whispered, "You can make more."

"Those were for tonight," I mumbled, once again completely ignored.

"Hurry up and grab a treat. We gotta get back to the school," Mari instructed her students.

The kid, Cath, glanced up at me and gave a half-smile as quickly as possible before looking away.

Ugh. Whose great idea was this anyway? At least when I enjoyed my retirement around here, I wasn't hurting anybody else. I was just existing in peace and quiet. Helping bees and hanging with my mom.

"See y'all tomorrow." Mari waved and bounced away, her blond ponytail bopping as she went.

"She is such a lovely girl," my mom said when they were all gone.

I snorted.

"She knows how to get things done," she added.

"You don't say."

She shoved me with her shoulder, just above my elbow. "Just wouldn't want to be on her shit list." She raised her eyebrows smugly and went back into the house.

I groaned and followed her. No way was I going back to that school. It was bad enough to know the whole town got more gossip for the mill this morning. I was the last person who would be wanted at the precious homecoming game. I wouldn't be going, and nobody could make me.

CHAPTER 5
MARI

I yawned into my sad turkey sandwich, wondering if maybe I had gone too far this morning. I had warned the kids not to step on the flowers at all. Mostly for Janice and not Leo. Leo with his stupid black curls and sleepy grin. He hadn't been what I expected. Maybe I'd watched too many videos of him on stage. I don't know what I thought he would do, really. Forcing people to do things against their will rarely worked, but I'd felt so desperate. Now I felt so silly.

Was this maturity?

Janice had been in support of the surprise visit, and she'd even gone so far as ensuring that their neighbor, Pin Dick, who happened to be my principal, wouldn't be home. But maybe it hadn't been a rational choice.

Rational just meant nonconfrontational and letting things slide. The world was filled with people making excuses not to have a real conversation.

I was glancing at the line of Keurigs, debating if I could sneak a cup from Coach Easton's machine without being noticed, when Clara slid into the chair next to me. "What's up with the grumpy face?" She set down a Tupperware container of what looked like pasta carbonara, blowing the steam that rose from it.

Clara and I were cousins once removed or some such. Our grandfathers were brothers. We had played when we were little until she was suddenly gone from my life. It was good to have her back in town, and having her sub at the school was an unexpected but pleasant surprise. We reconnected with the familiarity of old friends. She was also the only person I had initially told about my family's last-minute change of plans but I brushed it off as no big deal. With her big, complicated family, she didn't have time for any more drama.

"I was thinking about the driving force of greed and the broken systems of the patriarchy behind it." I sighed. My stomach growled loudly as I caught a whiff of cheesy bacon.

"How fun. No wonder."

"That looks yummy." I forced myself to look away from the pasta, my mouth filling with saliva. If I never ate another turkey sandwich again, it would be too soon.

"Leftovers from Sadie. I don't do the cooking thing."

"I feel that." I gestured to my bag of chips and sad sammy. "Aw, Sadie. I haven't seen your sister since we were kids. I think she was like twelve and I was jealous that she was getting boobs. How is she these days?"

"Great boobs." Clara nodded, and I laughed. "Married. Happy. Just like the rest of the sisters," Clara said with just a bit of edge. I wondered what that was about. "Except Gracie, obviously."

"Look at us, two single babes living our best lives." It almost sounded convincing. "Sadie lives next door, right?" I changed the subject before it got too morose.

"No, she moved but she's still close enough to make edible food very convenient. I like where I live. I like sitting on the porch drinking my coffee and working in the yard."

"And spying," I added. She'd told me her tales of *Rear Window*-ing and often delighted me with the antics around her block.

"Speaking of. What was with the wake-up call this morning? Not that I don't love our marching band. Go Black Bears."

"Go Bears." I told her about Janice's request to help Cath, and Leo's refusal to Devlin. "Maybe I had misdirected some of my frustration with my family . . . I've been accused of being reactive in the past. But it wasn't like I lit a motorcycle on fire."

"I see nothing wrong with your actions. A literal wake-up call. Here, you can have some." She shoved the dish toward me. "If I hear your stomach growl one more time, I'll shove a candy bar down your throat."

"Thanks." I took a giant bite, not even pretending to turn down the offer like a polite Southern lady. "And, right?" My response sounded muffled around my mouthful. I swallowed with a wince, a piece of bacon scraping my throat. "What else is Leo going to do?"

"Listen. I've seen that man, and I can honestly say something shady is happening at that house. He's what, our age? Thirtysomething?"

"I think he was three grades behind us."

"Oh yeah. Leonard. He was so weird and shy. And so painfully quiet. That kid Vander, who he was always with, did all the talking for both of them. "

"Shy?" Devlin had made it seem like Leo was arrogant. Weren't all drummers just a little too full of themselves? Distracted at best. "I don't really remember him from back in the day. He was just my teacher's kid."

"He was an odd duck. He's all grown up now, though, isn't he?"

I avoided her question because my brain was all too quick to replay the interaction and his strong shoulders.

"Still. No man is that concerned with gardening."

I shrugged. "Not my business. I just don't want Cath to suffer because he's a snob. But now I'm thinking bringing the marching band to his mom's house was a bit reactive. I was just so mad. And maybe I misdirected some of those feelings."

"Are you upset about your parents bailing?"

"I have unresolved feelings . . . I guess. Possibly." I sat back with a sigh.

"You really need to come to spaghetti night."

"I will." Even as I said it, I wasn't sure that I would. I wanted *my* immediate family to want to spend time with me. I didn't want to have to foist myself upon extended quasi-relatives. I felt so pathetic.

"Family can be complicated," she said softly.

"It's fine. They're busy. And anyway, the year will be hectic with all the bands I'm running. From here on out, I'm focusing on my students and Cath's audition."

I thought of Cath's parents, of the pride in their eyes. Despite their long shifts at The Mill and Donner Lodge, at least one of them made it to every show. They made it work for Cath, no matter what, so I refused to let her down. I was weirdly relieved to feel my anger for Leo returning. Spite was the ultimate motivator, no matter what any philosopher said.

Clara made a sound of acknowledgment.

"I'm at my best when I'm focused on my work. I don't need anybody else . . ." I trailed off before I could be accused of protesting too much.

A sudden image popped into my head. My finger pressed against Leo's mouth. The soft lips pressed between my fingers. The surprising jolt of electricity.

That must be what happened when you hadn't been intimate in a while.

29

Any sort of physical contact could get your motor revving. Didn't matter. Hardly the point.

Though, Leo's bedhead was cute, and his voice was a lot more gentle and soft-spoken than I'd expected. Not that he talked much. And what was with that weird fabric shift he'd been wearing? Was that a celebrity thing? It hinted at the drummer's muscular chest. His dark curls were long enough that he constantly tugged them out of his eyes just to blink when they fell back in. Of course, he was cute. He was a rock star. There was a sort of optical illusion that made even the scruffiest of men become hot when proficient at an instrument.

He was a great drummer, and people with that level of skill should share it with the world, or at least pay it forward. It was their duty. Wasn't anybody with extreme privilege responsible for giving back? Wasn't that how community and humanity worked? What got us this far? My frustration bubbled back up.

"What has needing other people ever done for anybody?" Clara asked with a touch of sarcasm.

"Nothing but taint that couch." I gestured to the cursed teachers' lounge couch.

"Is that why nobody sits on it?" Clara leaned forward, eyes wide with curiosity.

"Supposedly, it's where our previous principal had several indiscreet . . . fits of passion," I whispered.

"Really? I thought it was because a raccoon made a nest in there, and the couch will break if anybody sits on it."

I shrugged. "Well, whatever the story, do not ever sit on it."

"Noted."

Just then, the hunky substitute walked with pep into the teachers' lounge. He wasn't around very often, so when he was, everybody took notice. He also worked at the local car wash. The women of Green Valley had very clean cars.

"Hey," Clara and I said in tandem, dragging out the word.

He grabbed an apple from the fridge, washed it, and took a large crisp bite, devouring half the apple in one go. Clara and I watched unabashedly until he tipped a pretend hat, winked a blue eye, and left again.

We shared a look. "I know," I said.

"Whoever gets his attention—"

"I know. I heard he might be on some show, like an adventure thing." Clara leaned closer to whisper.

"What? No way."

"We'll see. As long as the producers make him lose his shirt once or twice."

"Oh, we shouldn't objectify him." My words were half-hearted at best.

"I'm trying to feel bad about it."

"You should. Also, I need to get my car washed. I just remembered."

We cackled.

For the rest of lunch, as we chatted, my mind wandered to the homecoming game tomorrow. If Leo would show up or if I would be let down by somebody else in my life.

CHAPTER 6
LEO

I thought about Mari for the rest of the day. The sharpness of her stare. The defiant way she held her own to me. Her takedown was a little bit sexy . . .

I admired her but wouldn't be going to the game, no matter what. The whole thought of it made my stomach turn. Just imagining what the people of Green Valley would say if I showed up in blue and gold to cheer on the Black Bears.

No way.

Let her blast the music until the neighbors called the cops or the parents realized their kids were off school property. She was all talk and a bullhorn. I didn't need her approval or her guilt anyway.

I had everything I needed right here. Thursday nights were for bunco. Janice and I set up card tables in the back garden. I'd hung string lights and had enough of those mosquito machines circling the perimeter that I could potentially wipe out the entire species. There was a nice breeze wafting the sweet smell of flowers toward the guests. I curated a selection of delicate, easy-to-eat snacks—like caprese salad kabobs—and tangy cocktails/mocktails made of fresh citrus. I was absolutely killing it here with my people. Who needed overcrowded tour buses and screaming fans when I had all the wisest matrons of Green Valley passing down generations of knowledge?

I smiled at the collection of Bunco Broads at my table.

"What's wrong with your son?" Maxine Barton asked, glaring at me over the rim of her glass.

Janice glanced at me quickly before returning to her rapid rolling of three dice. "He's happy."

I grinned at the rest of the table, feeling the threat of a blush, but forced it away. Even if most of the town hadn't accepted me, at least these ladies had let me into their circuit.

Maxine grunted.

The bunco rules were unclear, but I got the gist. And quite frankly, I was too afraid to ask any clarifying questions at this point. I rolled the three dice when they were passed to me and passed them to the left when I was told. I enjoyed the cadence of the rapid-rolling game pieces and the fast-paced play. I did *not* care for how intense the women got, especially if I took too long to go. I used to be able to drum roll faster than any other drummer I'd met, but apparently, when it came to dice, I was glacial.

The yard was set up today with three tables, each with four ever-rotating people. Twelve of us total. At my table, I had the pleasure of Janice across from me, and Maxine and Becky Lee Monroe, Maxine's current partner for the round, to my right and left, respectively.

I looked longingly to the other tables where Belle Cooper, Julianne McIntyre, Faye Brentmore, and Daisy Payton played with a few other women I only recognized in passing. It wasn't that I didn't like this group, but Maxine was harder to win over than the others. She didn't have the sweet Southern charm known in these parts, like Belle, my mother's ex-stepmom. Belle Cooper had eight ex-husbands, but her maternal care for me kept me safe from her grabby hands. She often checked in on my mom and me, even though all we shared now was a last name.

I widened my smile at Maxine until my cheeks hurt when I looked up to find her narrowing her eyes at me.

Daisy snorted as she shared a look with Belle Cooper at the head table.

"You need a job," Maxine said.

Guess who won't be getting sugar on her rim next round.

"Oh, you shush, Maxine," Faye said. "It's nice having young blood around here."

Maxine grunted as I tilted my head graciously at Faye. She was newest to bunco, newer than me, but she was quickly becoming my favorite.

"Young blood? My social life is more active than his," Maxine said. "He needs a job."

Janice remained awfully quiet at my side.

"I have the garden. Those plants won't grow themselves." I frowned and reached for my sweet tea. "Well, technically they do. Still."

"Less talking. Hurry and roll."

We went silent as Janice rolled for twos. She managed four points.

"It's not healthy for a young buck your age to be hanging with a bunch of old biddies," Belle Cooper added above the sound of dice clanging. "Bunco!"

Various sounds of displeasure went up from the other tables.

"Speak for yourself. I'm at the peak of my life," Daisy called, and several ladies cheered.

"This is fun. Everybody talking about me like I'm not here," I said.

"He needs friends. It's weird." Maxine was getting the spicy dip next time too. "He's too young to be hiding out like this."

"Hiding? Who said I was hiding? I'm having a social night right now. Who would I learn more from than the matriarchs of Green Valley?" I asked.

"Don't suck up."

"You don't want me here?" I gestured to the decked-out snack table. My years of providing the band with healthy alternatives on the road led to a secret calling of game snackage curation.

I kept my tone light, but with every comment, I grew more tense and too conspicuous in my big body. Maybe this wasn't the refuge in Green Valley I'd hoped for. Right now, it was feeling more like a pit of vipers.

"Your mother comes here to get away from you," Maxine said. "And now you've infiltrated here."

My heart sank.

"Mom?" I looked at Janice, unable to hide the worry that contorted my eyebrows.

The matrons of Green Valley did not appreciate me calling my mom by her first name, even though I always had. It was one of those inside signs of our close relationship that nobody else understood.

"Maxine!" she chastised the woman before focusing on the rolling dice, not quite meeting my gaze. "That's not true, honey. I love spending time with you. All day. Every day."

"Bunco!" yelled someone at another table, and Maxine cursed under her breath.

"Good," I said, then frowned in confusion. Why had she said it like that?

"I do think it might be good for you to get out of the house more. Maybe a hobby?" She focused on the scoring card.

"But. The garden." I gestured toward the yard. "Did I tell you about the bees?"

"Yes, love. You told me about the bees. But maybe something outside the property? Go into town?"

"I thought you loved me being back home?" I glanced at the others; this wasn't a private conversation, but they all looked away. Embarrassment burned the back of my neck.

Janice glanced nervously at the other ladies, Faye nodded subtly at her for encouragement. Had this been discussed before? Did nobody want me around? "Of course I do, sweetie. Of course. But you used to be so . . . driven. Music was your passion. I just hope you aren't hiding out here instead of living your life. You're so young."

"Hiding? I'm not hiding. Why does everyone keep saying that?"

"You hardly go into town," Maxine said. "You have a reputation."

Why would I go into town when I felt the judgment of every person who looked at me? Half of them thought I was still the weird punk who used to get beat up in high school for wearing eyeliner and black nail polish, and the other half thought I was a snooty musician. Nobody knew me. Except for Janice.

Except for now, it would seem that even she was eager to get rid of me.

"I guess . . . if I'm not wanted." I stood. I was all too aware of this familiar feeling.

Vander and the members of The Burnouts all staring at me. My chest heaving, hands fisted after throwing my sticks. Their exchanged glances, like they'd been talking about me . . .

"Honey," my mom cajoled.

"Sit down. We can't be down a person. Three more rounds." Maxine whacked my knees, and I collapsed back into the chair.

"I don't want you to leave," my mom said, holding my gaze. "I *do* think that helping other people can be healing. Stops you from dwelling on your own problems."

"You think I should help Mari?" I asked. "That's what your ganging up is all about?"

"I think you should help Cath. Imagine what a mentor could do at that age. You know how big everything feels at seventeen. I think it would be a lovely way to help the community and get out a little. Connect with some locals. Green Valley has changed a lot since you were in high school."

"We have a pole dancing studio now!" Belle said.

I wouldn't be thinking about the implications of that statement.

"All right, ladies, I'm getting older with every roll. Can we focus?" Maxine smacked the table, shaking the drinks. Around me, the game continued as I dwelled on my public razing. What was so bad about enjoying time off? I had been driven for most of my life, and look where that got me.

I was happy now. Or at least . . . content? No. Something else. It would come to me.

That wasn't what stopped me, but I certainly couldn't tell that to my mom, who only ever supported me. I had to keep the truth about what happened with the band to myself. I couldn't handle her reaction.

When I said nobody could make me go to the game, I hadn't considered that my own mother was sick of me being here. If the wisest set of the population thought I needed to leave the house, what did that say about me?

I would go to the high school football game just to show Janice that I was perfectly capable of leaving the house, even if it was my idea of hell. Just to show that I was well-adjusted and doing just fine.

I would hide under the bleachers like I used to. I wasn't going to talk to anybody. I would go for her. But only because Janice devoted her life to teaching kids, and I wouldn't besmirch the Cooper name. At least not in that regard.

CHAPTER 7
MARI

I swelled with pride as the Marching Black Bears made Green Valley look great during the halftime show in the game against Merryville High. I couldn't focus much on the game as I kept looking for a curly-haired man. The coach didn't seem happy. Not that Nick ever seemed happy. Poor Coach Easton was beaten down and worked way too hard. And that said something coming from me.

The marching band killed the halftime show. The air was electric; the crowd screaming louder at Cath's drum solo on the quads, backed up by the snare line, than they had at the one and only touchdown. The rest of the band wiggled their fingers in support as she hammered out the insane tempo. Her face remained unchanged with her success, but her eyes flicked up into the stands as if looking for someone.

Leo was nowhere to be seen. We'd set up Cath to show off to him, and he'd not even bothered. My chest seized with a familiar defeat.

That spineless little jellyfish.

I stood trying to summon the anger, trying to find a way to use it to catapult me into my next choice. My whole life felt like moving one foot after the other, trying to find my footing, acting without thought. Disappointment after disappointment.

But now, I couldn't muster offense. As Cath performed her incredible solo on the quad, I felt a crushing sadness. It wasn't enough that her parents were here, they were already stretched so thin. She looked up to Leo, idolized him, in fact. Not that I would tell him that. He already walked around with massive neck muscles from holding up that giant head. Metaphorically. To be fair, he did have good muscles and was perfectly proportioned.

I shook my head.

Cath needed a mentor. A helping hand. When I'd suggested Leo, she'd been more excited than I'd seen in ages. I wanted to give that to her. What was this guy so afraid of that the thought of a little girl made him hide out? I wouldn't take no for an answer. Her future was more important than whatever else he had going on.

The crowd went wild with cheers as the band finished. Clara came to my side as the band jogged back to their seats in the stands.

"They sound really good," she said.

"Thanks," I beamed, slightly breathless.

"Cath is just . . ." Clara started.

"I know. So good." I shook my head. "I'm going to go to jail. Sheriff James is gonna put me away."

Her head snapped toward me. "What happened?"

"Nothing yet. But Leo didn't show up, and I cannot be responsible for what I do next."

A knowing grin transformed her features. "Did you know I was a bit of a wild child in my youth?"

"I heard rumors . . ."

"It's the past, and I don't think about it. I spent a lot of time doing unmentionable things under the bleachers. All the ne'er-do-wells did."

"I'm aware." I had never been there. I was too much of a Goody Two-shoes and busy playing the flute. "Where are you going with this?" I asked.

"I always look there now. Just to see if the kids today still do it."

"And?"

"They do. But tonight I happened to see a shaggy-haired grown man hiding down there in glasses and toboggan," she said.

"Who wears a *beanie* in this heat?" We'd debated the term for a winter cap before and called a truce. Her time away had changed her.

"People hiding out."

"I'm going to get him and give him a piece of my mind."

"I'd hoped you'd say that." She grinned mischievously.

I stomped away and found the side entrance under the bleachers. Sure enough, tucked in the shadows like he thought himself a small-town Batman was Leo.

He had his phone out, thumb flicking through an app as he leaned against the metal supports. When he noticed a presence, he straightened and tucked his phone away. When he realized it was *me* stomping toward him, his eyes went wide. He lifted a hand to mess with his hair but dropped it when he found the beanie.

The rush of relief that flooded me at the sight of him must have been due to Cath. I would tell her that he showed up to watch her after all. That flutter in my chest was because he hadn't disappointed her.

"Look who's hiding," I said as I stopped in front of him. I'd perfected my unimpressed look in high school. It was hard-earned by having two older brothers who teased me relentlessly for any interests they deemed "uncool." Which were all of them. Thankfully, the look didn't take much since my mouth sort of fell into a downturned line, and my large eyes naturally narrowed. Ironically, when I was most relaxed, I came across as most pissed off.

Leo straightened and glanced up into the stands. "I'm not big on crowds."

"That's helpful for a career as a rock star."

He looked away. "I didn't think, uh . . ." He gave up the fight and tugged off the cap to run his fingers through his hair. "I just didn't want to make a scene."

"Yes, the big celebrity might steal the show," I mocked.

He frowned. "No, I just—" His mouth shut, and his pronounced Adam's apple moved up and down. He shook his head as if trying to find the words.

If it weren't for the fact that he was a professional performer, he almost looked nervous being here. Was he that afraid people would want to talk to him? Nobody in Green Valley would ask for an autograph or something embarrassing. *No offense*, I thought, *but most people couldn't even name a famous drummer outside Ringo Starr.* I still felt bad for my snark. I was jacked up on sweet tea and in defense mode, and he was here, wasn't he? Despite being notably reclusive since moving back.

"Is that why you're lurking?" I asked, stepping closer and softening my voice.

"Not lurking. Just enjoying the ambiance." He looked me up and down as he said it, then moved his gaze away quickly. I was in jeans and a Black Bears shirt, yet the look had me wondering if I accidentally left the house in only my bra. Being down here did something to me I hadn't expected. I was humming with adrenaline. Was this what it would have been like as a kid? All those people so close but nobody watching us. It did make me want to do something naughty.

Yes, thinking the word *naughty* made me "cringe" or whatever the kids said.

"Oh yes, like spring in Paris," I said.

I swallowed and glanced away and around. No cigarette butts, but graffiti from decades of burnouts and truants and an excessive amount of chewing gum. Seriously, hundreds of multicolored blobs. At what point would it impact the structural integrity of the seats? I looked back at Leo, who was still watching me expectantly. He wasn't a great conversationalist, but when I caught him looking at me, his neck flushed, and he looked away.

I studied him. He wore sweats and a well-worn Rush tee, but his tall, fit form gave him the natural vibe of a rebel.

"You look like you should be angstily smoking a cigarette and have a pack rolled up in the sleeve of your white tee shirt," I said.

"Was the last movie you watched starring James Dean by any chance?" he asked. There was the soft, rich voice. I had thought all drummers were egotistical, based on a lifetime of experiences with them: loud and obnoxious show-offs. But Leo looked like he hated taking up space. His shoulders were sort of hunched and his head tucked forward in an attempt not to come across so large. Even his constant fussing with his hair felt like an attempt to push himself down.

Interesting. Maybe he had been hiding down here, but not because he was afraid of a random fan.

I tried to find a comfortable way to lean against the inverse staircase, but I just ended up bonking my head on the corner of a step. I played it off, hoping he didn't notice.

He did.

He bit back a smile and said, "I do that a lot. My mom called me 'Lumpy' for years after my growth spurt." He gestured to his head.

I'd expected him to tease me, make fun of me, or use the opportunity to brag, but he'd deflected my embarrassment and shone it on himself. This was a far cry from the egotistical, flamboyant musician I'd painted in my head. In the shadow of the bleachers and with that self-deprecating grin, he seemed different from the man I'd rudely awoken.

This was Devlin's fault. He purposely wound me up so I'd go off on Leo. Except I knew myself, and I could have used any excuse to take my frustrations out on someone.

There was a slight chance I could be rash.

"I would really love to know what you're thinking right now," Leo said. He flushed and looked away as if he hadn't meant to say it out loud.

We'd stepped closer when I hadn't been paying attention. I pulled my ponytail off my neck, fanning it. It was unseasonably warm, and the hundreds of bodies above didn't help. You'd think it would be impossible to hear each other, especially as the game started again and people were yelling and stomping just above our heads. Yet there was an intimacy down here like we were in our own little bubble.

"I was just thinking if I found a long enough stick, I could jab Principal Pin Dick in the backside."

He chuckled. "Is that what you call him?"

"It suits him, I think. He's got that PDE—Pin Dick Energy."

This time, he laughed, and it lit up his whole face. Dimples popped out, transforming his features. These dimples inspired the online fan-made videos of him drumming, overlaid with music and special effects highlighting his incredible physique or the secret, shy grins he sent his bandmates as he played. Those zoomed-in shots when he thought nobody was looking, where his head dropped back and his focus took over, were the definition of sexy.

Lordy, he was attractive and there was nary a drum kit in sight. It must have just been the memory of watching those videos. The sweat dripping from his dark curls, glistening his abs—because, of course, he would take his shirt off during performances—the delicate way he held his drumsticks, firm but loose.

That finger dexterity though . . .

I stepped back as feet stomped with a roar of cheers above us. I cleared my throat to hide the burning and instant heat that flushed through me.

How could my body feel so much electricity for this man when my brain booed from the cheap seats and chanted, *Focus on the plan!*

I didn't think this sort of attraction was a real thing. I was the type that admired intelligence, compassion, and hard work ethics. This slacker was the antithesis of all that. Time to get this show back on track.

"What did you think of Cath?" I asked.

He stepped back as well to glance in the crack where he must have been watching the performance. "She's great." He tucked his hands in his jeans and lifted his shoulders to his ears. "That was never in doubt."

"Then you agree to help her?" I asked hopefully.

"It's not that. I-I don't think that I'm the best—" He took a breath in and out, unable to complete a single sentence. When he found me waiting, it was like he was trying to muster the words, trying to read something off me. He'd gone quiet again as something he'd seen on me held him back. He wouldn't just say no. He waited for me to speak. He wanted me to tell him that it wasn't going to work because he couldn't just say the truth.

I had thought we were warming up to each other, but his inability to be honest was infuriating.

I left my features blank.

"She's incredible," Leo finally said slowly and carefully. "But impressive drumrolls on quads won't be enough for somewhere like Berklee. How is she on a full set? How's her jazz drumming? All these things would be required on an entrance audition, right?"

Had he researched what sort of requirements she might have? Was that a tinge of hope I felt?

"She's incredible. On a full set too. Playing rock or jazz. Whatever you throw at her, she can do it," I said, attempting to keep myself relaxed.

He glanced to the side, and I felt him getting ready to make an excuse. I was starting to soften toward the dingus, and I didn't want to do something that might piss him off. I reached for my phone in my back pocket and searched the calendar for the next several weeks. "Come to dinner with me."

He stilled, holding my gaze, when I looked up from my phone. "You want me to go out with you? In public?"

"Next Saturday. At the Front Porch. The jazz quartet is doing a dinner show," I said.

"Oh. Right," he said, staring at the ground.

"We also have our first full symphony performance in October. That's a bit of a ways away, but that will be good. Oh, and we're performing at the Fall Festival. That should be fun. You should come to all of them." I locked my phone screen. His face had taken a greenish tint.

"I'm not sure about my calendar." He avoided my gaze as I put away my phone.

"It would be good for you to see her." I kept my voice even and proudly did not call him any names.

"You go to all of these?"

"Yeah, of course. I think you should try to make it. At least Saturday."

"To the Front Porch?"

"Yep. I'm not directing for this one, more like moral support. Make sure they get set up and everything. They won't need me while they play, but I like to be there to ensure it goes smoothly. And I want to talk to the owner about some donations. It's a free concert, but I hope they will consider donating after that. That's another reason I like to go. Feed two birds with one scone."

The words were flying out of my mouth before I could stop them. I couldn't help myself. This band, these kids, they were my life. I had to admit, Leo had a way of making me chatty. Maybe because he was as quiet as a church mouse.

That or I was more lonely than I thought.

44

Nope. We were not thinking about that.

"Scone?" His brows lifted with amusement.

"A less violent analogy," I explained.

He looked at the ground again, so I couldn't tell for sure, but I thought I saw a hint of a smile. "Good album name," he said.

It was my turn to hide a smile.

"Okay." He met my eyes. "I'll try to make Saturday work."

"And then?" I crossed my arms.

"Then we'll see." He was tugging at his hair again.

"Need I remind you of the marching band alarm clock?"

"Need I remind you of restraining orders?"

I bit my tongue to keep from grinning. "Fine. Just be there. And try to dress better."

His dark brows lifted as he looked down at himself. "It's Green Valley."

"It's our nicest steak house. If you insist on wearing Adidas slides and sweats, I'll pretend I don't know you. Not when I'm working my magic with the owner."

"Now I really have to go. If for nothing else than to see you sic yourself on someone besides me. Does the rest of the town know about your hidden dark side?"

"Oh, shut up." I turned and started to walk away before the kids started to wonder where I went. "See you Saturday," I called over my shoulder.

A thrill of excitement trickled down my neck. I clamped the feeling down, even as I wondered if I had any nice clothes that weren't all black business casual for performances. It might be nice to get a little dressed up. Just for myself.

CHAPTER 8
LEO

My feet made a boom-bap rhythm as I hopped/jogged down the back set of stairs to the kitchen. My mother's shocked face greeted me. To her credit, she tried to cover the surprise as fast as it arrived.

"Don't you look dapper," Janice said, taking me in from head to toe.

"Has it been that long since I showered?" There was a slight shake of nerves in my voice.

"Do you really want me to answer that?" she asked with a wry grin.

"No." I guess I had let my hygiene slip a little. Without hours of sweat-drenched practice, I hadn't felt like I needed to shower as often. My curls had been tangled and greasy, and my beard grew a little long, giving me a some-what feral look. It kept people from approaching me, at least, if I ever did have to venture from the house. For the *not* date with Mari—because it was clearly a work thing and nothing else—I'd tidied up my face and slicked back my hair as much as possible until the humidity would free the curls from their prison. I wore my nicest black jeans, and my shirt had a collar.

Mari had made a big impression on me in a short amount of time. I should have told her the truth about my history with The Burnouts at the homecoming game instead of agreeing to this meeting tonight. But there was something about the intimacy of our conversation and the look in her eyes that I hadn't quite been able to get the words out right. Clara, my neighbor and Mari's friend, had found me first under the bleachers. She wormed ideas into my brain about Mari, things like asking her out. The woman seemed to feel like she was taking on a big sister role with me. I didn't need any more people in my life. Not that it mattered. Asking somebody out required leaving the house. And tonight was an exception to my rules.

Not that it was a date.

"Can I ask where you're off to, or would that be uncool mom behavior? I don't know the rules when you aren't a teenager and it's your home," Janice spoke, breaking my internal spiral.

"First, I would be offended if you didn't ask. And second, it's *your* house. I just bought it." She glanced at my shoes, my nicest black Vans, and raised an expectant eyebrow.

"I'm going to the Front Porch. Mari wants me to see Cath's jazz drumming."

"You decided to tutor her? Oh, I'm so proud of you."

I avoided her gaze and glanced at my phone. "Crap, gotta go. See you later."

"Mari's single, you know," she added as I rushed to say goodbye.

"Hardly relevant." I kissed her forehead as she gave a knowing raise of her eyebrows.

I hurried out to the silver sedan we shared. The drive went fast, but it took me a few minutes to find parking. I had to resort to the overflow lot, cursing the gravel that made my shoes dusty.

With a steadying breath, I opened the door with sweaty palms and stepped in. It was nicer than I remembered. A rich, savory smell of grilled filets filled the air. Several sets of eyes took me in as I stepped into Green Valley's nicest steak house.

I tried to evoke the aloof manner of a drummer who had played at Coachella. I tried not to need anybody here's approval, yet I hadn't felt so exposed since I was *literally* exposed to Mari in my front garden under my mother's wrap.

"Name on the reservation?" the hostess asked after setting down the phone.

I raised my eyebrow. Was she serious? The back of my neck burned as I glanced around at the patrons of the restaurant. Several people looked up at me, one of whom I was pretty sure was my former boss at Pizza Hut years ago. He narrowed his eyes. Oh right. I had left without telling him I wasn't coming back for a final shift. This was a bad idea. I shouldn't have come out.

Failure. Loser. Loner.

My eyes snagged on a familiar face in the back of the restaurant.

A wave of relief hit me when I spotted Mari helping set the band up in the corner, tightly squeezed in next to the swinging door that led to the kitchen.

48

"No. I'm just here to help Mari, uh, Miss Mitchell, with the band."

"Okay, you can go back. I think she's just gonna sit at the bar. You can order there, doll." She looked at the tablet on her stand, pushing back her bangs. "Otherwise, if you want to get a table, I won't be able to squeeze you in for a good hour."

"No worries. Bar's great." I gave her a tight smile and made my way across the restaurant, refusing to make eye contact with any single person. It was the same when I was on stage. I would blur out the crowd by focusing on a fixed point above their heads. If I couldn't see them, they didn't exist.

What the hell was I doing here? Where had this compulsion to see Mari again come from? I wasn't toying with her. If anything, I was toying with myself. As much as I understood wanting to help the kid, Mari needed to know some facts before she entrusted her pupil to me. So then, why had I acted like I was considering it when, after tonight, she wouldn't want anything to do with me?

I had to come clean and end this charade once and for all.

Something had shifted between us when she found me under the bleachers. It was like we finally found the groove of our interactions. Or at least it had changed for me. Our first meeting hadn't been friendly, but if I wasn't crazy, our last exchange had almost been flirty. She had almost smiled at least once.

Being around her coursed an energy through me like the rush I hadn't experienced since I nailed a particularly intense solo after hours of practice and everything clicked into place. A sort of confidence that gave me reckless excitement about the endless possibilities of the future.

She made me feel young. Or at least hopeful?

She glanced up as I approached, and her eyes widened after her gaze quickly flicked over me.

An instant surge of adrenaline pulsed through me once our eyes met.

Well, crap.

Was she happy to see me? Or was she happy for Cath? Did I care?

I must have, because why else was I here? Had her perspective of me changed, or was I still the spoiled little rock star who wouldn't help out? What I wouldn't give to have her look at me like I had potential instead of like I'd skipped her class to smoke weed.

Her mouth opened to a surprised little O before quickly clearing her features. She held up a finger to me—not the middle one, thankfully—before angling back to help the bassist tune. I took the opportunity to get a good look at her. Sue me. It was the first time I'd seen her hair down and styled. It was longer than I would have expected, with lighter pieces framing the edges in the low light of the glass candles on every table. It flowed past her shoulders in feathery, soft waves.

She bent forward slightly to hear the strings that the bassist plucked over the background noise of the restaurant. A dark purple dress made of soft cotton clung tightly to her waist before flaring out over her hips. A deep cut in the front set the creamy skin of her cleavage on full display. I really tried not to ogle it in front of her students and the fine diners of Green Valley. Tried and failed. A portion of her legs were revealed where the material came together, and her calves were nicely shaped.

She was even more beautiful than I'd thought.

I swallowed, and something in the back of my mind that had been napping sat up and paid attention. A cartoon hound dog with droopy heart eyes, rapidly stomping his hind leg, howled, "Ayywoooga!" One more peek and I was done.

The jazz quartet was setting up. It contained a stand-up bass, an electric keyboard, a muted trumpet, and Cath with her drum kit. I lifted my chin in hello.

The teen's brows pinched together, and she glanced away. I'd already made a stellar impression. Was she mad that I didn't talk to her at the homecoming game? Had Mari not told her I saw her? Maybe I should have gone and talked to her? It didn't matter. After tonight, I was sure I wouldn't see any of these people again. And okay, now why did that cause my chest to lurch?

I sighed and stopped a few feet away. This was exactly what I didn't need.

"Hey, you made it," Mari said in front of me. None of the ferocity in her gaze that had been there like at our first meeting. She seemed almost breathless and, well, not happy, but maybe cautiously optimistic?

"Who could turn down such a casual, nonthreatening invitation?" I asked as she shrugged innocently. "You look nice," I said. She froze. "Sorry. Shit. I'm not—that wasn't me making a pass. I only know you don't have a boyfriend because my mom told me you were single. And Clara. Small towns." Her brows crept higher for every piece of information that slipped out of my mouth. This was why it was always better not to speak. Once the words flowed, there was no mystery, just buffoonery. "You know how it is. And the Bunco Broads basically have a running checklist of every newsworthy thing happening in Green Valley. Not that you came up last time. They've mostly been filling me in on all I missed in the past ten years or so. Speaking of, did you know Sienna Diaz married Jethro Winston?"

Her features smoothed into an amused smirk. I really wished I'd stopped speaking after I said hi. Wait, had I even said hi? Was this my first night as a human on planet Earth? What was my deal?

50

"Wow. You really were out of the gossip loop. A lot more has happened since then." She stepped closer as a passing server brushed by with a full tray over their shoulder. The scent of sweet cherries and almonds drifted to meet me. "Next, you'll tell me you didn't know Kip Sylvester was murdered."

My jaw dropped. "What?" Dropping my head to whisper, I hunched over her. "Guess the Bunco Broads are slacking." I wasn't sure if she was messing with me. Her tone was dry, and her face, close enough that I could reach out and touch it, was difficult to read for humor. Another server brushed by us, and we penguin shuffled even closer. I was blocking the main thruway from the kitchen and couldn't remember how to normally navigate shared spaces with this cursed, lanky body.

"I should let you get back to it. I'm going to go get a drink at the bar." So I'd stop blabbering.

"They're actually good to go," she said. "I was going to go order some food."

There was an awkward exchange as we both looked to the bar to find the only available seats close together near the end.

"Why don't you—" I started.

At the same time, she said, "If you want company—"

This awkward fumbling was so much worse than her two-faced rage at my mom's. That at least had me playing the cool rock star persona, not whatever the hell this was. Band geek goes on his first date?

Not a date, bro. I could almost hear Vander in my mind, chuckling at me.

Mari had seemed like another person at that first meeting. But then, I hadn't been a dressed-up goober worried about giving her the right impression. This was why giving a shit about what people thought sucked nuts.

"After you." I gestured to the high-back bar chairs.

I definitely did not watch her ass as she walked to her seat. I pulled out her chair without thinking. She tucked her hair behind her ear as she sat. "Thanks."

This wasn't weird at all. The evening took an unexpected turn. There was too much pressure now. The low-light ambiance wasn't helping. How was I supposed to tell her my shortcomings in such a romantic atmosphere?

"Drink?" the bartender asked, setting down cocktail napkins.

"Yes," we both said instantly.

"And a food menu, please. House red is fine for me," Mari said.

"Just a beer," I said.

The bartender blinked. "Which kind?"

"There's more than one?" I asked, surprised. That always worked in the movies.

He turned to point out several taps. "We feature a few nearby breweries."

"Dark lager?" I asked, getting knocked down at least three cool points. Here I was, back in Green Valley, worrying about seeming cool. I hated this uneven footing I felt in a town that never wanted me.

He nodded and left to get our drinks.

"It's changed a bit around here since you left, I take it?" Mari asked.

Her legs were crossed, and the slit in her dress went to her midthigh. I cleared my throat and focused on maintaining eye contact.

"I wouldn't have thought Green Valley would have gotten on the craft beer bandwagon," I said.

"Cities change, people change."

"Not that much."

Her mouth pursed just before she opened it to speak. Whatever she'd been about to say was interrupted by the stand-up bassist, a massive teen with a bobbing Adam's apple and ruddy cheeks. "Uh, sorry." His head barely lifted to make quick eye contact with my chin when he apologized before turning to Mari. "Miss Mitchell, my bridge slipped again."

"Not your fault, Nathan. It's these ancient instruments." She stood, tugging her dress in place subtly. "Be right back," she said to me. "Get us an app?" she asked.

I stared at the small bar menu, unable to decide what she would like best, not knowing if she was even vegetarian or had any other dietary restrictions. What if I picked something she hated? Better to give options.

After I ordered, I watched her fix the bass and re-tune it. As she was walking away, the trumpet player asked her a question that had her checking the mute, and then the keyboardist kept getting feedback from one of the microphones. She was patient and kind with each interaction, seemingly unbothered by the garbage instruments they were working with. The kids looked at her . . . like I looked at Dave Grohl the one time he walked past me backstage in Chicago—still one of the best moments of my life.

She ended up snapping a tempo to get them started. Her hips rocked, causing the light material of her dress to sway off her ass in a pleasing manner. After they got started, she backed away to let them do their own thing, encouraging them to listen to and play off each other as was required for jazz. They weren't half bad. The keyboardist was a little timid, and the bassist slightly ahead, but honestly, they looked and sounded pretty damn cool. Except Cath's drum kit seemed held together with duct tape and pure determination. It reminded me of my first drum kit, down to the collection of stickers on the side of the kick drum.

Wait.

I leaned closer, trying to see in the dark. There's no way the school still used the same shitty drum kit from when I went there.

My jaw was on the floor when Mari returned. She grabbed a mozzarella stick and fried pickle, barely sitting down before tossing a bit of each back. "Still better at Genie's," she said, double-fisting the snack food. "Whoa, did you order the whole menu?" She glanced at the spread of every appetizer on their menu currently jammed into our small bit of bar space.

"I wasn't sure what I wanted," I lied. I was glaring toward Cath.

The drummer looked up, her eyes widened, and she stumbled over the tempo before finding her footing again.

Shit, that glare wasn't meant for her.

Mari glanced at Cath and back to me. "Fix your face." I saw her hackles rise, waiting to defend her student. When I did, she asked, "What's wrong?"

"I'm trying to figure out if that's the same drum kit I used when I went there."

Mari turned to the band, who had just started with a slow, easy tune. The crease between her brow smoothed. "Oh, yeah. Probably."

"How is it even still in one piece?" I asked. Another wave of guilt broke over my head like a crashing cymbal, imagining my top-of-the-line kit sitting covered and unloved in the basement of Janice's.

"I don't know that it is one piece. Are you really that surprised, though? Funding for art and music is always lowest on the district's priority list. That's definitely not changed since you went here. If Principal Pin Dick has his way, all funds would go to the sports teams, and the music programs would be cut totally. He thinks it's a waste of time and money. Hence, twenty-year-old drum kits." She took another bite, doing the mouth huff thing of someone whose food was too hot. The woman ate like she was running out of time. Didn't anybody feed her? I would make sure she always had food, the way she was constantly on the run. After she swallowed with a wince, she said, "And broken music stands and barely any rehearsal space. Damn, these are good. Did you try those yet?" She pointed at the shrimp cocktail. I shook my head and grabbed one.

"That's why there are five different coaches, and one Mari doing every music class outside choir?" I asked as she shrugged. "How can you afford anything?"

"Begging."

I snorted.

"I'm serious." She leaned closer to whisper, "I'm close to selling my panties online. I'm kidding." I froze and felt the temperature of the restaurant go up five degrees. She waited a beat, then added, "Mostly. No. I just go around to all the business owners and ask for donations. We offer to put on shows and performances like this in the hopes that they are willing when I ask for donations. Which reminds me." She glanced at the bartender and waved him over. "Is the owner here?"

"Yeah, back in his office. Want me to get him?"

"Nah. Thanks, though."

After he walked away, she leaned closer to whisper again. I didn't mind. "Better if I go back there uninvited and catch him off guard before he can think of an excuse not to donate." The action caused her knees to brush against mine. Ever more electricity pulsed through me. I was definitely attracted to this woman, and more than that, the tenacity that fueled her.

"Vicious," I said after a swallow.

"Well, you have to be." She shrugged and grabbed a loaded potato skin.

I chomped on a shrimp, feeling more sick with every bite. It wasn't expired seafood that was the culprit. It was witnessing how hard Mari was working herself to the bone for this small high school band. And for what? Most of these kids wouldn't even think about music after they left school.

On the drums, Cath gently moved her brushes around the snare, eyes almost closed as she listened to the others around her. For every hundred students who just wanted an easy elective, there were the kids like Cath and myself. Kids who dreamed big and had souls fueled by music. Kids who had music so tied into their identity they didn't know who they were without it.

This couldn't be dragged out any longer. I needed to tell Mari.

"You said your family was supposed to visit?" my mouth blurted. That was not the plan. That was the opposite of the plan.

She glanced to the side before she took a large gulp of her wine, taking a moment to debate something. "They were supposed to come in last weekend. It didn't work out."

She'd said it lightly enough, as if passing on the weather report, but I had briefly glimpsed a tension to her shoulders when my mother had asked about them. Many Green Valley families were large and interconnected. Janice's former stepmother, Belle Cooper, had several ex-husbands, and there were so many Hill family members, nobody could keep track. Who would she have to rely on for help if her immediate family wasn't around?

"Sorry to hear that."

"It's fine. It's hard to coordinate our schedules." She cleared her throat.

"I'm used to being the pushy, sad woman who devotes all her life to her students."

"Not sad. Admirable," I blurted. It felt too honest. I quickly added, "Better than the washed-up musician who sits around being . . . what did you call me? An entitled, spoiled brat?"

"Something like that." She winced. "I'm sorry for all the name-calling."

"Not the marching band?"

"No, that was hilarious. But my anger may have been a little bit misplaced. I was just feeling—" She changed her mind midsentence. "I was just really tired."

I cleared my throat uncomfortably, deciding what to say to this news. I wanted to reach for her and tell her that her family had no idea what they were missing, but since she had been calling me names not so long ago, she may not take much stock in my opinions.

"Sorry. Way too heavy," she joked and finished her glass of wine. "So, tell me about your garden. You seem weirdly attached to it, but convince me it's totally normal behavior for a man your age."

She shifted the topic off her before I could ask more.

I would get around to telling her why I was here. Eventually.

But for now, the food was good, the environment was better, and the company was the best. We chatted for a while. I may not have convinced her why gardening was totally normal and not at all weird, but she didn't poke fun. Not as much fun, at least. Our knees bumped two different times before the quartet packed up for the night and left after saying their goodbyes.

Our knees bumped five more times after that. And one bonus arm touch. She lightly dropped her hand onto mine while laughing hard at one of my Bunco Broads stories.

Our plates and glasses had been cleared a while ago. We sipped decaf coffees and were running out of things to order. We sat so long that the Saturday dinner rush settled into a few tables of couples close together, arms wrapped around each other. This had been one of the best nights I'd had in a long time. Maybe my mom was right, and I was hiding out. Was Mari feeling the same? Or was this part of the charm she used to get her donations?

But if she was having a nice time like I was, what came next would suck even harder. The realization made me sick. I was about to disappoint this woman, and I never wanted to do that.

"So now all these moms are constantly finding excuses to come into the school and go to the car wash. Actually, our PTA volunteer numbers have never been so high." She laughed, finishing her story.

I chuckled too, but had only partially listened. Not just because the story was about a hot guy at her work but because the more charming and quick-witted she was, the longer she spoke, the harder it was not to fall for her. She was cool and tenacious, not to mention a total knockout.

"I need to tell you something," I blurted.

She held my gaze for a moment, eyes narrowing. "Did you know that your mom mentored me when I was in high school? I think you were in freshman band, so I didn't know you." The tension in my shoulders tightened.

I pushed down the words that had been about to spill out. "No. I don't think she mentioned it," I said dryly. I didn't love where this was going.

"She wouldn't, would she, as modest as she is?" She pushed away her empty mug and sat forward. "If it wasn't for her, I would have never even applied to college or pursued a career in music theory. She was so supportive of my moderate, at best, talent."

I shifted uncomfortably and glanced around the place. There was nobody to save me.

"It only takes one person to change the whole trajectory of a life. I'm sure you had someone who believed in you unconditionally and supported you."

"Same person, actually," I said with a huff. "She's . . . one of the most giving women I know."

"She really is. You see where I'm going with this, right?"

"I mean, it's so subtle, but I'm picking up something."

"Ah, and just when I thought you put your sarcasm away for the night."

"No, it's always there, lurking just below the surface." I tugged at my hair, realizing now that the curls were long since freed from their gel prison. "But I really need to tell you something. I can't help—"

"Oh, hell no." The anger I'd witnessed briefly had returned, and I braced myself.

CHAPTER 9
MARI

I t was the first time Leo had appeared genuinely scared, a reaction I'd grown accustomed to from the residents of Green Valley, but tonight, it bothered me. I blamed the anxious undertone to our evening on the fact that I'd worn this ridiculous dress on the chance he'd show up.

And then, when he'd stepped up wearing all black, hair styled, beard trimmed short, and looking like he made a genuine effort, my heart had stuttered, temporarily distracted from the goal. As the night went on and our conversation extended, his nerves grew.

He was going to tell me no, and I refused to accept that answer. I dragged out the evening as long as possible. Told stories about the kids, about the money struggles. It wasn't exactly torture to hang out with the guy, either. He turned out to be pretty funny, and his admiration of Janice was incredibly sweet. When he started a new story or was particularly excited about something, he'd grip his thick curls and tug them back. Or if he was getting ready to tell me bad news. Like right now.

"But I really need to tell you something. I can't help—" Leo started.

I looked up to see the owner of the Front Porch trying to sneak out the back door. "Oh, hell no!"

I grabbed my bag and stood.

"Wait? Where're you going?" He stood too, reaching for his wallet.

"I got it." I beeped my watch against the machine the bartender had ready and extended to me. "You get the tip."

Leo's eyes widened. "They take e-payments now?"

I rolled my eyes. "I have to go. He's leaving out the back."

Leo threw down a few bills that would have covered our meal and not just a nice tip. "Wait, I'll go with you."

"Don't worry about it. I'm not sure how long this will take. You can go." I sped away, through the kitchen, not worrying about the surprised faces of staff finishing their closing duties.

"Mari, wait. I still need to talk to you." Leo was right on my heels, reaching for my arm.

"Shoot. He's as slippery as an eel. That tight-fisted so-and-so," I mumbled into the rest of my cursing.

"Can you slow down?" Leo asked, bringing me to a stop.

"Not really. My only setting is wogging. Don't slow me down." I brushed him off.

He growled and continued to follow me. "I really need to tell you something."

"And I really don't have time to hear it right now." My excuses quota had been reached for the month.

The owner was already in his running car when I stepped out to the back parking lot. He glanced up at me and rushed to start backing out before even buckling, pretending we hadn't locked eyes.

"Oh, that *sonofa*!" I would chase after him. I would leech myself to his hood if that's what it took to get his dang attention. The students needed these donations. People needed to stop trying to get away from me.

Leo lurched forward to stop me by grabbing my arm. I twisted out of his grip easily.

"Now who's slippery as an eel." He hooked his arms around my waist, and I beat at his hands. "What is your plan here?"

I stopped struggling and turned in his arms. "Are you laughing?"

He chuckled more. "I'm sorry." He tried to clear his features. "It's just nice not to be the one receiving your wrath."

"I can't believe he just left. He saw me. We made eye contact."

"Maybe if you weren't chasing after him with that look in your eyes."

I stomped my heel, my anger making me shake.

"That's the look." He leaned back.

His arms were still locked around my hips. An awareness of spreading heat coursed through me. He swallowed as he took me in. My hands were fisted and tight to my chest. The effect had my cleavage pushed up. We both noticed that at the same time.

58

"I am so sick of people saying one thing and doing another. He said he would talk to me tonight about donations. I'm not just chasing him randomly." Anger burned me up, but I heard my mother's voice again telling me to control my temper. I ground my jaw and threw out my arms. They flopped to the outside of his embrace and now it was a loose impression of two people dancing. "Just another disappointing person in my life."

His mouth dropped open before closing again, jaw clenching. He looked at our tangled bodies and freed me to step back.

"Just out with it, Leo. Give me your excuses and reasons why you don't have time or resources. I've heard it all." Absurdly, the anger was morphing back into that gaping pain I'd felt alone in my apartment.

His head dropped, telling me that I was correct in my understanding of where this conversation was headed. What sort of man would toy with me— with *Cath* like this? Show up to hear her play twice just to make an excuse not to help her. How could he see her play at all and not believe in her?

He mumbled something.

"I don't understand you." I crossed my arms over my body. The fall weather had finally settled into the evenings, but my posture was more about the frustration leaving my body and being replaced by the familiar acceptance of disappointment.

"I was fired." He clenched his jaw, emphasizing a pulse at his temple. "I didn't quit The Burnouts. I was fired."

"Fired?" I blinked in confusion, recalling every rumor I'd heard in the months since he'd been back—artistic differences, big ego, early retirement— and fired wasn't one of them.

"Yes." He swallowed. "Everybody thinks I retired. I didn't exactly correct the rumors, for obvious reasons." His hand went to the back of his neck. "We all signed NDAs and probably you will need to now also."

I frowned at the ground. Wouldn't Janice have mentioned that? Or Devlin? But clearly, this was a confession few people knew about. Maybe I shouldn't have taught the kids to play his former band's big hit. It was funny at the time, but after seeing the embarrassment in his lack of eye contact, it was definitely a bad move.

"That's fine. About the NDA . . ." I said, still processing.

"Yeah?"

"I'm not a gossip just because I live here. You don't have to worry about me blabbing." I thought about my goss sessions with Clara at Genie's, but that hardly felt relevant to share at this time.

"Hmm, that look you just made makes me think you're lying."

"Thank you for telling me," I said. "I still don't get why you won't help Cath."

It was true. Whatever his reasons, his talent was there. And more importantly, he was here. He spun in a circle, groaning as he tugged on the back of his neck with both hands. When he turned back to face me, his cheeks were flushed. "I have no degree. I was fired from the only job I ever had, and I haven't played the drums since I was kicked out by my best friend." His chest heaved.

The back lot was abandoned this late. The sun had gone down long ago, but the one buzzing overhead light cast enough of a glow to see him perfectly. "That's it?" I asked after looking back at him.

"That's not enough?"

"Can you physically not play anymore?"

He frowned. "No. I probably could."

"And you aren't morally opposed to Cath playing?" I asked, my defenses on edge.

"No." He shook my head, confused. "Why would I be?"

I ignored that question. "I don't understand what the issue is, then."

"The issue is, you were right. I'm a washed-up rock star with no life plans and absolutely no skills. Who the hell am I to get this girl into college? I couldn't even get into college. I'm a loser. You know it. This whole town knows it. I'm the last person who should be helping Cath."

I never said any of that. I might have thought it though, and now I regretted my earlier assumptions as I studied the tortured man.

"Is that it?" I repeated.

"Again, is that not enough?" He huffed air out of his nose in a scoff.

"No. It's not. Quite frankly, I would only accept a few very legitimate reasons."

"Like what?"

"I'm absolutely not telling you that now."

"Mari. Come on, you have to see I'm not the right fit. I don't get why you're pushing this so much."

My determination surprised us both, but once I decided something, I wasn't easily dissuaded. Cath needed a tutor, and Janice thought this would help Leo. This was how I helped my community and gave back.

"I completely disagree about you being a loser. You have talent. You have passion. I've seen you play." His eyebrows moved up in surprise. "But none of that matters. More than anything, Cath needs someone to believe in her.

60

Someone who gets what it's really going to take. She's so close to something, but she's holding back in her playing, and I'm not there enough to help her get to it. She needs somebody who understands what it's really about."

"What what's about?" he asked.

I gave him an incredulous look. "The art. The music. That fire that burns deep and needs the constant source of fuel to grow into something huge."

His eyes moved over my face. His chest still heaved from his outburst, but his eyes gentled. He got it. He could pretend to be scared, but he knew exactly what I was talking about.

"Don't get me wrong, her parents are incredibly supportive, but they aren't artists. They've never had that burning desire to be great. That drive that pushes you to practice and practice until you're literally bleeding." My palms tingled, and I could summon that feeling of wanting something so bad it was all I could think about. My heart raced in my chest. "Music is everything to her. And once upon a time, it was everything to you."

"And look where it got me," he mumbled.

Now, I scoffed loudly. "Do you mean your years of successful touring with one of the biggest rock bands from Tennessee? Or the house that your talent was able to purchase for your mom? Is that what you mean? Because that's what I mean." He looked up, brow creased. "Get your head out of your ass, Cooper, and step up for this kid. She's already going to be at a disadvantage going into college. Especially if—*when* she gets into Berklee. So many of these kids come from a world of private tutors and music conservatories. She has raw talent, but she needs the passion and the drive. Like you once had.

"Be the person who she talks to about all this stuff. That part of your life may be over, but it's just beginning for her. And you have the opportunity to be that person who takes her to the next level. Help give this kid her shot."

If my words hadn't sunk in now, if this hadn't motivated him after he shared this burden, then there was no helping him.

"I'll see you Monday at three fifteen. Check in with the front office first, then meet us in the band room." I tugged my purse up higher on my shoulder. I had done everything I could. "Slash choir room slash sometimes dance and yoga studio."

I walked away with my head held high. Then I turned around and passed him again. "My car is actually in the other lot." I lifted my chin. I'd almost made it out of there with my excellent and powerful speech hanging in the air when he finally spoke.

"You'll be hearing from my lawyer," he said.

I froze and turned. Had I actually gone too far this time?

His mouth quirked. "I was serious about the NDA."

I nodded and left him standing out there. My body shook with nerves all the way home until I turned on my street. Only then did I let myself smile. It hadn't been a yes.

But it hadn't been a no, either.

CHAPTER 10
LEO

Most of the following Monday was spent staring at the clock. Even the garden was off-limits to my anxious pacing. I was too twitchy and wound up and didn't want to bring that bad energy around my plants.

By three o'clock, my pit sweat made it seem like I'd been practicing for hours and not sitting still, paralyzed by decision fatigue.

The memory of Mari's impassioned defense of music finally had me move off my bed. She understood the power of passion and worked so hard for her students that I would have to be a monster not to help, now that the truth was out.

I put everything on the proverbial table—the reason for my exit from The Burnouts—yet she was still convinced I was the person to help Cath get into the school of her dreams. I wiped my palms on my jeans and stood. *Just go. Meet Cath and come back to the safety of the house.*

Downstairs, Janice was shrugging into a light coat and reaching for the keys.

Worry spread through me, tingling the tips of my fingers.

"Where are you going?" I asked, my Adam's apple tight in my throat.

Janice pressed a hand to her chest. "For crying out loud, you startled me." She looked me up and down. "Where are you going?"

I glanced at my phone. I needed to leave now. "I'm supposed to go to the school to meet Cath. I didn't know you needed the car."

"Why didn't you tell me? I've been here all day." She sighed and looked at her watch. "I have plans in town. Can I drop you off?"

As if it wasn't bad enough to be going back to school, now I had to have my mom take me.

"Is it on the way?" I asked as I looked at my phone again. "I have to be there in fifteen."

"You won't be late." She still hadn't mentioned where she was going, but my anxiety was ratcheted even higher with this unexpected hiccup. I wasn't even positive I was going until I came down to get the car keys, but now this felt like a sign.

"No, no. Don't make that face," Janice said, reading my thoughts as only a mom could. "We have plenty of time. But let's leave right now. The roads are slick."

In the car, Janice put a hand on my jumping leg. "I think it's very lovely that you're agreeing to help Cath." She maneuvered carefully on the short drive into town, but I was so nervous, I couldn't unclench myself enough to respond.

Every time the sick crept up my throat, I replayed Mari's impassioned speech. She wouldn't have asked me if she didn't think I could help. This wasn't some elaborate ruse to lure me back to high school just to mock me. As rain beat down on the windshield, I was beat down with a hundred memories I'd repressed or replaced with The Burnouts' drum solos and screaming fans.

But now, even those memories of playing on stage were tainted. Was nothing in my past safe to think about? I didn't want to be back here, where all of my biggest insecurities made me feel like a loser. This place where I was bullied and laughed at. The place that had felt like a prison to my teenage self. If my mom hadn't been a teacher here, if Vander hadn't been there to have my back, it would have been so much worse. Why had I agreed to do this?

Mari. Well, Cath. Of course. But the thought of letting Mari down hurt worse than the pain of harmless memories. At least those were in the past.

Janice turned into the school zone way too soon. I wasn't sure that my knees would hold me up. This was ridiculous. I was a grown man who, by all outward appearances, was a huge success. I didn't need to hold on to the past like this. I just wished my body didn't act like it was being chased by cheetahs. Janice pulled up front to drop me off, and I stared at the entrance of the building. Wasn't it supposed to seem smaller now?

I hadn't had anxiety like this since backstage before a show. This clammy, fuzzy-headed terror made every obstacle seem insurmountable. This was why leaving the house was extremely overrated.

"Come on, now." Janice rubbed a circle on my back. Absolutely absurd that the small gesture had my throat tightening. "I haven't seen you like this in a while. Are you okay?"

I glanced over at her, and worry creased her brow. I could almost see her berating herself for encouraging me to get out of the house. If nothing else, I needed to be strong for her. She'd been my rock year after year; I wouldn't let my issues become hers. I forced a smile. "I'm okay. Just weird being back here."

Janice squeezed my shoulder. "Focus on all that you've accomplished. It's just a building. You're in control. And you're doing a really great thing."

I nodded, and she hugged me with one arm.

"Call me when you want me to come get you, okay?"

Hearing her say that in this place was like being thrown back in time. I was sixteen and being driven to school after sleeping in because my anxiety was so bad I couldn't get out of bed.

I nodded and jumped out of the car with a final goodbye, sprinting to the doors to avoid being soaked. Once inside, the sinking dread of these familiar hallways made my feet heavy as I made my way to the front office.

Once I was checked in, I was about to be escorted to the band room when Mari came wogging past—her words, not mine. I would never say wogging in real life.

"Mari," I called after her. She came to a halt, and I expected her shoes to make that squeal of tires braking too fast. To the office aide, I said, "Can she take me from here?"

"Of course, dear," she said with a smile.

"Where's the fire?" I asked Mari. Some of the tension I'd been feeling relaxed away at the sight of her.

"Leo? Oh. Hey." She glanced at her watch. "Lord, is it time already?"

"Yep." Wasn't I a chump for watching the clock the entire day when she barely remembered that we were supposed to meet?

This Mari was a far cry from the breezy, relaxed version I'd glimpsed after a boatload of appetizers and a glass of red wine. Her hair was tossed up in a knot on her head with a pencil holding it in place. Her eyes wouldn't sit still as they flicked through the mass of students exiting for the day. She shrugged out of a cardigan worn over a sleeveless silk top, fanning herself.

"Everything okay?" I asked, hands deep in the pockets of my jeans. My skin itched all over. Even though she was just a couple of years older than me, I had the same uncomfortable feeling I would have had being stopped by a teacher fifteen years ago.

Several passing students watched our exchange, and I pretended not to notice their curious glances.

"No. I've been running around like a greased-up pig all day. And now the flipping cherry on top is that Principal Pi—" She paused, remembering her surroundings. "Mr. Pindich told the football team they could use the rehearsal space to set up their free weights."

"Can they do that?"

"They do sometimes. And normally, it's—well, it's not great because they leave puddles of sweat and little cups of water everywhere, and it'll smell like feet for the next couple of days, but at least it doesn't impact our rehearsals. But I specifically booked the room for you and Cath to practice."

"Assumptive," I said.

"Optimistic," she countered. "But now it doesn't even matter because twenty stinky boys are currently doing push-ups in there."

"Isn't there a classroom we could use? Push some desks aside?" Look at me with all the ideas.

"That's what I was in the process of finding out. Worse case, maybe outside?"

"It's raining," I said, afraid to push her any further into her frustration.

"Of course it is." She tossed out her arms. "And theater club is currently using the performing arts center and I can't imagine they want a drum solo in the middle of *Guys and Dolls*. Oh shoot! That reminds me, I need to see what band kids want to be in the pit for that show." She pressed her fingertips to her forehead. "It's almost like one person shouldn't be doing the jobs of ten different people." She mumbled the last bit to herself.

A very bad, no-good idea was clawing its way out of my brain. I kept my mouth clamped tight.

"Cath has to be at work tonight by seven." She waved the thought away like it wasn't important right now. "One thing at a time, Mitchell."

This was it. This was the perfect time to back out of here and dust my hands of this whole thing. Except . . . what was this nagging feeling that was making it hard to breathe? Was this . . . guilt?

Ugh.

"And if that wasn't bad enough, her crash cymbal bit the bullet." Mari went on, a screw being twisted tighter in my chest, thinking of that decrepit old kit. "I mean, it's still usable, technically, but a giant chunk broke off. I swear I saw Miles and Cassius messing with it after performance band practice today. We're getting ready for the Fall Festival. You should come, by the way. They're going to do a whole thing. Oh, I already told you about that." She waved her hand again, wiping away another tangent from the air in front of her. I was genuinely scared to know what the inside of her mind looked like right now. "So now, I have to search through the instrument closet to see if, by some miracle, there is an extra cymbal in there."

Yes, I should definitely leave. I would only make things worse. I wasn't exactly a soothing balm to her nerves. There was nothing I could do here.

"Well, it seems like you have your hands full. I should probably get out of—"

Just then, Cath walked up. Outside of her marching band uniform and jazz night attire, she looked like any average teenager, or what I assumed teenagers looked like. I never hung out with them. She was in a giant hoodie, black leggings, and Converse shoes and gripped the straps of her backpack like they were the only thing holding her to the earth.

"Hey," I said with a wave.

She made a sound of greeting. Or was she clearing her throat? Jury was still out. "Hey, Miss Mitchell," she said to Mari.

"Oh hey, Cath. We're working on getting a room now. Don't worry."

"It's fine." Her cheeks burned as she glared pointedly at the floor.

"No. It's not fine. I booked the room. This is why we have a system in place." Mari's head shot to the left. "There he is!" She scurried after the retreating form of a man in an ugly brown suit.

Déjà vu.

Was my life now chasing after Mari as she chased after slightly scared-looking middle-aged men?

"Principal Pindich," she called. I swore his shoulders went to his ears before he stopped and turned around, a smarmy smile in place.

"Hello, Mary."

"Mariam," she corrected. "The rehearsal room was booked on the shared calendar. The JV team needs to move elsewhere."

"My hands are tied," he said.

Mari spoke again. "That's not good enough. Why even have a shared calendar if we aren't going to follow it?"

He sighed and tilted his head, looking downright condescending. "All right. Calm down," he said to Mari, whose ears were bright red and nostrils were flaring. I snorted softly. This was calm. Wait until she really got angry. But then he looked at me for the first time. "Women, right?"

The man was too stunned to speak. Was he looking toward me for commiseration? We were not on the same team, sir. We weren't even living in the same world.

"And you are?" he asked me. Thankfully, he didn't extend a hand because I would not be shaking it. He glanced at the visitor badge stuck to my tee. "Wait a minute. That hair, those gangly limbs. *Leonard.* You're the big famous drummer. Couldn't stay away from home sweet home."

"Something like that," I mumbled.

I wished I had a better comeback than that. For the next week, this would be a future shower conversation where I'd spit the perfectly caustic response to my body wash. He'd managed to cut me down with one barb. Too bad he couldn't use that precision on his overgrown pine out front.

Dammit, that would have been a good comeback.

"Well, let's hope you picked the right person, Mary," Pin Dick said with a final disapproving scowl at me. "Sorry about the practice. Maybe next time." He turned to Cath. "Michael, hope you understand."

Cath stared at the floor just in front of her feet and nodded once.

Pin Dick left without another word.

"What a dick," I said. I didn't even bother trying to be quiet because he scuttled out of there as fast as he could anyway.

"Hence the name," Mari mumbled, but her worried gaze was set on Cath. I was so taken aback by the outdated sexism and passive-aggressive bullying that it took me long after he walked away to process what he'd said.

"What's that guy's deal with names?" I asked, turning back to them both.

The ladies exchanged a glance.

"He never remembers my name. Or at least, he pretends not to. I've worked here for years now, but I guess he can't be bothered. Shows just how important he is," Mari said, oddly defeated. I'd expect her to She-Hulk rage out and chase after him, leaving potholes where she stepped. I was looking forward to it, honestly.

This morose acceptance was much worse.

"He's deadnaming me," Cath said stonily.

My mouth snapped shut. I already decided I hated the guy since my mother complained about his tree, and then even more the first night Mari talked about him. Witnessing him firsthand was rage-inducing. This was more than a small-dick, insecure man pulling his power around. This was absolute bullshit.

I had a taste of the anger that motivated Mari. The red-out of my brain, short-circuited decision-making.

I felt protective of Cath and Mari and the whole systematic injustice of assholes like this who crushed programs they never deemed worthy. I might not have much to offer, but I had some experience.

That settled it. I was a lot of things, probably most of them weren't great.

But I had been bullied my whole childhood, and I couldn't stand a bully. Mari and Cath seemed to inherently understand that giving him a reaction was exactly what he fed off. So then be it. I had an idea, and he could fuck all the way off.

I didn't want to be here, and I sure as hell did not want to have to see that guy again. He reminded me of every mediocre loser who wielded whatever power they had on those they knew were powerless against them. By using the name that Cath was born with and had not chosen, he was purposely hurting her. I would help Cath because I had the ability to, but then I would go back to my life of solitude.

"There is one other option." I heaved a sigh. And I was probably going to regret it.

CHAPTER 11
MARI

Leo was stone silent and still as I drove us to his mom's house. He wouldn't tell me his big idea, saying he'd rather I saw it first. It was agreed that the practice wasn't going to happen today, after all, despite my best efforts. Cath got a ride to work at Pizza Hut early, ever eager to pick up some extra cash. She'd been hard to read as she walked away, and I wasn't sure if she was relieved or disappointed with the turn of events.

I tugged the pencil free and let my hair loose. I had so much residual tension in my body from this day, I felt like I could snap. There was so much to do, and nothing felt like it was going right.

I tried not to feel defeated as the rain outside matched my mood: stormy and melodramatic. Some days, it felt like the world conspired against me. I wanted Cath to have everything she could possibly need to set her up for success, but if her and Leo's first interactions were any indication of what was to come, the months until her audition in late February were going to be an uphill battle.

Leo seemed to be faring no better to my right. He hadn't even made a snarky comment when I had to move stacks of paper, sheet music, and several travel mugs from the passenger seat. I'd managed to shove the bra into my gym bag of extra performance clothes I kept in the car just in case before he saw. He spotted my copy of the signed NDA at the top of the stack, and he frowned.

"I emailed it in. It's just my copy." I didn't want him to think I didn't take his privacy seriously.

"No. I know." His thumb tapped repeatedly against his knee.

"Are you okay?"

"Just wondering why you're so sure I can help Cath," he said.

He glanced at me with such vulnerability I was hit with a wave of compassion. I gripped the steering wheel tighter. Janice had suggested the idea, Devlin had the same, and Cath was totally on board, even if she was hard to read through her teenage angst. It would be incredibly shortsighted if I let my own biases get in the way.

"Why not you? Green Valley isn't overrun with proficient drummers," I said simply.

"And what if I don't help?"

"She's good enough to get in. I just want her to have perspective."

"What does that mean?" he asked.

"She's so focused on being perfect. I can't explain it, but my gut says you will help." Cath was so focused on technical perfection that I wasn't sure she even enjoyed playing anymore. Hopefully, Leo would keep her in touch with the joy of drumming as only another drummer could.

I didn't want him to feel pressure and risk him scurrying back into hiding. Whatever he wanted to show me was related to Cath. I thought Leo was a shallow, easy-to-read guy, but the man had depth, and I wished I could hear his thoughts.

Leo was silent until we pulled up to his driveway. Rain crashed in unrelenting waves against the windshield. "You can just park in front of the garage. We might have to move your car before my mom gets back."

I nodded and did as directed. I shot a glare at Pin Dick's house as I put the car into park. I couldn't even let myself think about that interaction because of how angry it made me. But guys like him only ever wanted a reaction, and he wouldn't get that from me. A towering pine shared the property line next to the driveway and caused a pause in the relentless splatter of rain. Only the occasional drop plopped loudly onto the windshield now.

"Should we make a run for it?" I asked.

He hadn't yet unbuckled, still seeming distracted and bothered.

"Is he always like that?" Leo asked.

I assumed he meant the principal. "Pretty much."

"How do you handle it? How does he get away with it?"

"Guys like that manage to always come up on top." I glared at his house, an average ranch style that looked perfectly normal from the outside, with no sign that an absolute jerk lived inside. "I believe the only thing I can do is prosper despite them. When Cath plays Carnegie Hall or whatever makes her happy, I will be more than happy to rub that in his face. So maybe I am a little spiteful."

He looked at me closely, swallowing as his gaze roamed over my features. Did my eye makeup smear? Or was that look something else . . .

"I hate bullies," he said.

"Me too."

He nodded once. "Okay. Let's go in. We can run to the side door and into the kitchen."

He counted to three, and we sprinted to the side of the house. We were breathless and laughing by the time we slid to a stop to close the door behind us. Leo shook his curls out like a dog, and I held up my hands to block the spray.

When he looked up, his gaze moved behind me. His eyes widened in happy surprise. "Oh, hey, Janice."

Leo's mom blinked in surprise from where she'd been filling a cup of water at the sink.

"Hi, Mari. Leo," she said and covered her shock with a friendly smile. "I thought you were gonna call when you wanted to get picked up?" She wore a silk robe, which she tugged closed, hiding a flushed chest.

"Change of plans. You weren't kidding. That new principal is a real piece of work."

"I've heard." Janice frowned. "I'm glad I never had to work with him. Though his predecessor wasn't any better."

"Weren't you going out?" Leo asked.

I looked at Leo as the tension in the room grew. Did he not see her flushed cheeks? Or the way she kept glancing to the stairs that led to the second floor?

He tilted his head. "Why are you wearing a robe?"

Captain Oblivious.

"I love a rainstorm bath," I said quickly. "Nothing better than hearing the rain fall as you soak."

Janice nodded gratefully at me. "Yes, dear. I suddenly didn't feel well and thought I'd come home and take a bath."

"Oh no," he said, genuinely buying the excuse. "Can I make you anything? Soup? Tea?"

"No. No. I'm fine." He pressed the backs of his fingers to her forehead as she protested. "Oh, stop I'm fine."

"You do seem warm." Leo spoke in an attempt at stern. "You go take it easy. We won't be long."

"Leo just wanted to show me . . . ." I trailed off because I didn't know.

"Beatrice and the kids," Leo provided.

Janice's eyebrows shot up. I was more confused than ever. Did he have a secret family? A pet cat that had kittens?

"You'll be going to the basement, then?" Janice asked.

And . . . my confusion grew.

"Yes, but we will be quiet. Don't you worry."

"Wha—" I lifted a finger as though to ask a question but nothing came out.

"Oh, pishposh." She waved him away. "Take your time."

"We will," I said. Even if I had no idea what was going on, I could help Janice by getting Leo downstairs quickly. "Enjoy your bath."

I sent her a final smile before I followed Leo to a door off the kitchen and she made her way to the stairs going up.

Leo flicked a light switch that illuminated a set of old wooden stairs heading into the basement. "Watch your step. These are steep and have no handrail."

I followed him closely as we descended, my eyes adjusting to the mostly dark area as I pondered what had just transpired upstairs. Janice had been single as long as I had known her, or at least incredibly private.

"Do you think your mom will ever date again?" I asked gently.

"Janice?" He laughed. "No. No. I don't think so. Janice was never a big believer in relationships."

I rolled my eyes behind his back. Men were so oblivious sometimes.

"Though I definitely think she's hooking up with someone now," he added.

The surprise of his comment caused me to misjudge the last step. He turned in time to catch me before I face-planted. I was in his arms, and the height of the step put me at eye level with him for once. His dark eyes moved over my face. We were so close and that heat was back. He smelled *good*, even wet from the rain. Masculine and fresh and a hint of sweaty.

I found my footing, and he gently set me back on the ground. "Thanks," I said. "I wasn't sure if you had any thoughts on all that." I pointed at the first floor.

"She wasn't exactly subtle up there, was she?" he asked.

I sucked in my lips. "You may want to start knocking before you come home," I said. He wasn't as clueless as I'd thought. Leo continued to defy my expectations of him.

He huffed a laugh but also squished his face up in a wince. "She clearly isn't ready to talk about whoever is upstairs, and quite frankly, I'm not sure I want to hear it. I don't know if that makes me immature, but there it is." He tugged at his damp curls, which had begun to fluff out. "As long as she's happy." He sighed. "I guess there can be complications with having your mom as your best friend."

I couldn't help the little tug on my heart. That was so damn sweet. And only a tiny bit weird. "I'm sure she'll tell you when she's ready."

"Mama's boy struggles," he teased himself and then added, "Good album name."

I snorted. I loved commitment to a bit.

He nodded, holding my gaze for another second. "Well, anyway." He gestured to a massive black shadow in the corner and said, "There's Beatrice and the kids."

"Is she a grill?"

He chuckled. "Not quite." He went over to the dark shape, flicking another light on the way.

The metallic *sizzle* of cymbals filled the room as he whipped off a dusty sheet.

I gasped. "Wow, they're beautiful."

Tiny dust motes danced in the stream of light provided by the overhead lights directed onto the drum kit. I half expected a harp to start playing heavenly notes.

"This makes much more sense than the ideas my brain was coming up with. Wait! Are these for Cath to borrow?" I asked as I grabbed his arm excitedly.

He rubbed the back of his neck. "I thought . . . since they're just sitting there . . . Cath could use them."

I shook his arm. I couldn't contain the joy bubbling out of me. Leo half grinned as his top half wobbled back and forth. Cath was going to be so happy. Playing on a kit like this would only help her skills.

"The only thing is," he said, "I don't want them at the school. Not to be a dick, but I really only want her to play them. And it wouldn't be fair to the other kids. That's why I wanted to check with you before I suggested it." He swallowed with difficulty, waiting for my reaction.

"Leo. This is incredible." I held his gaze and poured my sincerity into it. "Thank you. Are you sure? This set has to be worth . . ." I literally had no idea. "These look very fancy."

There was no doubt in my mind this set cost more than my used Toyota.

"Uh, yeah. I'm not worried about Cath using them. She'll respect them."

She absolutely would. Another bubbling of joy fizzled through me. I wanted to wrap my arms around Leo. Not only did he have this amazing set, but . . .

"So that means you're going to help?" I asked with stars twinkling in my eyes.

He shrugged and looked at the ground. "I'll do my best. I figure, we probably can't practice here. Because of various complications of a student and non-faculty," he said. "I'll ask Devlin if we could use his place, but it's a bit of a drive."

I balled my fists to keep from attacking him with a hug.

"That's a good idea. Though lessons with you aren't on school time, so it's no different than if she were getting private lessons from anybody in town. But I agree, better safe than sorry." I appreciated that he was aware that his quasi-celebrity didn't automatically mean the school board would approve. "I'll ask Ben Huntsford too."

He gave a look like he wasn't sure who that was.

"He owns Big Ben's Dulcimer shop. He lets out a room for practice."

"Oh, right." He looked at his feet. He really didn't seem to love the idea of involving any other people in this arrangement. Ben was okay, but I would have to make sure he didn't make a scene like he had when Sienna Diaz turned up at the Front Porch with Jethro Winston.

"The biggest issue will be moving them. It would be best to have one spot and keep them locked up," I added.

He tugged at his curls. "I'll be honest, anywhere would be better than the high school. I would prefer to never step foot in that place again."

I frowned at him. I doubted this was about signatures or being recognized. Or at least not in the way I had imagined he'd been worried. This was something else. He looked like he was about to crawl out of his skin when we were at the school, and talking about it now put a crease in his brow.

Leo was shy, and that was a startling realization to have about the former rock star. I reviewed all our interactions through this new lens, finding it made a lot more sense than my preconceived notions. He wouldn't be the only one having a conversation with Devlin.

"Don't worry. I'll figure something out," I said, adding it to my mental to-do list. "I really appreciate this, Leo. I cannot tell you how much this means to me. What it will mean to Cath."

Leo looked at the concrete floor. "We better pack these up."

I nodded hesitantly. I wanted to ask why they were set up to play if the dust cover was on them. He stepped forward.

"Will you play for me?" I asked before I meant to or realized what I was saying.

His shoulders went to his ears. "Nah."

When he didn't elaborate, I cleared my throat. "Sorry—"

"You can try them if you want." His hands were back in his pockets.

"Really? I'm not very good. Think Meg from The White Stripes but even worse."

He chuckled. "Now I have to hear you."

The lights in the basement flickered as the storm outside whistled through the HVAC system and shook the pipes.

"Wild storm," I said, suddenly nervous.

He nodded but reached for some sticks on the snare and handed them to me. I stepped forward with reverence. I didn't want to sit down and try to play. I really couldn't do much more than hold the most basic beat, but I didn't feel ready to end this moment. The sounds of pouring rain added to the moody atmosphere of the basement.

I didn't get behind the kit, instead choosing to whack the ride cymbal in front of me. It stung my palm and hurt my arm more than I expected. It rattled throughout the basement just as lightning flashed outside the ground-level window.

"Whoa. I am Zeus!"

He chuckled, and I realized he had moved right behind me. "You don't need to hold on so tight," he said.

"Why is everyone always—"

"To the stick," he clarified as he reached around to loosen my grip. "You have to let the sound waves travel freely."

He moved ever closer, not touching anywhere but where he loosened my fingers from their death grip. Yet the whole back of my body warmed as though he'd pressed himself against me. A flash of heat spread up my back, knowing he was close enough to hold me if I moved back an inch. I imagined him pressing himself against me and into the wall. His hands trailing up my arm to take the stick away and toss it to the floor. His other hand roaming up my sweater and—

Jesus, save me, what was happening?

I wasn't interested in a relationship; the idea felt exhausting, but my body was on a totally different page. It was reading an erotic novel. Especially as his long fingers deftly wrapped around the stick, toying with it. He mimicked the motion he wanted me to perform, loosely playing with it.

"Like this," he instructed quietly. "Listen to the difference in the sound now." His smooth, deep voice trembled the hairs on my neck.

I did as I was told, and the air vibrated differently this time.

"Yep. Right. Good job."

Those words pulsed a shocking wave of desire through me. Obviously, the attraction had been there since I first looked him up. And sure, maybe I'd been in awe of him before he even came back to Green Valley. It wasn't every day that a GVHS alum made it in the real world. And the more time I spent with him, the more I respected him, but this was not about me and Leo. This was about Cath and her future.

"When you hold on too tight, your arm absorbs the impact." He hadn't stepped away. Were his breaths coming faster, or was it my imagination? Any second now, I would move from this position.

Lightning might as well have struck us for how charged the air felt.

What if I leaned into him, letting his rich tones vibrate through me as an example of sound waves? I wanted something of his to move into me. I needed to see his reaction. To be alone in this state of tightly coiled tension would be unbearable.

I turned my head to find his face inches from mine as he watched me hesitantly. His pupils dilated, and his mouth parted. My heart jumped up my throat. His eyes moved to my lips and, holy crashing thunder, was that the storm or my heart racing? The way he looked at me differed from the lascivious gazes I'd known since puberty. He looked at me like I was precious and confusing, like he was as surprised to find us in this position as I was.

If he lowered his lips to mine, would I stop him?

A flash of lightning came instantaneously with a house-shaking clap of thunder. I jumped so hard that I dropped the stick and gasped. He instinctively wrapped himself around me to protect me from some imaginary danger.

"It's okay," he whispered, holding me tight. "Just the storm."

It was unexpectedly lovely to be held and protected.

Upstairs came another crash of something dropping, followed by Janice's shout. We shared a look of fear.

Leo didn't hesitate. He sprinted up the stairs before I'd even exhaled. I still felt the weight of him as I followed, unsure if I was grateful for the interruption.

CHAPTER 12
LEO

I 'd never appreciated my long legs more than when they propelled me up the stairs to the first floor.

Janice's shout caused a panic in me like nothing else. My hammering heart was now erratic.

"Are you okay?" I yelled as I made it into the kitchen.

Janice had a hand to her chest and was leaning over the large basin sink to look out the window. On the floor, the teakettle spilled steaming water. She turned around as I entered.

"Yes, oh my, I'm sorry for yelling. Just scared the good Lord into me."

I went to her, grasping her shoulders to look her up and down. "You're okay, though?"

"Yes. Yes. I'm fine. Lightning hit the tree, I think." She patted my hand.

"I'll clean this up." Mari had come up and was kneeling to pick up the teakettle.

"Oh, you don't have to. Thank you," Janice said.

I tossed a dish towel onto the water before going to the window. "Shit. I think we need to call someone. The tree is smoking."

"Is it on fire? We have a volunteer firefighter crew just up the road," Janice said. She already had her phone to her ear.

That was news to me, but with the heavily pouring rain, I wasn't too concerned about the fire spreading. I was concerned about my garden and the heavy branches falling.

I ran out the side screen door to look down the driveway. Rain pelted every surface, creating a deafening cacophony.

"Be careful!" my mom called after me, and I stopped just before I went into the storm.

Bright light flashed across the storm-darkened neighborhood, followed instantly by another crash of thunder. It shook the air molecules and raised the hairs on my arms.

Janice gasped.

"I should move my car so they have room," Mari said. She was already running past me and out into the storm.

"Wait, no—" I reached for her as she zipped by me, but she was too fast.

She covered her head, but rain plastered her body as she splashed through the water pooling in the driveway.

"Don't let her go out in that," my mother called before reporting the situation to whoever was on the phone.

"I know," I said, exasperated. Everything happened so fast, delaying my processing. I shook my head. "No!" I yelled to Mari.

Above her, the still smoldering pine cracked. Water streamed into my eyes as I peered to the top of the tree where heavy branches shook in the gusts. A particularly large limb was seconds from breaking off.

I looked back at my mom, whose hands covered her mouth.

"Mari!" I yelled again, but she couldn't hear me.

Terror bolted through me, and I ran without thinking. She was seconds from reaching her car door as I ran full speed and tackled her like I'd ever watched a single game of football in my life. I tucked her to me as my arms wrapped around her waist, using my body as we fell to cushion her. That, of course, meant I took the full brunt of the impact.

"*Oomph.*"

The air was knocked out of me, but I still managed to hold on tight to her writhing form.

"What in the—" She flailed and tried to break loose. Water poured from the skies, filling my nose, eyes, and mouth. Water seeped into me from the ground. It was as though I was drowning from all directions.

"Stop. Fighting. Me," I coughed out.

"Stop whatever you're doing!"

"I'm being heroic."

"Well, don't be. I need to move my car if they're supposed to help."

She twisted to get a leg over, straddling to peer down at me. Her whole soaking body sat on mine. It was so soon since the touching in the basement.

Why couldn't I keep myself from chasing after this woman? I held on tighter to her wrists and tugged her back to me.

"It's not safe," I growled. Didn't she understand how close she was to danger?

She fell forward, collapsing to rest her chest on mine. Her gaze moved over my face.

"Leo. It's okay." Her voice had softened with whatever she saw written on my features.

I frowned and squeezed her closer. This maddening woman.

"It's okay. I can wait," she said.

She'd barely finished speaking when we heard the groan and crack of a massive tree ripping in two.

Our heads snapped in the direction of the sound, and we watched, as though in slow motion, as the top half of the tree seemed to separate itself from the base. A branch—more like another tree—the length of a car and just as thick had detached. It fell down and down until it landed with a crash on the roof of Mari's car.

The unexpectedly loud sound caused us to flinch into each other as bits of debris flew at us. My arms cradled her head and her rib cage. When the dust settled, so to speak, Mari stared agog at what had been her car but was now considerably less car.

She blinked rapidly, water dripping off her lashes and off her nose. Her blond hair looked dark, plastered with rain. Her whole body convulsed with a shudder.

"My . . . car." She looked back at me, mouth parting. My hands were still wrapped tight around her as her head came to my chest, and a wail escaped her.

Had I imagined an outpouring of gratitude and "You saved my life!"? Maybe. Yes, it was harrowing, and I was still in shock that I had acted without thinking and the right thing had happened.

But if I had imagined that scenario, however brief, I was wrong.

"I could have moved my car!" Mari thrashed loose of my grip and scrambled, slipping and crawling to her feet.

"I saved your life."

"My car is pulverized!"

She ran to her car and attempted to tug free the new Christmas tree decal, but it wouldn't budge. Her hands slipped off soaking pine needles, cursing me. Cursing nature. Cursing me again when I got to her.

"Mari, we have to go inside. It's still dangerous out here."

PIPER SHELDON

Her shoulders slumped, but she let me drag her inside.

My mother met us immediately with towels. "Oh my goodness, are you okay?"

"Yeah." I didn't add that Mari had lost her mind since Janice could clearly see that for herself.

I kicked out of my shoes and then bent to pull off Mari's. She'd stopped fighting me at least but stared straight ahead, water still dripping off her blue lips and shivers racking her.

Janice fussed and made sure we warmed up.

"I'm going to get fresh towels. Why don't you get some dry clothes for the two of you, and I'll wash what you're wearing?"

I looked down at both of us covered in mud, bits of grass, and pine needles.

"Good idea." I stripped out of my clothes and down to my boxers so I wouldn't drip on the stairs. When I glanced at Mari, she still shivered in her towel and stared straight ahead.

"I'll be right back. Don't move," I demanded.

She made a sound, and I ran to change and grab her some extra clothes.

Less than a minute later, back in the kitchen, I was relieved to find she'd listened to my instructions.

I handed her the clothes I brought. "You can change in there." I gestured to the half bath off the kitchen.

She nodded and shuffled away, leaving a trail of water behind her. While she changed, I cleaned up the remaining mess and reset the kettle for tea. My hands shook as the adrenaline slowly seeped away. That had been so *damn* close. I couldn't fully process just how close that had been.

When Mari walked out of the bathroom a few minutes later, I had to look away before my arms reached out to grab her and hold her to me. Seeing her in a favorite tee and a pair of my shorts made my heart flip and my stomach hurt. I longed to touch her all over and check for any damage. I wanted to strip her and kiss every inch of her body to make sure she was okay. I wanted to take any pain away and replace it with pleasure.

There was no doubt in my mind I had developed feelings for Mari. Feelings much deeper than shallow attraction.

I had cornered her in the basement, and the memory of what I had been about to do flooded me as the iceberg of adrenaline melted away. I'd almost kissed her.

This attraction to her was the last thing she wanted. Another "disappointing person" in her life. If ever there was a man to ultimately let her down, it was me.

She slumped into a chair and collected her long hair over one shoulder. She deftly braided and tied it off with a band from around her wrist.

"Sorry about all that"—she thumbed with minimal enthusiasm toward outside—"almost getting myself killed nonsense."

"Are you okay?" I asked, my voice still shaky.

The floor creaked above our heads, where Janice moved around upstairs.

"Yeah. I reacted without thinking. Very on brand for me. It felt very important to move my car at the moment."

"To be fair, it did get crushed by a giant branch. Maybe that was the rush?"

She smiled, but it faded away quickly. "Yeah, but thanks to you, *I* wasn't crushed. Sorry for beating you up for it."

"I've managed worse. Was anything important in there?" I had a weird burst of post-adrenaline panic at the realization we had been minutes away from putting the drum kit in there. So maybe it had been a good thing I couldn't keep myself away from her? In the game of what-ifs, it was very easy to win whatever side you wanted.

"No, actually. Not really." She tossed her braid over her shoulder and sat up straighter. "It's not the car. The car is whatever. I have insurance. But this is just another thing I don't have time for." Her fingertips went to her temples to rub circles. "It's another way for the system to beat me down. The car is my independence and my way to help Cath. It's really starting to feel like something is out to get me. It was a freak accident, yet it feels like a sign." She stood, arms punching down in determination. "Okay. Enough. I need a plan. The Winstons will likely have a loaner I can use while this gets fixed."

Just like that, she'd shaken off her near-death experience. Maybe she should process it before she got to work, but she was ready to go.

"Pishposh. You can borrow ours," Janice said, appearing out of nowhere.

Or maybe I'd been too ensconced in watching how Mari moved in my clothing. Either way, I jumped when Janice had reappeared magically at my side.

"You mean the one car I'm already sharing with you?" I asked.

I could not possibly risk any more time with Mari. My feelings for her were growing too quickly, so any alone time needed to be avoided at all costs. How hard could that be? She was busy, and I was a hermit. I had not agreed to spend time with Mari. A few months to help out Cath and come out on the other side unscathed. That was the new plan. Even if part of me thought the new plan was shitty and just hovering around what I actually wanted.

"Who's sharing with whom?" Janice asked, crossing her arms. "And anyway, where do you suddenly have to be?"

I opened my mouth to argue, but she had a solid point.

"Though it does remind me. I don't have anybody else insured except us two." My mother patted my head. "Looks like you'll be driving her around."

Mari and I both started to object at the same time. I turned to her. Wait, why was she objecting?

Oh, right, being escorted around by the town's biggest disappointment.

"What about you, Janice? We can't even use the car until this is all cleaned up, it's currently blocked by the remnants of the tree."

"Actually. The car is *not* in the garage." Janice made a scene of cleaning up the spotless counter. "I had a friend drive me home. When I started not to feel good." I carefully did not look at Mari, already sure what look I'd find. That look that sounded like *mm-hmm*. This was most definitely the same friend that was either still upstairs or had snuck out when we were in the basement. "And I can always get a ride from the bunco ladies as I need. Or walk. It's good for me."

I suspected this same friend would be driving her around, and she was all too happy to have the ready excuse to spend more time with them.

"I couldn't. And it's fine. Like I said, the Winstons will have a rental." Mari nodded, determined.

Weirdly, the more determined she was not to let me drive her, the more I felt like insisting I didn't mind.

"It's not a big deal," I said.

"It is more than you think. I have to be at school by six thirty for zero hour."

I groaned. "In the morning?"

"Yep. And rehearsals after, not to mention appointments in town almost every night."

"Maybe we should just let her get a rental. She needs her freedom."

"No." Janice shot me an all-too-familiar look. It garnered no arguments. To Mari, she said, "Leo will drive you. He'll have to be going to town more often anyway to help Cath. Good. So it's settled."

Mari opened her mouth, nothing having been settled, but the fire truck siren coming up the street cut her off.

CHAPTER 13
MARI

The morning following my car being pulverized, Leo pulled up to my apartment building promptly at 6:15 a.m. like I'd asked. I'd waited at the bottom of the stairs, ready to go. There was no way I wanted him to see the pathetic apartment I called my home.

After the volunteer fire crew made sure the tall pine stopped burning, they'd helped clean up, and Beau Winston towed away the remnants of my car. Pin Dick arrived home just in time to argue that it wasn't his fault. He insisted his insurance didn't even need to get involved. Leo glared at him until he gave up his information.

I had to hope it wouldn't be totaled, but regardless, I needed a car quickly. This rideshare thing was not a long-term solution. After just a few minutes alone with Leo, I'd been distracted by his shy smile, gentle voice, and strong fingers. I couldn't be trusted.

Leo was borderline comatose this morning, mumbling, "Hey," as I got in the car.

Our close calls yesterday had been on my mind all night. I thought for too long about those capable fingers, the strength of his arms as they banded me in place, and his surprising ferocity as he saved me. And after, the fear I saw in his eyes as he checked me over for injury and the gentle way he'd removed my shoes and dried me off when I'd been too shell-shocked to do anything other than stare. The anger he showed when he didn't let Pin Dick weasel out of his responsibility.

Ultimately, a literal tree crushing my car as he'd been about to *maybe* kiss me was a sign from the universe.

Stay focused. So that was what I would do. This attraction was fun, but it would pass. I was stronger than my desire.

"Daisy's is on the way. Want to get a coffee?" I asked, clearing all the repeating thoughts with a plan. I needed some breakfast too. I had no food at the house, but that wasn't new. Usually, I had time to stop and get something.

Leo grunted.

"I think that was a yes. I'll run in, just pull up."

There was a small queue as Rebecca poured my coffee and handed me two of the daily specials. She raised a brow and nudged her chin in the direction of the waiting car outside.

"Long story," I said, following her gaze.

She'd hear enough from Daisy after the next bunco night.

I thanked her and made my way quickly to the car.

We each ate our donut in silence. By the time we got to the school, Leo had drunk half of his to-go cup. His blinks weren't as slow, and his frequency of yawns was cut in half. "Go ahead and pull into the teacher parking lot," I instructed. "The front office doesn't even come in for another hour. Yeah, here's good."

He parked and turned in his seat expectantly. "What time should I come get you?"

"I can get a ride home from Clara." Though even as I said it, I remembered that Clara already had her hands full playing chauffeur for Gracie and her sprained ankle. "You don't need to worry about it. I know this is a pain. There are probably a dozen better options."

He yawned behind his hand. "It really isn't a big deal. Also, there's no arguing with Janice once she's decided."

I knew that firsthand.

"I always admired that about her." I sighed and relented.

"I'll drive you until it no longer works." He shrugged as if the extra time together didn't matter to him at all. Well, how nice for him. If he wasn't worried about it, then neither was I. We were adults, after all, with fully developed frontal cortexes designed for smart decision-making.

Maybe mine had been damaged at some point, and that was why my temper often got the best of me? Food for thought . . . for another time.

"Five should be good. You can pick me up at the field," I said.

He ran a hand down his face. "That's almost a twelve-hour day. When do you take a break?"

"There's tons of free time between classes. I make it work," I said. It was sort of true. "Do you want to come in and check out the teachers' lounge? I could show you the mysterious cup that everyone refuses to clean?" I wasn't sure why I'd offered, but I wasn't ready to say goodbye to him yet. So much for pointless cerebral cortexes.

He shot a look at the building, and his lip curled. "Nah. I think I'm going to go back to bed."

"You really don't like being here, do you?" I asked.

"It's not my favorite place." He tugged at his curls and took a breath. "I never really fit in here. I was bullied. Pissed off teachers with my complete lack of attention span. I couldn't wait to leave . . . Now I'm back." He mumbled the last bit to himself.

"Nothing wrong with coming home."

He shrugged but didn't speak. Another person who wanted nothing to do with Green Valley. He hated it here, so he probably couldn't wait to leave. Of course, I was attracted to him. Something was deeply wrong with me.

I grabbed my stuff and opened the door. "Thanks again. I'll see you later."

He looked like he was about to say something. I waited until he nodded with a tight smile before I left with a wave. I glanced back one last time and caught him watching me walk away. He looked away and focused on putting the car in reverse.

I bit back a smile. Maybe not totally unaffected.

As usual, the day flew by. I hardly thought about the almost kiss with Leo as plenty of other distractions occupied my mind.

It was after-school marching band rehearsal before I knew it.

I was dizzy and starving by the time we ran through the Fall Festival routine. Mouth watering, I eyed up a granola bar poking out of a backpack.

I chugged from a water bottle as we took a break.

"Who's the creepy dude staring at Miss Mitchell?" a sophomore called, tucking their trumpet under their arm and pointing at the parking lot.

Several heads turned to see what he was talking about.

Arms crossed and leaning against the side of the car was Leo. His head was down as he played on his phone.

"Was that the guy who dropped you off this morning?" Ruby asked with a mischievous twinkle in her eyes.

"Wouldn't you like to know," I said.

Cath narrowed her eyes at Leo. I had explained to her about the car situation earlier but not about why I had been at his house to begin with. The drums were his surprise.

"Oooh." Several people yelled and catcalled.

I held up my hand and closed my fist to bring them back to attention. "I was going to wrap five minutes early, but you know, I think we have time for one more run-through." The whole group groaned, and I smiled. "Okay, let's start from the top."

We ended up going five minutes over, and by the time I'd helped everyone off to the instrument room to pack up, it was almost twenty minutes later than I'd promised Leo.

As I walked out to meet him where he still waited, my heart picked up at an excited pace. My lady bits decided that now would be a good time to remember how it felt to straddle him, after suppressing those thoughts all day.

"You better stop that right now," I mumbled to myself.

"What?" he asked as I got closer.

"Nothing. Ready?"

"Whenever you are. Do you need help with anything?" he asked as he opened my door.

We both looked at his hand holding the door in confusion. He let go and went around to the driver's side. "Nah. My students have it."

"They sound good," he said after he got in.

I preened. "Thanks. They're really tight this year. I'm excited for the Fall Festival tomorrow."

"They'll be ready."

"Are you going to come?"

"Maybe." He started the car. "I left a message for Devlin about the rehearsal space. I haven't heard back from him," he said, clearly changing the subject. I was happy to hear that he'd taken the initiative to do that. I had worried that he was going to put it off until I had to call Devlin myself and ask for another favor.

"Thanks for doing that," I said. Before Leo backed up, he reached into the back seat to grab something. When he twisted back around, he handed me a Tupperware container along with napkins and plastic cutlery. "What's all this?"

"Just some leftovers," he explained. The tips of his ears were red.

I gasped in excitement. My stomach gurgled, and my mouth watered before the lid was even off. "You're an angel." I inhaled the aroma of what looked to be chicken, rice, and grilled veggies. It was incredible. "Would you judge me if I shoved my face in here and ate like a pig at a trough? Manners be damned."

He grinned as he checked over his shoulder for oncoming cars. "I would expect nothing less."

I awkwardly wrangled the container to balance it on my knees and dug in. He'd even cut the chicken into bite-sized pieces. I moaned and shimmied my shoulders as the food went down. After I swallowed, I said, "This is amazing. Thank you."

"No big deal. I noticed you didn't bring food this morning, and based on how you ate at the Front Porch, I got the impression you don't cook for yourself much. I had extras from cooking for Janice anyway."

I winced as I swallowed a too big bite down. "You made this? You cook?" I asked, not hiding my surprise.

"I got into the habit while touring." He shrugged his large shoulders. "The options for eating on the road are terrible. I needed to fuel myself and the guys, with how much energy we burned during the shows." I remembered the videos of him. Sweat dripping down his neck and glistened his chest.

"It's a high calorie burning activity," I said robotically and shoved another bite in my mouth.

"It turned out I actually enjoyed the cooking. One of my favorite things was trying to figure out what local ingredients I could find and cook in the small kitchen of the tour bus. I got creative." He shot a glance to read my reaction.

For my part, I had a piece of red pepper currently sticking out of my mouth and rice stuck to my lips.

He smiled as he turned back to watch the road. I chewed and swallowed like a normal human.

"Man of mystery, you are. You'd think one of your favorite things would have been all the Burnnies or the adoring fans or the fame and, I dunno, the money."

He cleared his throat and tugged his hair with his free hand. "Burnnies are a myth."

I pulled up my phone and read from Urban Dictionary. "'Named for the band and an assumed play on Playboy Bunnies, The Burnouts' groupies were notorious for dressing up scantily at their shows and creating an online sensation via their fan videos.' Y'all had groupies."

"Vander was always the draw. But we never cared about all that."

"Listen, I've seen the thirst trap videos. You definitely had Burnnies. You had your own hashtags."

"Is that right?" He flicked a look at me.

"I've said too much." I shoved more food into my mouth to keep myself from divulging any more.

"Taking you back to the apartment?" he asked, still blushing and willing to change the subject.

I wiped my mouth and cleaned my mess. "Actually. Can you swing by Main Street? I hate to ask for anything else, but I don't need to go home and eat first now." Not that I had any food at the house. "I need to talk to a couple of people. You don't have to stay. I'll just walk home after."

"It'll be dark," he said sternly.

I opened my mouth to argue that it was Green Valley, but he shot me a look reminiscent of his mother. "You can wait in the car, then," I suggested.

"I planned on it." He scoffed as though any other idea was laughable.

CHAPTER 14
LEO

"I 'll drive you until it doesn't work anymore. I loved cooking for the band. I'll wait while you go in." I mocked myself out loud as I sat in the car, watching Mari's retreating form.

And what a retreating form it was. All I had to do was ensure that I spent less time thinking about her and ways to touch her, yet the second my mouth opened, I was scheming the exact opposite. I cooked her a damn meal. What had I been thinking?

I knew.

If I had thought seeing her in my clothes was a magical sight, watching her inhale the food I cooked for her changed something in me on a cellular level. It certainly never excited me to see the goobers from The Burnouts shoveling down my food. I'd only known Mari for a short time and already I felt like my whole world was flipped upside down. I was meant to be home and relaxing until Cath and I finally had our first session.

And wasn't I a chump? Sitting here as she walked down Main Street. This was what happened when you got involved in things. You then had to leave the house and interact with people.

Groaning, I rubbed my temples. How did people live like this?

Mari made her way to the Victorian mini mansion on the corner lot, across from where I'd parked. The sign outside said Monroe & Sons. I squinted and leaned closer to get a better look as a large man came forward to greet her. I frowned as they shook hands. The man looked like he could play Superman;

he was that good-looking. I tried to remember what Becky Lee had said about her sons during bunco. They were all married now, right?

I should probably go in there, just in case. He seemed professional enough, but I couldn't hear what they were saying. I unbuckled and was about to open the door when my phone vibrated.

"Hey," I answered Devlin's call, keeping my eyes on Mari and the Monroe brother.

"Hey, man, sorry I missed you."

"No worries. I'm calling for a favor. Since you owe me."

"Is that right?" Devlin asked on the other side of the line in a cocky tone. "Does that mean you have decided to help Mari and Cath?"

"I'm working on it. Only, there's difficulty securing a place for us to practice. Any chance you would be open to a few nights a week at your new and improved studio?" I asked.

Mari threw her head back and laughed. I squeezed the phone in my hand.

Devlin cleared his throat.

"Sorry. What did you say?" I asked.

"I was going to call this week anyway." Devlin's voice took a gruff edge.

"Yeah?" In the shop, a dark-haired woman appeared at Mr. Chiseled Features's side. It was Molly Cooper—related to me only in name because of Belle Cooper's previously mentioned now deceased husbands. The Monroe brother, who must have been Garret now that I thought about it, looked at Molly like she hung the moon, squeezing her close. Tension melted out, and I focused back on the conversation in my ear.

"I got a call from Vander," Devlin said.

I froze at the mention of my former best friend. Devlin also knew Vander from our time at camp and they had remained friends over the years. Apparently, even now. A different sort of jealousy gripped my chest. "Oh?"

"The Burnouts are wrapping up their tour. They want to record their next album before Christmas and asked if they could come use my studio."

I swallowed. "A new album," I repeated numbly.

That part wasn't a surprise. The Burnouts' tour had been massively successful since I'd been booted. *Because* I'd been booted, depending on who you asked. But the shocking news in all this was that Vander was the one who reached out.

Vander back in Green Valley didn't make sense. If I had been eager to leave this place, he'd been even more determined. He'd always been the ideas guy with the big dreams and life outside here. I wanted it too, of course, but mostly, I wanted to get away. Vander hated it here and swore he would never come back.

"Why Green Valley?" I asked, trying to hide any reaction.

But truly. What the hell was Vander playing at? Thousands of studios in the country. Some of the best in the world, just over in Nashville. Why had he chosen to come here? We hadn't exchanged a word in six months after talking every day since we were kids.

To laugh in my face? To rub in how successful the group has been since I was kicked to the curb?

"He said he wanted to get back to his roots. Hoping the Smokies will inspire them," Devlin explained.

I grunted. Likely excuse.

"I wanted to make sure it was cool with you before I agreed," Devlin said.

Why had he cared what I thought? I wasn't the one recording an album. It wasn't like I could say no without looking like an absolute jerk. It wouldn't matter. They could be up at Devlin's massive cabin on the lake, and I would be safely not leaving Janice's house. Even just driving Miss Mitchell had been enough for one day.

"It's fine." I absolutely would not be using the studio now. "But I guess that means we have to find a different place for Cath and me," I mumbled.

I glanced up to see Mari hugging Molly goodbye with a smile on her face.

"Not necessarily," Devlin said cautiously. "It's not like they'll be in it twenty-four seven. We could schedule it so there wouldn't be an overlap. There's just a chance you might bump into each other, that's why I wanted to warn you. I'm happy to let y'all use the space, though."

I grunted noncommittally. "Yeah. I'll see what Mari says."

Mari strolled happily back toward the car, her long blond hair sashaying with her hips. She was alit with victory, so I assumed the talk with Monroe & Sons went well.

She was breathtakingly beautiful. What would it be like to be the person who kept her happy and fed? Who would be the lucky asshole who would eventually get to be that person who met all her needs? Not another disappointing man.

"I'm really happy for you and Mari," Devlin said. My jaw was clamped tight. Otherwise, I would have worried I'd been thinking out loud.

I flinched. "What do you mean?"

"I heard about what happened with the marching band. I did try to warn you she had a way of getting what she wanted."

"Yeah, weird how she seemed to think I was a spoiled punk who refused to help out," I said, remembering that bone I had to pick with Devlin.

"I have a new baby. I'm not sleeping well. When I talked to her, I may have miscommunicated parts of our conversation."

"How about that," I said flatly. But couldn't muster any sort of real anger. Not when Mari, with a coy grin, had lifted her hand to give me a thumbs-up. I held up a hand and gave one back, feeling considerably more dorky with the action.

"Sometimes we just need a little push in the right direction. Take it from somebody who let their past rule them for way too long," Devlin said.

I grunted again like I was impersonating him. Who was letting their past rule them? Not I. I was retired. There was a difference. Mari turned toward the direction of a contemporary boutique that looked to sell a mishmash of expensive candles and lotions.

Seriously, what had happened to this town?

Just then, a motorcycle came roaring down Main Street. It was so loud several people glared. Not everything had changed. The Iron Wraiths still made a scene wherever they went. The biker slowed by Mari as she crossed. He checked her out, not even trying to be subtle as he whistled at her. My hackles rose, and I turned off the car, body tense.

Mari ignored him but switched to come back toward Janice's car. Smart woman. I willed her on, *Ignore him. Come back to me.*

She held my eye contact even from twenty feet away. I poured my thoughts into that stare.

"Mari can be highly motivated. But she's good people. I hope you guys will learn to work together," Devlin said as I kept my focus straight ahead. "Don't let her tough demeanor scare you off."

"She's not so scary," I said as my words drifted.

Recognizing he wasn't getting the attention he wanted, the biker mouthed what might have been very bad language and threw a cup over his shoulder. My heart sank.

The scene unfolded in front of me like a bad dream. In fact, I'd had a nightmare last night where I was chasing after Mari, but when I called her, she wouldn't turn around. I'd been trying to warn her about something, but she was on a mission, wogging away from me. The same sense of impending doom from the dream suffused me now.

The biker, with the Iron Wraiths emblem embossed on his leather vest, missed whatever his goal had been. I optimistically assumed he had been trying for the trash can that Mari just happened to be passing as he threw his giant Styrofoam cup, only missing her by a hair. But Mari had not interpreted the event in the same way.

No. Stay focused on me, I willed.

She did not do that.

She stopped midstride and spun on her heel. She looked at the cup. Looked at the biker. Looked at the cup.

That familiar burning rage transformed her features.

"Shit. Devlin. I gotta go—" I was already launching myself out of the car.

Mari bent and picked up the trash with revenge in her eyes.

CHAPTER 15
MARI

The half-full, sticky cup—aimed directly at the retreating back of the asshole biker—was about to leave my fingers when an arm came out of nowhere to rip it from my grasp.

"Mari," Leo hissed as he tossed it into the trash. "That was a Wraith."

I saw red. Anger pulsed my temples, and I had no clear thoughts. "Oh, I know." I chuckled without humor. "I was gonna hit him dead center on his precious little vest."

"And then what?" Leo's eyes were frantic and wide.

"This isn't your problem." I stomped my foot and wiped my hands on my jeans.

"You really think starting shit with the local biker gang is your best idea?" he asked, a vein throbbing in his temple as he whisper-yelled.

A few passing pedestrians had glanced over when they heard the bike ride through and my accompanying shout of rage. They stopped to watch the drama unfold as I'd prepared to launch the cup. "He shouldn't get away with that," I growled back.

He looked around again and tried to bring me to the car. I dug in my heels. I wasn't done here.

"Do you have a death wish? Why am I always pulling you away from danger?" He mumbled the last part to himself.

"I would prefer if you didn't!" I shouted, and I heard a cackle of laughter from across the street, but I didn't break my eye contact with Leo.

His shoulders rose and fell as he took a deep breath in and out.

"Mari, can you just—"

"Do not finish that sentence with 'calm down.'" I hated that my voice shook with pent-up emotion.

"I wasn't going to." He held up his palms to me.

"I'm so sick of people telling me to calm down. To be quiet. To let shit like that slide. It's because nobody is making a scene or standing up to these . . . these *bullies*, that awful stuff continues to happen." My body thrummed with pent-up energy; it begged to punch or scream.

"I'm starting to think this isn't just about the litterbug," Leo said.

I shook my head. "I'm sick of people treating the world, people, like they're disposable. Nobody tries anymore. Nobody takes the time to make things right."

Leo blinked at me and then let out another long breath.

I'd been so happy only seconds ago. I'd caught up with Clara's best friend, Molly, and her husband. I'd secured further donations. And when I'd walked out to find Leo watching and waiting for me, I had a frisson of hope. This could be my life. I could have my students and band while a thoughtful, sweet man made me meals and waited for me with that goofy half-smile.

And then that Wraith roared through, and it was like a switch had flipped instantly. A reminder that I couldn't have those things. Just like with the crashing tree, every time I started to let myself think about a future where I wasn't alone, the universe delivered a sign.

It wasn't healthy to get angry so fast, to flood with such venomous rage that I couldn't think straight. I should be quiet, mind my manners, let things slide. But with every passing year, I struggled to remember why remaining passive was so important.

The older I got, the louder my inner voice wanted to scream out at all the injustices it saw.

"I have an idea," Leo said. "Let's get out of here."

Of course, he just wanted me out of there. He wanted to return to the safety of his house and get far away from me. He hadn't even wanted to come out in the first place, and I was living out his nightmares. The more I stood up for what I wanted, the less attractive I became, and that was the crux of an aging woman. I couldn't keep anybody around me.

I wouldn't have to set boundaries with Leo because my natural human-repellent was doing just fine. "You can just take me home. Or I'll walk. Whatever."

I shoved past him. The anger that made me feel like I could flip a bus deflated, leaving my shoulders hunched.

98

"Mari." He jogged to keep up with me. "Actually. My idea is something else. Can you trust me enough to come with me without asking a hundred questions?"

I stopped and chewed my lip. He wanted me to come with him? Wasn't I glad for the boundaries? But his curls were all mussed up, and his brows were contorted in hope, and ultimately, poor decisions were what made life interesting.

"Okay," I said. "But I can't make any promises about the hundred questions."

"I'll take it." He pulled out his phone. One hand tugged his hair as the other scanned something. "We should make it, but we have to go right now."

* * *

A little over an hour later, inside a nondescript concrete building, Leo and I wore matching jumpsuits, helmets, gloves, and safety goggles.

The teenager running the Rage Room handed me a sledgehammer after going over the rules and safety precautions.

"You're good to go. You have thirty minutes. Rage away," she said and left the padded room filled with junk.

"I've heard of these but thought they were a joke," I said, glancing around. Several glass bottles sat on a ledge, but an old box TV on the table called to me. "I can't even decide where to start."

Leo fidgeted with his goggles, grinning happily. He looked hot. How could he possibly pull off a silk caftan, or jeans and a tee, or this look? Not fair.

"The whole point is not to think. Or at least don't overthink," he said.

I frowned in confusion.

"Pull up a memory that pisses you off and let it rip. That biker throwing his drink. Or Pin Dick," he suggested.

I hefted the sledgehammer, testing the weight of it. "Or Ben Huntsford."

"Who?"

I huffed a laugh. "Really?"

"Oh yeah, the dulcimer guy. Wait, why him?"

"He left me a voicemail today when he knew I wouldn't be able to take the call. He said he couldn't help Cath because it would be too loud." I scratched an itch under my helmet. "I think he just doesn't want her practicing there."

Leo frowned.

"At least we still have Devlin as an option," I said. "He's good for it, even if it isn't as convenient."

Leo picked up a crowbar. "Well, screw that Ben guy. Muster that classic Mari rage. Go balls to the wall." He gestured all around.

Classic Mari rage.

I glanced down to look at myself. In this too-big jumpsuit, helmet knocking around on my head, I suddenly felt a little ridiculous. I felt like a child.

"Time's a-wasting," Leo said. "Wait. What's wrong? I thought you'd love this."

"I do in theory. But being here, I feel so ridiculous." I'd had too long on the drive up to Knoxville to cool off.

"Ridiculous? It was my idea."

"Or maybe childish? Grown women shouldn't be acting like this. I should learn to control my temper," I said.

"Why control it?" he asked. "Just acknowledge it."

I lifted my chin.

"Do you think maybe you're holding on too tight?" he asked.

"This again." A flash of him standing behind me, holding my hand that gripped the drumstick.

"You're this ball of pent-up rage. Bouncing around in this perpetual pinball machine of life, never fully free to go off. It must be exhausting."

"Excuse me?"

He went on, "I don't pretend to know what it's like to be a woman in this world. I've never been catcalled. At least not by a sleazy biker. And I imagine that's only the tip of the injustice iceberg. But 'should' is a dangerous word."

When I didn't say anything, he said, "Emotions don't have value. Good or bad. They just are. They need to be acknowledged before you can let them go. Maybe if you ever had your feelings of anger validated, you wouldn't need to feel like going to extremes to be heard."

My mouth fell open.

"That was . . . shockingly profound."

I frowned in thought, recalling the many times I was told to be quiet, smile to seem nice, or make myself as small as possible to even avoid being noticed. I felt the need to make a scene because I never felt like anybody was listening to me. It was that same helpless feeling as when I was young, and my brothers would talk over me. Or when I tried to talk to my mom about something and she'd say, "There's a plan for everything" and "Don't get so worked up about it."

"I never had this temper before when I was younger," I admitted. "In the past few years, it feels like . . . like I can't pretend anymore."

"Pretend at what?"

"To be nice. And sweet. Maybe I'm just an angry person." My throat felt tight. How else could I explain this temper that seemed to rule me lately? "I'm just not nice."

"You're an incredible and giving person, Mari. I think bad shit happens sometimes, and you were never taught how to express your anger. What would happen if you were allowed to be angry?" He tapped my sledgehammer with his toe. "Let's see." He eyed the room. "Or I'll call dibs on the TV."

I roughly pushed him aside. "Nice try, little drummer boy. That's all mine."

Chuckling, he spread an arm wide, proffering the room. He stepped back as I swung the hammer above my head.

"This is for Pin Dick!" I slammed it down with all my might, thrilled with the satisfying crash that accompanied it. The hammer bounced off, shock waves moving through my arms. "Ouch," I said.

"That's it," Leo said, going to the opposite corner.

"Yes! And gross bikers messing up our town!" I screamed as I twisted to hold the hammer like a baseball bat and swung it into the glass screen. The screen shattered, sending debris everywhere.

"There you go!" Leo called over the crash.

Then he got to work on his own side. I didn't watch but heard him smashing glass.

"This is for sports always being picked over music!" I swung down again, a large panel breaking off the side to reveal circuit boards.

"This is for moving to different cities and not even considering me." I smashed down on an old plastic wall phone that sat on the table. It exploded in tan and black pieces, a bell ringing in the chaos. I hadn't even realized I was still upset with my family's last-minute change of plans. I was so mad to have not even been an afterthought in their decision-making.

"This is for leaving me here all alone while you got to live your big, important lives in different states!" The hammer cracked a sturdy but outdated laptop in half. "For only calling when it's a holiday!" *Whack*. "For never remembering my birthday or asking how my life is going!" *Thunk*. "For starting new families away from Green Valley and never remembering your roots!"

I stopped when I couldn't see anymore. My vision blurred, and for a second, I panicked, thinking a chunk of plastic had gotten through the goggles. Then a tear rolled down my cheek. I touched a fingered glove to my face and looked at the damp spot on my finger in confusion.

I *was* crying. But I had just been so mad. I'd been pulsing with anger. And now this? It was as if acknowledging the anger made the floodgates burst open. I started to sob, shoulders shaking.

"Mari?" Leo stepped to me but kept his distance. "Wait, are you crying or laughing?"

I lifted my head and was grinning like a maniac. "I'm really not sure."

Absurdity at the situation had morphed my gaping sadness into laughter. Now, I was both crying and laughing so hard I wasn't even sure what I felt. "I don't know what's happening."

Leo's shoulders relaxed, and he popped a dimple. "Listen, I'm no doctor. But there's a *chance* you might have some pent-up emotions that needed to be let loose."

I scoffed a wet laugh and shook my head, clearing the last of whatever the hell that all was.

"That was wild," I admitted.

My whole body shook with what felt like every passing emotion. Adrenaline coursed through me, and now this shaky post-emotional euphoria was settling in. I felt like I could float off the floor. I felt better than I had in years.

"That was incredible," I said to myself in awe.

It was just destroying stuff, but it felt like so much more. I felt free to be myself in whatever form that took, even if it wasn't always pretty, nice, or quiet. I was loud and wild, and I took up space.

Leo was panting as he looked around the destroyed room. "We went through the stuff a lot faster than I thought." He wiped his brow. "I can pay to get more junk in the room if you want to keep going. Cheaper than therapy, at least."

He grinned at me, and it tugged something deep in me. That familiar blackening out of rational thought. I only saw the world in glimpses. Leo's lips. Leo's dimples. Leo's curls.

"That's not what I want." I hardly recognized my voice.

I tugged off my gloves. I pushed off my helmet and tossed my goggles to the side. I shook out my hair, and with every action, whatever Leo saw on my face caused his smile to melt away.

He swallowed, his gaze moving all over my face and body.

"What are you—"

I launched myself at him.

CHAPTER 16
LEO

Mari was going to kill me?

As the light changed in her eyes and her features grew feral, I realized it might be too late to save myself. It was my turn to be the person she launched herself at.

I'd been genuinely trying to help her. I understood the need to smash through some big emotions, and it'd been going well, until she started crying. More than crying, body-shaking sobbing.

Or was it laughing? I still wasn't clear because the two emotions turned out to be startlingly similar on her.

Whatever it had been was entirely wiped clean as her panting slowed down, her shoulders rose, and her breaths evened out. Her pupils were blown out, and her throat worked a swallow as her gaze moved over me. She looked like she wanted to eat me up.

Even though divesting herself of her outerwear took several seconds, my body was incapable of moving. Fight, flight, or freeze? I now knew where I stood.

And it was directly in her warpath.

I barely had enough time to toss aside my crowbar before Mari moved. She hopped into my arms, wrapping her long legs around me and shoving off the rest of my protective headgear with her hands.

Feral had been the right word.

"What is happening?" I panted out as she grabbed my face, her gaze moving frantically over my features.

"I don't know," she admitted, trembling in my arms.

"I think we should explore it," I said.

I walked until her backside rested on the table, making sure there was no sharp debris. She squeezed her legs, bringing me closer yet. My quickly growing arousal would be apparent against her soon.

I really hoped I wasn't misreading this situation.

"I want to kiss you," she said.

"Thank God," I said.

Our mouths clashed together roughly. Trying to get a handle on myself, I squeezed her thighs and forced myself to calm down. I pulled my head back slightly, and she chased after me, our lips never disconnecting.

I smiled against her soft mouth. "It's okay. Just . . . slowing."

She made a needy sound that shot to my cock. There was no doubt she felt it now as she ground against me.

"Fuck," I said, turning my head and wrapping my fingers into her hair with one hand.

The other hand was busy running up her side and waist. The jumpsuit made it hard to touch her skin, but I was nothing if not determined. I searched for a snap or zipper that might let me feel the heat of her skin.

Our kiss softened but wasn't any less urgent. Our tongues found each other quickly, and our mouths moved perfectly in sync. We read each other like musicians who'd been playing together for decades. When she took, I gave. I tilted her head in my hand, exposing her neck to me, and kissed down the side. She gasped out my name, and all thoughts vanished.

We couldn't get close enough. I didn't have enough hands to explore her with. I finally found the godforsaken zipper and began to tug it down.

"Uh. Excuse me," a voice called out through the speakers. "Your time is up in five minutes. We're about to close." It was the teenager that had let us in.

Mari leaned back, and her wet, swollen lips parted. I took a long, slow lick across them.

"Just so y'all know, there are cameras in there," the girl added.

Mari licked her lips, tasting me as her eyes widened. A flush burned across her cheeks.

"Sorry," I called out. "We are, uh, just wrapping up."

We separated and took off the protective suits. We exchanged the occasional look, and I really wished I could hear Mari's thoughts.

"Sorry about that," I said to the worker as we left out the front door.

"It happens a lot." She didn't glance up from her phone as she pointed at a sign I hadn't noticed before. There were several just like it when I looked around: Cameras Recording at All Times. With a graphic of a black camera and red flash.

Mari was silent until we got in the car. Then she threw her head back and laughed.

I worried she might freak out, but laughter didn't feel *great*.

"I cannot believe I did that!" she yelled into her hands now covering her face. "I guess we can just chalk that up to the heat of the moment," she said. "I'm sorry. My impulsiveness still manages to catch me off guard."

"I hardly think that's something to apologize for. A marching band at seven in the morning? Yes. That? No."

"It's not okay! I attacked you. I didn't even ask for consent. How humiliating. I completely lost control. I didn't mean to send the wrong signals. You don't deserve to be the person I work my stuff out on."

It was like I'd been punched in the gut. Something weighed on her. I'd heard her cursing *somebody* while she pulverized her aggressions into smithereens, but I wanted to understand how she felt about me separately from that.

But it wasn't about me. Whatever Mari needed to get out of her system, the outing had been a success.

"Apparently, it happens a lot." I started the car and cleared my throat. I was embarrassingly hard still.

"Maybe I should think about investing in that unlimited pass." She let out a long sigh. "Gosh, I'm still sweating. That was . . . incredible. Thank you. I've never let loose like that."

I glanced over at her. Her head was back against the seat, a little bit of hair stuck down from sweat on her temple. She still had a mark on her nose from the tightness of the goggles. And she was beautiful. My feelings for her were rapidly pulling me under. I kept waiting to find a time when I wasn't attracted to her, but with our every interaction, she became more alluring.

I needed to get a grip.

I began the drive back to Green Valley. The fall hours meant it was already dark, and the car grew quiet. I began to wonder if she'd tuckered herself out completely and checked to see if she was sleeping. As another car passed, briefly illuminating her face, I was surprised to find her still watching me, sleepy eyes and hands curled under her cheek. She'd brought her knees up to her chest and leaned against the partially reclined seat. "I could fall asleep," she said softly.

I took no small amount of pleasure knowing she felt safe enough to be that relaxed.

"We've got a while yet," I said. "You can take a nap."

She made a soft sound and went quiet. My heart thudded in my chest, and I gripped the steering wheel tighter. I felt fevered and anxious. My body sensed something was coming and was trying to prepare me. I wanted to go home and not leave again.

Maybe if I didn't see her, or touch her, or smell her, I could quell this rising panic.

"How did you know that's what I needed?" she asked in a sleepy voice.

Something about the words and the way she said it had me clenching my jaw. An image of her sprawled out on a bed, knees parted, cheeks red, satisfaction curling her lips . . . *How did you know that's what I needed?*

I always know what you need.

I shifted in the seat, adjusting my jeans. "Just a hunch. Janice was a big proponent of therapy before all the cool kids did it. When I was young, I'd always felt so apart from everybody else." I cleared my throat, not quite ready to go into all my issues. "When the bullying started, she wanted to make sure I could process everything. I didn't tell her the worst of it, but she must have sensed something. Plus, I regularly got to smash loud things together, and that helped with a good amount of teenage angst."

"Anytime you get mad, you also get practice."

"Two birds, one scone," I said, and she chuckled.

"I'm sorry you had such a rough time in high school."

I shook my head. "It wasn't all bad. I had my mom."

"And your band, right? I think I read online that you two were best friends since you were kids," she said.

"You read online, huh?"

"Well, I needed to learn about the man who might be tutoring my student."

I'd assumed it had been her idea to seek me out, but something in her tone made me wonder if that wasn't the case.

"I had Vander. We were inseparable and going to leave this town once and for all, so I had that to motivate me whenever I got teased for wearing black nail polish."

"I'm so glad times are changing. There is zero tolerance for so much of the garbage that was just 'part of growing up.'"

"As it should be."

"Exactly. But still. I'm glad you had Vander. It helps when you're young."

"It was everything."

I couldn't think about Vander and The Burnouts now. Especially knowing they'd be here soon. A tug of guilt at the reminder of the conversation with Devlin. And now Big Ben's was off the table.

"I'm sorry," she whispered, but I wasn't sure what for.

I narrowed my eyes at the road. Vander was such a fresh bruise. Even six months later, I couldn't poke it yet.

"Are Noah and Jonas past boyfriends?" I asked, desperate to shift the focus.

"Ew. What! No?" She straightened off the seat. "They're my brothers. Why would you think that?"

Brothers? "In the midst of your raging, you said those names among the rest. I just assumed they were."

"Oh. I guess I didn't realize I was so vocal."

I swallowed down the useful thoughts that tried to pop up when she said that.

"You know, it's weird," she said. "All sorts of stuff came up that I wasn't expecting. Including my brothers, apparently. There's a small chance I have some thoughts about that," she said sarcastically.

"Where are they?" This was the family that had stood her up. I couldn't understand it.

She let out a long breath. "Noah, he's the oldest. He's in New York. He and his partner, Asim, are corporate lawyers." She turned and looked out the window. "And Jonas, he's the middle. He and his wife, Alice, live in North Carolina with their two little kids." She spoke like she read from a cold-call script. Like she'd said it a hundred times. "They aren't too far and come down for the holidays if they aren't with Alice's family."

"You aren't close?"

"We used to be," she said. The loneliness that seeped through her words broke my heart. "Or at least I idolized them growing up. I would survive off five minutes of their attention for months, waiting like an addict for my next hit. I would listen to the music they listened to. I would try to befriend their friends and act cool so they wouldn't be embarrassed to have me around. But they were older. I was just starting high school when they left the state to go to college. First Noah, then a year later, Jonas. They got real jobs and never looked back. That's just the way of it, isn't it?"

I thought, *Not always,* but the tone shift warned me to keep my comments to myself.

"I've never understood why everyone is so quick to forget their roots. Like this town means nothing. It's no worse or better than any other town."

I cleared my throat uncomfortably. It was hard not to wonder if this was partially about my own return to Green Valley.

"Some people just need to find where they fit," I offered lamely.

"Yeah. I guess. It's scares me how something that was such a big part of their lives for so long could be abandoned just like that," she snapped. "Didn't they miss it here at all?" Maybe this wasn't about the town. "Was this place so forgettable?"

"You are anything but forgettable, Mari Mitchell," I said in a tight voice.

She made a soft sound like she didn't believe me and turned her head away. I wanted to pull the car over, grab her shoulders, and kiss her until she believed me. I wanted to implant the taste of myself so deep within her that she would trust my truth.

I wanted to tell her that I couldn't *stop* thinking about her, no matter how hard I tried. That if there was any sort of justice in the world, I'd be able to get her out of my mind for even just a few minutes a day. But ever since she'd shown up on my lawn, she was the only thing that occupied my mind. My internal metronome was set to the beat of her heart.

We were silent as I took the exit for Green Valley. Nothing I could say would make her believe her worth if she didn't feel it in herself. But I could show her.

Maybe I was adrift in my life right now, but I had a purpose for the first time in a long time. Mari didn't want a relationship, but she could use a friend, and, I guess, so could I.

I could make her happy, and there was no better purpose.

"I talked to Devlin today," I said, pulling up to her apartment building.

"Oh?" If she thought it was weird I hadn't mentioned it earlier, she didn't say as much.

"He said we could use the studio."

"Thank you. Oh, amazing." Mari launched herself at me for the second time that night, squeezing my chest.

I closed my eyes and inhaled her joy. I could avoid Vander and the band. I could help out Cath. I nudged my chin along her hair. This, right here, made it all worth it.

CHAPTER 17
MARI

I f ever there was a sign the universe was conspiring against me, it was confirmed the morning after our trip to the Rage Room.

I woke up from a fitful night of confusing and stressful dreams. In one, I ran into my brothers, having found out they were back in town, but they didn't tell me. I yelled at them, literally screamed, saying exactly what was on my mind at that moment. I woke up angry and sad, wondering why my brain fixated on something outside of my control, something I hardly ever thought about.

Lying in bed, I felt the stress of that dream settle heavy in my bones. My body ached like I'd done a booty boot camp and not smashed a bunch of junk. Today was the Fall Festival, and Leo was set to pick me up in two hours to meet the marching band outside town in the field where the Headless Chicken Festival was held. The inside of my eyelids burned, and the bed was so comfortable it was nearly impossible to roll out and into the shower.

I turned on the water and stood, blinking as it warmed up. Shivers racked my body. I don't know how long I stood there staring, but steam had filled the bathroom when I zoned back in. The hot water felt like needles on my neck, and goose bumps covered me.

After the shower, I zoned out again as my brain debated wearing all black or something more casual and appropriate for a muddy field. A knock on the front door confused me from where I sat on my bed, facing my closet.

The towel was still wrapped around me when I answered.

Leo's eyes widened, and he cleared his throat before focusing on my face.

"You weren't downstairs. Usually, you're waiting outside for me." He stumbled over his words, eyes flicking over me again before he looked pointedly at the ceiling above my head. "I wasn't sure if I should have come up or waited . . ."

I could have said several things, but all of them felt like too much work. Instead, I nodded and blinked. It felt so nice to have my eyes closed that it took an extra second to open them again. I turned back and shuffled away. After a heavy pause, I heard him come in and close the door. "Are you okay?"

"Absolutely. Big Day," I said, trying to rally myself. "Fall Carnival. The whole of Green Valley should be there to hear the Brown Bears perform."

"Black Bears."

"That's what I said." I stepped into my room and dropped my towel. The cotton felt like sandpaper on my back. I shivered and looked longingly toward my nice, happy, warm bed.

Okay. Clothes. I could do this.

"Are you talking to me? Whoa!" There was a scramble of footsteps and a loud thump before my bedroom door slammed shut. "I'm sorry. I didn't know. I will . . . I'll just wait in the living room."

Time zoomed in and out, slowed down, and sped up. There was a sense of urgency that my body was not worried about. I found the clothes I'd picked out the night before—thank you, past Mari—that I'd forgotten I'd laid out. I sat on the bed to pull up my panties and jeans. It took another minute to get my bra situated. The clothes scratched like sandpaper, too stiff and cold.

I lay back on the bed, pulling the comforter to cover my top half. God, it felt so nice.

"Mari? You said you wanted to be there by ten, right?"

"Yes," I called, and it felt like so much work.

"Okay. We should probably leave soon. Can I help you?"

"Oh, you'd like that, wouldn't you." I sat back up, and the room swam around me.

Leo sighed audibly through the door. I needed to rally. A little coffee and food would help everything. My stomach churned unpleasantly at the thought of Daisy's, and that's when I should have realized something was really wrong.

I finally finished getting dressed and found my bag, making my way to the front door.

"Ready," I declared, feeling rather proud of myself.

Leo tugged on his hair and looked me up and down. "Shoes?"

I looked down at my feet. I sighed and felt my shoulders slump. The idea of lacing up my boots was unbearable. I frowned as my chin trembled.

"Okay. No worries. You sit here." Leo led me to a chair at the breakfast table. I slumped into the seat.

I extended my legs, and he laced up the boots one at a time. This was the second time he'd taken care of my footwear. He was either a sweetie or had a weird foot thing. I patted his head. No. He was just sweet. "Thank you."

He'd finished tying my boots and was still crouched, an arm on his knee. His brows were pinched as he frowned up at me. I liked the way he looked at me. Not right now. Right now, he looked like he was trying to do math. But normally. Or when he'd pulled back to look at me during our kiss. That was a look I wanted to frame.

"I think you should consider staying home," he said.

"Why?" I asked.

"Mari, I don't know how to tell you this, but you're sick."

I reeled back. Had he heard about my other dreams? The dreams that were stressful in different ways and involved his deep voice, his wandering hands, and my gasps of pleasure. "Am not," I said.

"You are. You should go back to bed."

"I can't. I have to get to the field, help the band set up, and ensure everything goes okay. I absolutely cannot be sick."

To prove my point, I stood abruptly.

The ground tilted and came up to meet me. His arms were around me before I hit it. "That proves nothing." I smoothed my hair into a ponytail. "Let's go. I don't want to be late."

Leo worried his bottom lip. I'd kissed those lips. And it was wonderful. Thankfully, I wasn't thinking about that anymore.

He cleared his throat and tested my ability to stand on my own. Success. Oh, I was holding on to him still.

He looked at me again, debating something. "Leo. I'm fine. Let's go."

"Is there anything else you need?" His gaze moved around the barren walls and sparsely furnished apartment.

"Tragic, I know. I'm not home much."

"This is nice." He picked up and shook the snow globe sitting on the counter. The only sign of life in this place. In it was a picture of my parents, brothers, and me at Disney World, on one of the few family trips we ever took. We smiled happily with our dorky matching shirts, and me with my gap-toothed grin. It was a perfect memory. Soon after that, Jonas and Noah got too cool for family trips.

I didn't want to look at that snow globe. I just wanted to get out of here.

On the drive out, I'd tried to sit up as straight as possible. The truth was, the ache in my spine had gotten worse, so that my whole body had a draining fatigue. I was freezing cold, but the air coming out of my nostrils was burning hot. It wasn't looking good for me, but I just had to get through today, then I had a full day off tomorrow.

I could handle this.

"Or you could just sleep," Leo suggested.

He shot a look at me. "I had not realized my internal thoughts went external," I said and clamped my mouth closed to keep my teeth from chattering.

"You've been mumbling since I got to your place." He put the car in park. There was a gravel area for parking, and it was filling up fast. I saw a few students walking with their instruments toward the makeshift stage near the entrance. I couldn't let them down.

"I can make it through a few hours," I said.

Leo turned and pressed his fingers to my head and sucked in a breath.

"I shouldn't have let you leave the house," he said.

"As if you could stop me," I mumbled.

"That's what I thought you would say." He bent his fingers to press the backs of them against my cheeks.

I fought the overwhelming urge to close my eyes and lean into him.

"You're on fire," he whispered.

I pretended to lick a finger and tapped it on my shoulder. I made a sizzling sound.

He groaned a laugh. "Think of it this way, if you have a fever—"

"I do not—"

"Which you absolutely do. Do you really want to be around your students? Let alone yelling at them, potentially spewing your spit into their faces."

My hand froze on the door. He had a point. Dang it. "I hardly spew," I protested weakly.

I imagined trying to summon the energy to conduct them when I could barely hold my head up. Or walking around the festival, talking with all the residents, shaking hands, spreading whatever this was to the innocent bystanders of Green Valley.

"I had so much I wanted to get done today." I let my head fall back against the headrest. I wanted to summon the familiar anger that usually motivated me to get moving, but I couldn't even muster that much.

I closed my eyes and noticed how they burned. In fact, now that I started to acknowledge his point, I allowed the rest of what I'd been blocking in. I felt like absolute garbage.

"They're going to be so disappointed. They've been working so hard." I curled up into a ball in his passenger seat.

He reached across me to tug a handle, and the seat leaned all the way back. He was so warm and cozy that I wanted him to fold me up like origami and stick me in his pocket. A second later, he was lifting my head and tucking a sweatshirt under me. I shivered. "See. Can't be a fever. I'm f-f-freezing." I wrapped my arms tight around myself.

He swore under his breath. "Is there anybody else who can help get them set up?"

I shook my head. "I don't know. Don't think so." I shivered again. I heard the sounds of him moving around but was having a harder time focusing. This was getting worse rapidly. At what point would I need to be quarantined?

This was the end for me.

"You're not dying. Just really sick." He tucked a blanket around me, making sure no part of me was uncovered.

"Oh, that's nice." I sighed in relief. "Of course you have an emergency blanket in your car."

"Everybody should. I won't be judged by the woman who has more clothes in her car than food in her apartment."

"Touché." I yawned, jaw cracking.

"They're self-sufficient. Maybe they're fine on their own," he said.

I shook my head. "They're like little ducklings. They need their mama duck."

He chuckled. "What about Devlin? He's a conductor."

I imagined the big grumpy man as a mother hen to a bunch of little ducklings.

"That's true. In fact, he'll be with the SOOK now," I said.

"Shit."

"It's okay. Just go tell them I'm dying and it's been an honor to teach them."

"Not dying." He sighed. I peeked an eye open to find him staring out the window. He tugged anxiously on his hair. Crowds were gathering and pouring into the entrance. "A lot of people came out for this."

"People love fried food and questionably safe rides." Both of those things sounded horrendous, and I regretted mentioning them. If I wasn't so lost in my own wallowing, I would have felt bad for Leo. He'd only agreed to drive me, but now he'd be stuck going out into the crowds of the people he had been avoiding for weeks to deliver bad news to *my* students. "I'll go tell them, and then I'll come back." I tried to sit up.

His strong arm braced me, preventing me from moving. "Nice try, Typhoid Mary. It's fine. I'll go tell them."

At least if these were my final moments on earth, I had the feeling of his arms against me.

"You went from 'I'm not sick' to 'dying' really fast," he said, a soft tug to his lips. "Just stay here."

Gravity pulled my lids down. "Maybe I'll close my eyes just to see what happens."

"Good idea." Leo made a sound of distress before taking a steadying breath. "Okay. Okay. I'll be right back as fast as I can."

I nodded.

"I'll leave the keys, but lock the doors after me. I don't think it's cold enough that you'll need the heat. Want me to leave the car running just in case?"

I shook my head. "I'll start it if I need to." Sleep was already pulling me under. I could take a few minutes. They would be okay.

"Be right back," he said. A second later, the car rocked gently, and his door shut.

I had just enough energy to hit the lock on the door before I succumbed.

A few minutes later, I sat straight up. "I'm okay," I said, realizing a car door shutting had woken me.

Leo winced. "Sorry. I was trying to be quiet. You didn't even budge the other times I checked on you."

"How did you get in?"

"Janice had her keys."

I nodded, processing being conscious. "Were they devastated?" I scrubbed my eyes with my palms. The fever didn't feel as bad, but it was that sort of temporary halting of symptoms that told me I wasn't in the clear yet.

"It was fine," Leo said. "Are you okay? Lie back down." He gently pressed my shoulder, and I relaxed back against the seat. My eyelids felt sticky and hard to keep open.

I vaguely remembered someone shaking me awake and forcing me to swallow medicine with water. "Did you give me medicine?"

"Yes. You should really reevaluate how willingly you take drugs without asking any clarifying questions."

"I live on the edge," I murmured.

My head turned from side to side. We were still in the parking lot, but it was packed now. People coming and going. The festival was in full swing, lights bright and music playing. "Dark already," I said, confused. I had just barely closed my eyes.

"Yeah. Sorry. It took me longer than I thought. But just relax. I'm going to take you to Janice's now."

"What? No, I can't get her sick."

"Don't worry. She got the spare room ready."

"I'm a burden," I said and felt a mortifying quiver of my chin.

"Hardly. I don't—Janice thinks you shouldn't be alone. I'm willing to bet you don't have medicine or any sort of sustenance at your house."

"Is mustard sustenance?"

"No."

"But you'll get sick."

"I toured in a van with four other dudes for years. I have the immune system of a street dog."

"That's a weird example. Are they known for having strong immune systems?" I asked.

"How about a kindergarten teacher?"

"Better than a high school band teacher, it seems."

"Also, after yesterday"—he hesitated—"if I was going to get sick, I would know by now."

"Ah, yes. When my face attacked yours." I gasped. "You got me sick." I tried to punch him, but my wrist just sort of flopped against his arm and fell into his thigh.

His muscles flexed under my hand before I pulled back.

"Nobody has been sick around me," he said. "You're the one constantly surrounded by germ-riddled youths."

"Good album name," I said, rather proud of myself for the joke, even in a time like this.

"Nice."

I groaned. "I can't be sick. There's no time for this."

"Funny how the body doesn't care."

It didn't take long until the medicine reprieve faded away, and I didn't have the energy or the will to fight the point anymore.

The thought of going back to my apartment, lacking all but condiments, to spend my final days held little appeal.

"Take me to my final resting place," I said and closed my eyes.

"You're not dying."

CHAPTER 18
LEO

Once Mari accepted her fate, not one of death but of being sick, she protested minimally on the drive back to Janice's house. A bone-deep exhaustion settled into me after the day I'd had. I couldn't think about it, couldn't really comprehend what had happened. The plan had been to send her regrets and get her in bed ASAP, but standing in front of the students in their little dorky band uniforms, knowing how hard they'd practiced, I couldn't let them down.

I just sort of blacked out. I would process all that later. Now, I had to take care of Mari.

With the car in park, I turned to Mari, with her cheeks bright red and brow creased in pain even as she slept on. I went around to her side of the car, opened her door, and gently rested a hand on her shoulder. Heat radiated off her through the blanket.

"Mari? We're home. At Janice's, I mean."

Her pitiful murmur made my throat constrict.

I took a rallying breath and bent to scoop her up. The angle was awkward, and my back would be angry tomorrow, but her walking was not an option. She moaned and placed her burning head against my neck as I adjusted her weight in my arms. It felt nice to carry her across the threshold of this house. It felt so nice to take care of her in general.

Janice was still at the Fall Festival, meaning I fumbled my way through the dark house alone, narrowly missing corners as I navigated to the guest room. I quickly transferred Mari from the emergency blanket she'd been wrapped in to under the thick comforter. She sighed as she nuzzled her way deeper into the sheets.

I stood, hands on hips, to arch and stretch my back. It couldn't have been that late, but if I laid down, I would instantly fall asleep. Instead, I went around the house, gathering any supplies Mari might need. I'd made note of the last dose of medicine she'd been given and set the alarm on my phone for when she'd need another.

I had just set down a glass of water on the nightstand, quietly in the soft glow of a single night-light, when Mari's soft voice startled me.

"Leo?"

"I'm right here." I could just see the shape of her arm reaching out. Her hand found mine, and our fingers tangled. She was still so hot to the touch; a flash of worry coursed through me. What if the fever didn't break? What if I wasn't helping her?

"I'm sorry about today. I'm sorry I'm so, so much." Her voice, slurry with sleep, caught in her throat.

"Mari." Anger swelled in me at whoever had made her feel that way. I knelt next to the bed and brushed her hair from her face. I was surprised to feel the dampness of a tear on her cheek. "You aren't too much."

"I am. I know I am. But I can usually handle things myself. I didn't mean for you to get caught up in it all. I'm sorry I got sick. I'm sorry I'm so upset now. I'm—"

"Shh. Stop. You haven't done anything wrong. People get sick. People need help sometimes."

She didn't respond but attempted to stifle a sniffle. Mari never shared this side of herself. Usually too strong and motivated, full of energy and life, to be so fragile and scared. Later, she might laugh at how a virus brought her down, but right now, nothing was funny about her fear. I would have done anything to take away her pain.

I stood when she reached out for me.

"Wait. Don't go. I'm so tired of being alone." She said it so quietly I almost missed it. I heard the desperation and vulnerability behind it. I shut my eyes, swallowing with effort. I knew what that confession cost her. I understood too well how it felt, claiming to want that utter solitude but knowing it crushed like a physical weight in the dark of night.

"I'm not going anywhere," I said.

I walked around to the other side of the bed, shucked off my shoes and a few layers, then opened the blanket and got in. The heat from her was like a furnace, yet her body was subtly vibrating with shivers and possibly over-wrought emotions.

Without hesitation, I pulled her to me and endured the heat as her muscles relaxed and her shivers stopped. Eventually, her breathing evened out, and the tension eased from my clenched jaw.

I must have fallen asleep at some point because when I woke up with a start, we were face-to-face. She blinked dreamily at me. She had the comforter covering her mouth, so in the soft light, only her eyes were visible, glassy, and not quite back to normal. But maybe better?

"I'm alive," she whispered.

"I did tell you."

She clucked her tongue at being wrong. Her gaze traveled around as much as it could without her moving her head. "This is unusual. Nice but weird."

Should I have not stayed here? Had I assumed too much? Maybe I should have sat in the chair and stood on guard. But the bed was so comfy . . .

"What?" I asked tentatively.

"Being taken care of. I forgot how nice it can be."

This family of hers wasn't much like a family at all. Who did she have? Who would she accept?

"It shouldn't be unusual. You should have people lining up to take care of you," I said.

I heard the sigh from under the blankets. How could her own family leave her all alone? Weren't they worried about her at all?

"You should go. I don't want to get you sick." Her words came out muffled from behind the comforter.

"I'm telling you, immunity is my superpower."

"Good album name." Her eyes creased with a smile.

My heart beat like it was hit with one powerful thump on the bass drum. "Joking at a time like this."

She blinked. Then blinked again, only this time her eyes remained shut.

I pushed the hair from her forehead. She was clammy and not back to normal temperature. "Mari? Don't fall asleep yet. We need to take another dose."

"Boo," she moaned with eyes still shut.

She sat up and let me administer the medicine before falling back to be re-tucked in. I studied her, features melting into relaxation as she went back to sleep. It was too easy to take care of her. It was as natural as finding the tempo. I needed to get out of here and into my own space to remember that this was not real.

I snuck out of the room and went to the kitchen. Janice was just coming home. It was the middle of the night. My mother really did have a vibrant social life.

"How's our girl?" she asked with a worried tilt of the head.

Our girl.

"She's okay. This fever is intense." I rubbed the back of my neck. My whole body felt wound tight and like I could sleep for a day straight, but I wanted to check on her again in a few hours.

"Hopefully, that means it'll pass quickly," Janice said.

I yawned on a nod. I could hardly stay upright.

"You were really great today, darling."

I made a sound somewhere between a thanks and a grumble.

"It's so nice to see you out and about again. So many people came up to me to mention you today. They said you were great with the band too."

I blinked in surprise. She was probably used to the people in town approaching her for different reasons. At least I could be a source of pride for her for once. "They're good musicians. Mari is a great teacher."

"That she is. But you are good too. It's great to see you helping Cath and this town. Mari." She said Mari last, purposefully.

"I'm still not sure what Mari thinks I can do for Cath. This arrangement seems like . . ." *Another way I will fail.* "I just don't see how I can help. But she's so determined I can." I shook my head.

My mother glanced to the side, her brows crinkling in concern. I shouldn't have burdened her with my fears. My job was to take care of her now, after she'd taken care of me my whole life.

"We all believe in you," she said as I was about to change the subject. "Don't put so much pressure on it. Just try to enjoy being out and about again."

"Yeah, okay." But it didn't feel that simple. I kept waiting to understand how I'd gotten caught up in this turn of events but couldn't find any answers. The only thing in my life that made any sense was being around Mari. That felt necessary, or *inevitable.* "I'm just gonna take a quick shower."

"Good night, son," she said.

"Good night, Mom," I said with a wink, and she smiled.

* * *

Mari

I had survived.

It was hard to tell how much time had passed. I slept on and off for what could have been a day or weeks. Probably somewhere in between.

Leo came to check on me often. He provided cool compresses for my head and forced soup down my throat—metaphorically—when I was well enough to sit up. Being conscious never lasted long, and our brief conversations faded like dreams upon waking.

"What's it like on the outside?" I asked during one of those visits. The blinds were closed. The house was quiet. There was no way to tell what time it was.

"The world is still spinning," he said in a deep, sleepy voice.

"You're not sick?" I found his face in the dark and pressed my hand to his forehead.

"Nope. And neither is Janice." He grabbed my hand from his head and brought it down, but didn't let it go. "A few of your students were out sick."

"Ah, 'tis the season." I squeezed his hand, and he squeezed mine back.

When I woke again, the room was brighter, but the house was still silent. I was a new person. The fever had left, and I didn't have any residual pain, except the general weakness that came with too much sleep and not enough food. I couldn't find anybody at home to ask, but a text from Leo told me where the linen closet was and to help myself to whatever.

He was off somewhere, and I only felt the smallest pang of loneliness. Not that I'd expected to wake to find him holding vigil at my bedside. That would be silly.

In the bathroom, I was mortified to find my gaunt, pale face and greasy, tangled hair staring back at me. A mysterious, unpleasant odor that came with fever sweats permeated me. Leo had seen me in the disgusting condition I'd been in, and that was mortifying.

I took the best shower of my life in the guest bathroom. As I let the steam revitalize me, I thought about how this was for the best. The kiss at the Rage Room was by far the most exhilarating intimacy of my life. Which may be pathetic, but true.

Leo was a rock star. That kiss probably didn't even make his top twenty list. None of it mattered. It was an emotionally chaotic release of tension. I wouldn't worry about it. And I definitely was not. Now that I felt better, it was the furthest thing from my mind.

After my shower, I changed into some of my folded clothes that sat on the dresser of the spare room I'd been using. After stripping and changing the sheets, I opened the window to let in some fresh air. I had a new lease on life and needed to move around. I wandered the house to straighten up. I would never take my health for granted again. Maybe it should have felt weird to walk around like I lived here, but I felt strangely at home.

"Ah, I'm dangerous. Stay back!" I held up my hands when I discovered Clara, of all people, in the kitchen.

"Calm yourself. Leo said your fever broke," Clara said.

"Where's Leo? What're you doing here?"

"Which of those should I answer first? And sit down. I promise not to get sick."

I was still pressed back flat against the opposite wall, but eventually scooted along until I sat across from her in the breakfast nook.

"Why are you here?" I asked.

"I brought you soup."

I glanced questioningly at the pot warming on the stove. "I'm not really—"

"Sadie made it."

"Oh, yummy." My stomach rumbled loudly, and I went to scoop myself a bowl.

"I also came to fill you in on the classes I subbed," she said.

The bowl clattered as I barely stopped it from dropping. "It's already Monday?"

"Tuesday."

"Whoa." I shuffled back to the table and hunched over the soup. The relief of survival was quickly being replaced by the stress of all that needed to be caught up on. Two days of class and rehearsals. Two days of preparation for Cath's audition. Not to mention the schmoozing and begging for funding I had planned to do at the festival.

"Leo wouldn't let me near you, but from what I saw at the festival, you were completely out of it," she said.

"You were there?"

"Yep. He asked me—more like made me—go check on you a few times. I tapped on the window to get you to let me in, but you were passed out, mouth open, snoring loud enough to hear through the window."

"I am beauty. I am grace."

She snorted and took a sip of coffee from her ever-present travel mug. I was desperately wondering where Leo was, but I didn't want to be obvious.

The brush of his strong fingers pushing my sweaty hair off my forehead.

And also, how long had we been at the festival if I had to be checked on? I vaguely remembered it being dark when we left, but that meant we would have been there for hours.

Nothing made sense. Time wasn't real. We were on a floating rock, barreling through space.

Too far.

"How was subbing? What did you do with my band classes for two whole days?" I asked instead of inquiring about Leo.

She fussed with the top of her travel mug, avoiding eye contact. "Not important. I kept them alive, and that's what matters." She waved away the question. "And don't pretend you don't want to know where Leo is."

I narrowed my eyes but didn't have the stamina to argue with her. "Fine. Tell me."

"He's at Devlin's with Cath. They're having their first practice. Janice went with them just in case a teacher needed to be there. We weren't sure. Also, I think she just wanted to see Devlin's place."

"They are practicing?" A little flutter of joy suffused me, knowing that Leo took the initiative to schedule their first session.

"I thought it was weird too. Especially with The Burnouts stuff," she said, misreading my reaction.

"What stuff?" What did a tutoring session at Devlin's have to do with Leo's old band?

"Well, just with how things ended. I know nobody really knows why Leo left the band, but the fact that everybody is so tight-lipped about it made me assume it wasn't a mutually wanted separation."

My still cloudy head didn't understand the connection. I shook it.

"Because they're in town recording at Devlin's studio," Clara said. "You didn't know that?"

My jaw dropped. "The Burnouts are back in town? How did you know that and not me?" It was hurtful to think that Leo had shared that information with her but not me. I had imagined we'd created a sort of friendship . . . even if I was always getting him into predicaments and launching myself at him in fits of rage.

"You know, small towns. I found out from someone who heard from their cousin . . . yada yada." She flipped her wrist out.

So Leo hadn't told her. But it still didn't explain why he would agree to work at Devlin's studio. Anytime the band and his past were remotely mentioned, even in passing, Leo quickly changed the subject or got quiet. I knew he had been fired, and the NDA kept my lips tight, but he hadn't gone into why. Was there bad blood with his former best friend? Vander wasn't a part of his life now. Outside of Janice and the Bunco Broads, I don't think he had friends.

And now he and his mom were at Devlin's with the band?

"You could have stayed with me, you know. We are technically family," Clara said gently.

I waved away her offer. She didn't want someone like me around. "I wouldn't have wanted to get you sick. Plus, I didn't really have a choice. He just swooped me up to whisk me off to his country seat. I feel like Jane Bennet at Netherfield Park," I said.

"Poor you and the hot man who's taking care of you and tutoring your student."

"When you put it like that, you make it sound like he's doing it for me." Heat burned up my neck to hear it put that plainly.

"Isn't he?"

"Doubtful. Leo hates leaving this house," I explained. "I bet his mom guilted him into it. She has superpowers greater than even my own."

"Really? Is that what happened at the festival?"

"When I was so sick, he literally quarantined me in the car?"

"No, not that. The stuff with the performance band," she said.

"What stuff?" I squinted my eyes, trying to put together the few memories I had from that day, but so much of it was a blur.

"He was everywhere. He was stomping through the whole place, shoulders hunched and on a mission. I was distracted . . . with my own stuff—"

"What stuff?" I asked. "Can we use more nouns and verbs?"

"Later." She waved away my question. I would be finding out what that was about. "Every time I looked up, there he was. He helped the kids set up their instruments and get them all tuned."

"What?" I sat up straighter. "I just asked him to call the whole day off."

"That's not what happened." She shrugged. "He even conducted them. Well, tried to. It was sort of a mess, but he did good enough. But afterward, that was nuts."

"Oh, God." My stomach tightened.

"All sorts of people from town went up to him and started asking him about how he was and all that. Then he was talking up several shop owners. I even saw him giving it to Ben Huntsford. He looked pissed. Leo. Not Ben. Ben looked like a kid caught pushing his sister."

"Leo? Leonard Cooper?"

"Goofy, shy kid turned rock star, yep."

I tilted my head and looked to the side. "Would we say goofy?"

"He was all limbs when I was in high school. I'll admit he's much more proportional these days."

"He's so hot. What are you talking about?"

Her eyebrows shot up. "Is that right?"

"I mean objectively. One look online and you'll see all the fangirls go crazy over him."

"Right." She gave me a knowing look.

I countered with, "Are you going to tell me what 'stuff' you were up to at the Fall Festival?"

Two could play at that game. She held my gaze, opened her mouth, and closed it again. "Anyway. Leo managed to book another gig in town for spring and get some donations."

My jaw dropped, and my heart started to race. *This man.* "I can't believe he did all that," I whispered in awe.

"I was as surprised as you are. Hasn't been seen for years and now he's on stage and schmoozing the crowd and acting like he was running for mayor. If a baby had been proffered, he probably would have kissed it."

"This makes no sense." I looked around his kitchen as though I could find the answers. "He didn't need to do any of that. I don't understand."

"Somebody has it bad for you."

"No. He . . . No," I sputtered.

She was teasing, but learning all this made me feel weird and anxious. Leo was such a good guy. I may have painted him with the wrong brush at first, but ultimately, he wanted to do the right thing, and I'd made him do all the things he hated. It would make sense that I was falling for him just as I was making his life a living hell. Why did I do this to the people in my life? Why did I push them so hard and make them hate being around me?

I groaned and dropped my head.

Thankfully, I was a natural human-repellent. People didn't want someone like me around, so brash and demanding. We would get through the next few months of his tutoring Cath. And honestly, after the past few days spent in the disgusting condition I was in, there was no need to worry about that inconvenient sexual tension because Leo would want nothing to do with me.

CHAPTER 19
LEO

The past few days had been more stressful than when The Burnouts opened for Sunshine Capone and played sold-out arenas. Way too much peopling. I wanted to hide in my garden, but even I began to feel the pressure of Cath's upcoming deadline. Mari cared so much, and I wanted to help her. I couldn't help how much her cares were becoming my cares. Every day that passed, the closer Cath was to her audition, and there was no more avoiding it. I didn't get to talk to Cath much at the clusterfuck that had been the Fall Festival except for when I briefly made plans to meet her for the drum lesson today. She had been guarded and short but at least willing to meet. Thankfully, Janice agreed to come, and we swung to get Cath on the way up to Devlin's house. The ride was awkward except for the stilted questions my mom threw her way.

I'd brought the drums up during my break in caring for Mari yesterday, and good thing because all of us would not have fit in the car.

I was constantly battling myself. I, equal parts, wanted to check on Mari and find excuses to be away from her. I couldn't be trusted around her.

It wasn't enough that I couldn't stop worrying about her, but at the festival something had taken over when she got so sick. It hadn't been me. It had been the spirit of Mari operating me like an avatar. But I was paying for that burst of energy, and my social batteries were almost all out.

Cath had perked up as Devlin gave us a tour of his renovated studio. She asked loads of questions and chatted more than I'd ever seen her. At least she was getting more comfortable. I, on the other hand, could not stop glancing over my shoulder. My ears were pricked, waiting to hear the voices of my former bandmates.

I was exhausted and on edge. I itched to get back to the house. And not just to see Mari, who thankfully had been sleeping when I left. Her fever broke in the middle of the night, and I was able to get a fitful few hours of sleep. People got sick all the time, but seeing such a force of a woman knocked down to that level was harrowing.

"Here's the studio restroom." Devlin gestured to a small bathroom off the main recording room with a toilet and a shower. "This is a new door. With a lock. Here is how the lock works."

"I think we would probably figure it out," I said.

"I'm showing you anyway. If you use the bathroom, lock the door." Devlin scowled.

Janice and I exchanged a look. "Somebody likes their potty privacy," she whispered to me as Devlin and Cath moved on.

"That was super weird," I agreed, wondering what the story was there.

Devlin finished the tour and led us to the padded drum room. "I'll be working on some mixes in here, but call if you need anything." He pointed at the mixing area behind glass.

"And there is the drum set." I gestured to the kit.

Cath didn't move for several seconds after Devlin left. She glanced up to Janice, who sat just on the other side of the glass, playing on her phone. She gave Cath a thumbs-up when she looked up to see her looking her way.

I didn't rush Cath. I'd been there before.

The first time I saw this set, I had a similar reaction. Complete awe. We'd both come from the same humble drum beginnings. She was probably not sure where to even start.

"Why don't you take a seat?" I asked.

She looked at me and then back at the set. "I don't want to."

I swallowed and blinked. Okay, maybe I'd built up the scene in my head a little bit too much. I would grandly reveal the drums, she'd gasp, and maybe an unshed tear would sparkle in her wide eyes.

I hadn't expected her not to want to play them.

"Why?" I asked, tentatively.

"They aren't mine. It's like using someone else's toothbrush." She tucked her hands into her sleeves. Another barrier to protect her from me and my *apparently* gross used drums.

"That's not true. It's more like using a perfectly good instrument that someone is offering you because the shitty ones you used broke. There. That's a better analogy."

Her gaze looked up and away; her lips sucked in. She didn't roll her eyes, but I got the impression she was trying not to. She mumbled something.

The longer my set sat there, unloved and unplayed, the more agitation grew. I wasn't exactly in a super patient mood to begin with. I hadn't expected an award for my idea, but I had thought a little enthusiasm—not teenage angst.

"Say what?" I asked.

"I'm not a charity case," she said louder.

I stilled. "Is that what you think this is?" Was it charity? It didn't feel like charity; it felt more like Mari held me at emotional gunpoint. But had Cath misinterpreted my self-consciousness as not wanting to help her?

"You don't even want to be doing this. Miss Mitchell basically forced you."

"I—" I started. I wanted to be a rational adult, and that was never my strong suit.

What did I remember from being a teenager? Let me dig back in the long, dusty vaults of my brain. I remember being hated by this town and feeling like the whole place couldn't wait to get rid of me. I remembered hating how every freaking adult talked down to me like I had no clue how the world worked. And okay, maybe I didn't know how the world worked, but nobody wanted to be treated like a dumb kid.

"I'll level with you," I started again. "I didn't think this arrangement was a good idea," I said. Cath stiffened, her body retreating even farther into the hoodie. "But that has everything to do with me and my shit and not you."

She ground her jaw but looked at me. I took it as a sign to go on.

"I don't know if you know this, but I used to live in Green Valley. I left the second I turned eighteen and was in a band for a while. The Burnouts? Ever hear of them?"

Cath blinked at me like I was clueless. Obviously, I sounded like an ancient, out-of-touch grown-up speaking about the music of years gone by.

"Well, anyway. The Burnouts are moderately big. And I toured and everything for a while. Until I came back here." I scratched the back of my neck. "I don't know the first thing about college auditions or sheet music. Shit, I don't even know if I hold my stick the right way. If anything, you'll probably teach me more than I could show you."

I'm just going to fail.

My mouth snapped shut before any more fears could dump out.

"Sorry for the overshare," I added. "And for swearing. I know you don't care, but as an adult, I feel like swearing is something I should be more aware of."

This time, Cath bit back a smile.

"Do you even know what Mari—er, Miss Mitchell—wants me to work on with you?"

Cath shrugged. This was off to an inspiring start.

"Listen. If the drum thing really grosses you out or whatever, I could ask Devlin if he has an extra kit we could use. But you aren't charity. If anybody here is a loser, it's me. Not the virtuoso percussionist."

"I never said I was a loser," Cath said and took a tentative step toward the kit.

"Okay, good. Then we're clear that I'm the only loser here." I shook my head with a sly grin.

"Crystal." She dropped her bookbag behind her, sat on the stool, and bounced a little on it, staring at the set, one piece at a time. Then she stood to twist the stool a little higher before sitting back down.

"Need sticks?" I asked at the same time as she twisted to pull some out of her bag.

"It probably needs a good tune. I think I have—" Again, I was cut off when she held up her finger. She did a run of the drums, hitting each one in turn, eyes closed, and then did it again. The hairs on my arms stood on end. I hadn't heard these beauties for a while, and all the memories came rushing back. Even after all this time sitting alone in the dark, they still sounded pretty good. The tension might need to be brought up on the snares, but otherwise, I was shocked at how good they sounded.

I had been just about to suggest I tune them when Cath leaned to the side again and dug in her bag. A second later, she whipped out a small silver drum key and began to tune by turning a few screws on the snare, then the toms, ever so slightly. Without missing another beat, she ran the drums through again, and they sounded perfect. She even managed to catch what I hadn't been able to.

She looked up at me expectantly as I picked my jaw off the ground. It took me years to ear tune, and she just did it in seconds.

"These are nice," she said, and it felt like a boon.

"Okay. Good. Uh, where should we start?" I asked.

"Isn't that what you're supposed to tell me?"

My hands still had the forever calluses that would shape my fingers, but the skin on top would blister the first time I played again. If I played again.

"Have you ever seen the movie *Whiplash*?" I asked.

Her eyes widened. "No. I tried and turned it off. It gave me stress dreams for a month."

"Yeah. Same." I scratched the back of my neck and sighed. "I guess, just start at the beginning. Do you know what you'll be asked to do?"

She nodded.

"All right. Let's hear it."

Cath played through four different rock and classical songs and then *improvised* a jazz bit. The whole thing was awe-inspiring. She was incredibly impressive. But as the songs went on, especially during the jazz set, I could start to see areas for improvement. Maybe that wasn't the right term. She was technically perfect, but she held back a piece of herself. But it was only her first time playing for me.

We wrapped up and made plans to meet again. I'd finally relaxed and realized I wouldn't be running into Vander or any of the other guys by the time we got ready to leave.

I found Devlin in the hall as Janice and Cath went upstairs to say hi to Devlin's wife, Kim, and the kids.

"You're sure that it's cool I keep my kit here?" I asked him.

"Beatrice and the kids are always welcome. You won't miss them? In case you want to practice?"

"Hasn't been an issue yet."

I flinched at the sound of a door opening and closing at the top of the stairs. My heart raced, wondering who would come around the corner, but nobody did. I'd rehearsed a thousand different things to say to Vander if I saw him again, but my mind blanked out with the burst of fear.

"They won't be here today. I made sure of it," Devlin said, following my gaze.

I felt my cheeks burn and nodded at the floor. "You didn't need to do that."

"It all worked out. How do you feel now about Cath?" he asked.

"Good. She's a real talent. Still not really sure what I'm doing here," I confessed.

"Just keep up with it. Maybe you'll find an area where you can help."

"Hmm. Maybe. I'm just tired." I scrubbed a hand over my face. "It's been a weird few days."

"I heard you were something of a celebrity on Saturday."

"How do you always know the gossip?" I asked.

He shrugged an eyebrow. I didn't even know a shrug could be conveyed through that small motion but here he was. "Small town."

And all these "friends" he supposedly had.

"The whole thing made no sense. One second, I was just trying to get away, and the next, I was on stage helping students and talking to people. It was an out-of-body experience."

"You didn't like it?" he asked.

I thought about it. "It wasn't awful, so long as I kept my focus on the kids. A few people in town stopped to talk to me and were clearly trying to sniff out some sort of gossip about my past, but I was actually so busy it was easy to make excuses to break away." I paused to finally analyze how I felt. "It was okay. I was so worried about what Mari would think when she got better. I didn't want her to hear that I'd messed everything up."

"It's okay to care," Devlin offered.

I realized if anybody could relate, it was Devlin. He'd had a one-hit wonder as a teen and spent years running from his past. "Being in town was weird. Everybody here hated me when I left, but now they couldn't wait to talk to me."

Devlin nodded in understanding. "A couple of things going on there, if I had to guess."

"Enlighten me."

"You're the big fish, right? There will always be those who are impressed by success. Or whatever they deem success to be. Just like there will always be the people who resent you for it."

It confirmed a hidden fear; I only had value to people if I was a *somebody*.

"But also, and probably more likely, we project more onto people than is actually there. Most people only care about themselves and what's going on in their world. Chances are people were just excited that Mari was getting some of the help she desperately needs."

When I first met Mari, I thought she didn't need anybody, but the past few days had shown how fragile her system of self-sufficiency was. Everybody needed help. No woman was an island.

I nodded and saw my mother's head pop in the doorway, her eyes asking if I was ready to go. "You've gotten wise in your old age, Devlin," I said.

"It's fatherhood."

"Is that right?

"Yes. I'm too exhausted to have any sort of filter or deal with any bullshit."

I laughed and clapped him on the shoulder. "I'll let you get back to your family. Thanks again for helping us out."

"See you next week."

After we dropped Cath off, Janice and I came home to a quiet house. There were signs that Mari had been up and about; the guest room had been straightened, the kitchen had dishes drying on the rack. We found Mari asleep in the living room. She had a book on her blanketed lap and her head tucked into her arms. She wore the clean clothes that had been waiting for her and her damp hair was braided over her shoulder. I was relieved to find her color returned to normal and her breathing soft and regular.

"You're staring," Janice said with a grin.

My shoulders lifted and settled with a deep breath. "Yeah." My whisper came out louder than intended in the silent room.

Mari blinked and sat up. "Hey." Her eyes were warming, finding me first. It caused a burst of protective longing.

"Sorry." I winced as she blinked herself fully awake. She noticed Janice and gave a sleepy wave.

"It's okay. I was waiting for you." She set the book down and stretched her neck, head tilting side to side. To Janice, she said, "Thank you for helping out and letting me stay here. I can't believe how many days I was out of it."

"Not a problem, dear. We're glad you're okay. Leo was happy to look after something other than his garden."

I looked at my traitorous mother. "The garden needs less attention this time of year," I muttered.

"How did it go with Cath?" Mari asked.

"It was good. Devlin's studio is incredible."

"Even with his weird fixation on locking doors," Janice added.

Mari looked confused but smiled. "Good. And she sounded good?"

"Yeah, it was great," I said.

Good. Great. What were we even talking about? I could feel the presence of my mother like a sentry in my periphery. I'd spent so much time around Mari lately, but this was the first actual opportunity since our kiss to have a conversation that wasn't in a fevered haze, and I was back to not knowing how to articulate any thoughts.

"I should probably get back home. You just got back and I hate to ask you to go out again—"

"Oh no, you're staying for dinner. Leo is cooking," Janice said, interrupting Mari.

I didn't show how happy I was at the demand. Instead, I shrugged sheepishly.

Mari tried to protest, but Janice held up a finger. "Pishposh. You can stay one more night. Just in case this bug hasn't quit you yet."

Mari smiled at the ground. "Thank you."

"Why don't we relax while he gets started," Janice said. "I can fill you in on the drama you missed Saturday."

I walked toward the kitchen, even though I was exhausted. I didn't mind throwing a quick dinner together. I glanced back to where Janice and Mari sat on the couch in the lamplight. Mari threw her head back and cackled.

"I bet the PTA moms loved that," Mari said as Janice grinned.

A warmth spread through me at the sight of Mari here, comfortable and laughing. It would be so easy to wish for a life like this.

CHAPTER 20
MARI

D inner was a relaxed affair consisting of tomato soup and the best grilled cheese I'd ever had. Comfort food could cure the world.

The three of us chatted easily about the happenings around town and about Cath. I updated them on the lack of updates about my car, though Cletus suspected it was likely to be totaled. I couldn't even comprehend what that would mean for the next few months of hectic holiday scheduling. Janice gave me in-depth details about Devlin's impressive house and studio layout. I was anxious to ask more about Leo's former band and if there was any trouble. Poor Leo put in a thought here and there but tried to hide several yawns.

After dinner, Janice insisted he call it an early night, and the two of us quickly cleaned up the kitchen. Janice gave me a hug good night, and I yearned to linger in her arms. No matter how old you are, having a mother's embrace soothed. Being here, I was in a home, not just sleeping in a cold, empty apartment. There wouldn't be anybody missing me at my place. There wasn't anybody worrying about where I was. It felt *too* good to be here. I could easily slip into a life that wasn't mine. And where would that leave me after Leo wasn't forced to be a part of my life?

Janice went to bed, and I tried to sleep but only stared at the ceiling for hours. After sleeping since Saturday, my body was restless, and my mind raced with everything Clara and Janice had told me about Leo. How could I possibly express my gratitude to him and what he'd done for me and my students? I gave up trying to sleep a little after midnight. I left the guest bedroom in search of a book in hopes it might lull me into a few minutes of sleep.

I started as I rounded into the kitchen to find Leo in his boxers, chugging a glass of water by the sink. He hadn't noticed me yet, and I worried I might startle him, so I waited until he set the glass down to make my presence known. His hair was mussed with sleep, and his muscular, long limbs were on full display. His Adam's apple worked as he swallowed his last sip with a sigh. Apparently, he wasn't the only thirsty one.

I softly cleared my throat, and he spun toward me. "Didn't mean to startle you," I said softly, stepping closer. Janice's room was upstairs, but the house was so still that talking any louder would have felt like shouting.

"Did I wake you?" he asked. "I've been accused of 'clomping like a horse' when I come down the stairs."

I shook my head. "No. I was up already. I've hit my sleep quota for the year."

He nodded, hand moving to his hair, making it stand up even more wildly, before dropping it again.

"Thank you for housing me," I said. "And making sure I didn't die." I started counting off my fingers. "And helping Cath today. And apparently helping at the Fall Festival. I don't even know where to start with all that."

"It wasn't a big deal."

"It's a big deal to me. Clara told me all that you did when she came over earlier. I can't believe you did all that."

"It wasn't really a choice any more than blinking or breathing. I just thought about what you needed and moved," he said simply. As though this were a completely normal thing to confess. People didn't act on my behalf. They certainly didn't do it naturally. If my bidding was to be done at all, it required brute force.

I held his gaze as he spoke. My heart began to beat faster.

"I would have been lost without you. Everybody would have," I said.

"It would have been fine." He leaned back on the counter, gripping the top. The tendons of his forearms flexed.

"Thank you." I wanted to ask why he'd cared so much to help when he hated being in Green Valley, but the air was too heavy to find the words.

"You're welcome," he said with shy modesty, finally accepting my gratitude.

"And how was Devlin's today? Really?" I pushed because it felt like there was something he didn't say with his mom around.

"It went fine. Cath is almost perfect."

"And?"

He narrowed his eyes in thought. "I'm still thinking about that. Something is holding her back, but I need to figure out what."

I nodded. "I agree. I couldn't figure it out either. I think she's already good enough to get into most schools."

"But she needs something extra to get into Berklee," he finished.

"Exactly." I stepped closer until I leaned on the island across from him. Even though we had a few feet between us, our toes were almost touching. "And Devlin's place sounds cool."

"Very cool."

"Was anybody else there?" I asked.

He raised an eyebrow. "Word is out about The Burnouts, I take it?"

"Clara told me. How come you didn't mention it?"

"Didn't really think about it." He was short and lying to me. I hadn't realized how much I took Leo's openness for granted until seeing him lie to me cut deeper than I thought it would.

"It can't be easy seeing them," I said.

"I'm hoping that I won't," he said sharply.

"Did things end that badly?"

"Why are you pushing this, Mari?" He laughed it off, but it sounded dry and sarcastic.

"I'm sorry." I was doing it again. Inserting myself, pushing him. "You just seem upset. I thought maybe you wanted to talk about it." I risked a glance at him to find his gaze on my legs. When he noticed me, he glared at the ground instead.

"I got myself fired. How could that be anything other than bad?" He scrubbed at his eyes. "Touring with my best friend was all I ever wanted, and I screwed it up. But more than that, I ruined the best friendship I ever had," he confessed.

A familiar pain I felt in myself was reflected in him. I longed to hold him. "You haven't spoken at all?"

He shook his head. "I made sure of that."

There didn't feel like there was anything I could say to help. He seemed so lost and alone. Like how I was when there was a break in work and I had nothing to distract me.

"I'm sorry," I repeated. Why had I pushed him? Why did I wish so hard that he would share with me? What was my hope?

"No. I am." He sighed, and his shoulders dropped. "I'm exhausted, but can't sleep, and that pisses me off."

"This is you pissed off?" I came to his side and nudged him with his elbow. "Trust me, as someone with anger issues, this is nothing."

"Too bad the Rage Room isn't open right now," he said.

He tried to laugh, but his shoulders slumped. This wasn't smash-up-things anger, though. This may not be anger at all. Hurt and sadness rolled off him.

To go from a life of such excitement and glamour, living his dreams every day, to hiding out in the town that he ran away from, no wonder he seemed so lost. No wonder he hated walking around this place, seeing what must feel like constant reminders of his supposed shortcomings and what he ruined.

I'd been so selfish to push him for my own agenda. It was never about him being too good for this town. He tried to tell me that so many times, but I couldn't see his hurt past my own. I was the Hector Projector here.

"I'm sorry," I repeated.

"It's the past."

"No. I mean, about me. About being so . . . God, when I think of what I put you through these past few weeks. The marching band, driving me around, pulling me away from danger. I've been incredibly selfish."

"You were doing it for Cath."

"That's what I told myself. But I wasn't thinking about you. And that's so messed up."

"It's not messed up to care. I have been . . . existing. Since you've gotten here, I feel like I'm living again."

My heart jumped into my throat. "The fear of death will do that," I tried to joke.

He chuckled half-heartedly.

"It's more than that," I went on. "I've pushed you so hard. Asked so much of you. The stuff with your band. And then at the Fall Festival. I can't ever repay you. I'm already in your debt because of what you're doing for Cath."

He scratched the back of his neck, running that same hand around to tug at his curls. "You don't owe me anything. And with Cath . . . I don't know that I'm even really helping. I don't know what to do there."

"I have faith in you. And as far as everything else, I can chill out a little. Control myself, my temper. I'll be better."

"What temper?"

"Come on," I said with a disbelieving look.

"Your passion is not a temper. You don't have anger issues. I think people have just told you that for so long, you take it to be true. You're a physically active person. You're highly motivated. But you aren't some ticking time bomb."

"You've literally pulled me away from people."

"Yeah, but I've also seen you hold back when it matters. With Pin Dick. That guy is the worst. If you were really overly emotional—whatever that even means—you wouldn't be able to deal with him. You wouldn't be the force that you are to this town and for this band. Just because people don't know what to do with you, that isn't your problem."

"I-I always felt like something was wrong with me. That I should be one of those very calm Southern ladies. I want to be better." *For you*, I almost said.

"People who care about you only want you to be yourself. You don't have to change yourself to be chosen."

An internal alarm went off. I wanted that to be true, but time had shown me the opposite. What it would be like to be chosen by a man like him. But it wasn't on the table, and this wasn't about me. I was meant to be comforting Leo.

He reached again for his curls. I brushed his hand away, stepping forward to tug on a lock. "You have such good hair. All this bounce. Totally the opposite of mine." Our bodies were inches apart.

He cleared his throat on a swallow. "Janice always jokes that I got my curls from her."

My confusion must have been clear as he added, "Because I'm adopted." He watched my face closely for a reaction to his confession.

My gaze searched his as I moved closer. "I didn't know."

"Not a lot of people do," he said simply.

How had Leo and I gotten to this place? Once strangers in a small town, now whispering confessions to each other in the middle of the night, our bodies only a breath away.

"Thanks for sharing that with me. Do you know your birth parents?" I asked.

"Nah. Janice never let me feel like I missed anything," he said.

"She's a wonderful mother."

"She's done everything for me. I literally wouldn't be here without her."

I smiled at his sincerity, thinking again of how she'd asked me to help him. How she'd raised this incredible man all on her own. I fell into him without warning to hug him.

It took him a moment before he lifted his arms to hug me back. My front pressed to his bare chest. It was incredibly intimate. It was peace.

He nestled his head against the curve of my neck. The brush of his prickly chin tickled, sending shivers tingling along my spine. I relaxed and luxuriated in his arms, hoping he found comfort too.

His skin felt hot and soft against my lips.

"Mari," he whispered.

I stilled when I realized I'd been subtly running my lips against the muscles of his shoulder.

I'd been taken over by lustful instinct. His hands slid down my arms to grab mine. He laced our fingers together, and the innocent action spread heat through to my core, overwhelming my senses. I wished he would press himself against me. I wished I could feel him hardening as I softened.

"You said you didn't want this," he said.

I hid my face. My cheek burned against his warmth. "I did say that."

"It's confusing to me," he admitted, and it was like cold water.

I leaned back to look up at him. His dark eyes were narrowed with regret and lust. He wanted this; he wanted *me*. He released my hands to tangle his own in my hair, tilting my head back to look at him. His gaze moved, never still, all over my face and neck. His chest rose and fell fast against me. I held on to his back as I studied him. The beat of my heart felt so heavy that it shook my quick breaths.

"I could kiss you. I would love to taste your lips again." His voice strained as he spoke. His nose ran along the shell of my ear, and I gasped. "But I can't have you regret it. Or think it was a mistake."

I nodded, unable to speak. I was torn between giving in to this desire and listening to my rational mind that told me I would regret it. I always regretted needing somebody.

His mouth hovered over the junction of my neck. He exhaled again, lips almost but not quite touching my jaw. My mouth parted to breathe him in like a shotgunned hit. He tilted his head to the other side. Nothing touched me, but his presence was as tangible as if he'd been licking me.

I wanted to be the person who could let my body lead in this instance. Why was it so easy every other time, when my mind clouded over in anger? Why did I still resist when it would only bring pleasure?

Because Leo would get hurt. *I* would get hurt.

I closed my eyes and brought my arms into my body, curling my fingers against his chest. "You're right."

His exhalation was sharp and pained.

"I didn't mean to confuse you," I said, throat tight.

His forehead dropped to mine.

"If it helps, I'm so confused too." I felt so vulnerable, so exposed to Leo like I'd never been with anybody else. "I never meant for this . . . I never meant to make you feel *used.*"

His arms went back to wrap around my shoulders.
"I only ever meant to help Cath," I said, exhausted.
"I know." He kissed my temple.
I closed my eyes and wished I was a different person.

CHAPTER 21
LEO

November arrived and brought with it a new rhythm of life.

I had done an exceptional job of playing the professional.

At least outwardly. I couldn't control my thoughts or dreams.

The midnight chat in the kitchen was a confusing combination of gratitude and sleep deprivation on Mari's part. I wanted her. I had incredibly deep feelings for her. *And* I was patient. To me, Mari and I were more than a fling that would be shameful in the light of morning. But releasing her that evening had been one of the most difficult things I'd ever done.

Three weeks ago, just before Halloween, she got the news that her car was officially totaled and was written a check by the insurance company. She had yet to drive to Knoxville to look at cars.

"It's just too much of a time eater. And this is still working," she had said, repeating my phrasing from when I first started driving her.

It was more convenient as she, Cath, and I had to drive up to Devlin's house a few times a week. She'd gotten in the habit of staying there to work on various tasks as Cath and I sat in the drum room to rehearse for two hours. There was a comfort in looking up and seeing her lost in thought.

We had made it clear that we wouldn't be crossing any physical lines, but we could still enjoy each other's company. And enjoy it, I did. I liked her peppy morning energy and our daily stops at Daisy's. I still hated mornings, but it wasn't as bad getting up in the mornings when you had somebody to get up for. I loved hearing about her and Cath's days as we drove up to Bandit Lake.

After Halloween, Mari was busier than ever, preparing for the end of the year and all the associated holiday performances.

Every morning, I picked her up to take her to work; she smelled sweetly of whatever shampoo she used, and she chatted happily. Every afternoon, we either went up to Devlin's for Cath's practice, or I picked her up later in the evening, and she would come over for dinner.

She protested at first, but soon, the offers of free, consistent food were too much to resist. It became a routine. Some nights, Janice was there; others, she had plans. I secretly enjoyed those nights the most. I doted on Mari and cooked for her. Most weeks the only night I didn't see Mari was bunco night. Try as I might, the women wouldn't budge about letting her in.

"You were the only exception," Maxine said. "I told y'all this would happen. It's a slippery slope. You let in one, and they bring in all their friends."

"Who are *they*?" Janice asked.

"Your son and all his youthful ilk. Can't we have anything just for us?"

I let it go, and Mari insisted that she always had plenty of things to do anyway.

After bunco night, I would call her and fill her in on what I learned. She'd insist she didn't care to hear the local gossip, but we would stay up on the phone talking for hours. She laughed at my terrible jokes and filled me in on what else I had missed around town in the past decade or the antics of her students.

My absolute favorite part of the new routine was learning about Mari and sharing music with her. I didn't have much, but I did have a massive music knowledge base. I'd share new-to-her artists from all different decades and genres. Occasionally, she'd share music with me, and we'd discuss how and *if* our favorite songs would translate to marching band sets.

I thought about her all day when she was in school. I thought about how luscious she felt pressed against me in the kitchen that night. I cursed myself for having the appropriate restraint. But having her in these glimpses was better than not having her at all. And if she gave too much too soon, my gut told me she wouldn't have agreed to be driven around.

The lessons with Cath were becoming something I looked forward to. Slowly but surely, she was opening up to me and even unleashed a sarcastic barb from time to time. I took that as a compliment, since sarcasm was a teenager's love language. I'd not seen any sign of Vander and the band and stopped looking over my shoulder every lesson. I suspected Devlin had something to do with that.

The vibe was off today. Cath was quieter than normal, and Mari kept shooting her worried glances. When Mari tried to get her to talk in the car, she only received one-word replies. The harder she pushed, the more Cath retreated into herself. Eventually, I lightly put a hand on Mari's knee and shook my head subtly. She sucked in her lips and nodded.

Now in the drum room, with Mari on the other side of the glass, Cath was half-heartedly playing the same jazz selection she'd been playing for weeks. She was technically perfect, but her energy was not there. If I knew better terms and words for music, I'd be able to pinpoint what was wrong. I wasn't making anything better.

"Okay. Stop," I called midsong.

Cath froze before lowering her sticks. "Why?"

"What's going on?" I asked her.

She glanced at Mari, who sat behind the glass. When I turned to look, Mari felt us watching her and lifted a hand. We waved, and Mari went back to typing on her laptop.

"Don't worry, she can't hear us," I said.

"Nothing. Just tired," Cath said, gaze focused on her snare.

"We don't have to do this today."

"We're already here."

"Okay." I paced in a circle. "Okay. Let's just quit with the audition stuff. It's boring as shit."

Cath snorted. "It's not so bad."

"Okay, you're right. It's not bad, but you aren't feeling it and that's coming across. It's clear that you could play these songs in your sleep. I'm pretty sure that's what you're doing right now. If I can feel that, the committee will too."

Cath frowned. "What do you mean?"

"You've been to concerts, right?"

"Obviously."

"Do you think the drummers up there care if they're technically perfect? No. Because it's more about the show and taking the listeners on a journey. Stop playing to the teachers. Or to me. Play like you're on a stage playing to all your adoring fans. Your job isn't to be a star student. It's to be a star." I was starting to understand what her playing lacked. I wanted her to be excited to play, to be filled with that fire I had once.

"Nice speech."

"I'm serious. What are you afraid of?"

Cath beat the sticks against her thigh. "I just want to play what I'm supposed to. Get into college and start my life. That's the plan," she said.

"Fuck the plan. You're what, seventeen? Here's a secret: nobody has a plan."

"Miss Mitchell does."

"Mari is the exception. Just play something you'd play if nobody was here."

Cath cracked a tentative smile. "What should I play?"

"The first thing that comes to mind."

She pursed her mouth in thought, looking into space for the answers. After a minute, she went to my phone, which was connected to the sound system, and selected a song. Her foot tapped as she counted off a beat in her head. After a second, she started to play, sticks hitting the cymbal and snare in tandem. The drum intro to "Rock and Roll" by Led Zeppelin was instantly recognizable. She even came in on the pickup to the fourth beat. Few drummers knew that correct entrance. This kid was so damn good.

"Nice choice!" I shouted. It was a high-energy song. The drums pulled the whole band through, as they should. The longer she played, the more her face remained impassive. She was still holding back. "Come on. Get into it," I encouraged. I stood and moved closer to watch her. She was good but still acting like she thought she should. She glanced at the window where Mari was still working, not paying attention. Was she worried about what Mari would think?

"More," I said.

She played louder but in the same energy, her face scrunching with the physical exertion of keeping the steady, almost Chicago shuffle–like melody.

"More!" I yelled.

Something was off, and I couldn't figure out what.

I opened my mouth to shout when she slammed down on the cymbals, grabbing them so they stopped ringing through the air. "If you say 'more' one *more* time, I will scream."

She was panting, and her face was bright red.

"Sorry." I shook my head. "It just needs . . ."

"More? Yeah, I got that. Can you be more specific?"

My ears rang in the silence. I took a breath. What did I mean? "It's a feeling. Are you feeling it? Are you really listening?"

"I thought I was." She glanced again to the window. This time, Mari was watching us, the first furrow of concern on her brow. I smiled and gave her a thumbs-up, and she went back to work. "This isn't why we're here. We should just get back to the audition stuff," Cath said.

"Hang on." What about Mari being here was throwing her off? "First, just try to listen to this."

I went to the sound system and queued up the song to play through our headphones.

"It's meant to feel like a return to rock and roll. That urgency. Like just trying to catch up with that driving feeling."

She raised her eyebrows. "I played it how it goes."

"Technically, yes. But those accents in the intro, you hear how they are different once the guitar kicks in. That's that feeling of rushing and rocking. Do you want to try it again?" I asked her.

"No." She crossed her arms. "I can't understand by hearing, obviously. I've heard this song a bunch. That's how I learned it," she said.

"But—"

"Just show me." She tossed out her arms.

I froze, a sudden tingling in my palms. "I-I don't really—"

"How am I supposed to learn without seeing?"

"That's the point, just listen to the song. The angst, the energy."

Cath's foot tapped, but her arms were crossed. She started to play along but fumbled a few times.

"Just show me!" she shouted over the music in our headphones.

I glanced at the glass, but Mari was on her computer, not looking. I wasn't sure if that made it better or worse.

I paused the music and stared at the kit. I could play. I could do that. Not a big deal. "Uh. Okay. Just. Okay."

Cath stood and handed me the sticks. I adjusted the stool and sat down.

Except it was a big deal. I wasn't ready. A wave of nerves tightened my stomach as I tested the set, knowing they sounded fine. I was delaying.

Cath looked hopeful, stars in her eyes. "You really want to hear me?" I asked.

She shrugged. I sighed, understanding that to mean *hell, yes*.

"So, I can't read sheet music. But if this song had some, this is how you would play it, right?" I started to play. Years of muscle memory didn't let me down. The song came right back to me.

"It sounds good," she said, her sleeves tugged over her hands.

"It's not bad, but listen to the song and the message and what's happening. Obviously, you won't be playing with a band, but the point remains the same. You're not trying to prove that you're technically perfect."

"I think that's exactly what they want."

"But you can already do that," I said. "Try to play like you're the engine of a car. You're keeping the tempo, but you're setting the tone."

I started again and, this time, closed my eyes. I let the memories of playing countless times on countless stages pour over me. I let myself hear the screaming fans and feel the electricity of the band playing in perfect sync. We'd been fueled by the rage and injustice we'd felt to be trapped in Green Valley, misjudged and undervalued. I remembered the first time we'd played this song, and it felt like everything had led to that moment. Robert Plant reminded me how good it was to get lost in the music.

I was sweating and moving my body. I wasn't thinking, only feeling. It was good. It was so good. God, I missed this.

When I ended the outro, I sighed, opening my eyes. Cath watched me, smiling ear to ear.

I cleared my throat and stood. "Do you feel the difference?"

Cath nodded.

My hands throbbed as I handed the sticks back to her. I couldn't help myself. I glanced up to the glass to see if Mari had been watching, but she wasn't there. I squashed down a pulse of disappointment. The point was not to play for Mari; I told Cath as much. The point was to play for myself, for the music.

And I had. I almost couldn't believe how good it had been.

I was panting and sweating. My hands smarted, but I felt amazing. I missed this. I missed the rush. I missed the adrenaline and power of playing.

Cath readjusted the stool and settled behind the kit. She glanced at the window and over to me. I gave her a thumbs-up. This time, the intro was noticeably different right out of the gate. Her playing transformed. Goose bumps spread up my neck.

"Holy . . ." I mouthed.

Her eyes were closed, her body barely able to contain the energy pouring out. Her accents were just perfect. Cath played with the emotion I'd been wanting this whole time. It was like a switch flipped. I didn't do this. This was here the whole time, but she had been purposely hiding it for some reason.

"That's exactly what I meant," Mari said, suddenly at my side.

"What?" I asked her.

"When I said you would know what she needs. *That.* She's totally in her element."

I shook my head. "This wasn't me."

Cath continued to go and was incredible. I felt something that I hadn't felt for a long time. That feeling of magic when music filled the room with its energy and transformed everything. It was that muse, that kismet.

It didn't seem possible that I could have contributed to anything so powerful, but had there been something about my playing that let Cath feel free enough to share?

I swallowed the tightness in my throat. And studied Mari's profile. She'd believed in me from the beginning. She'd insisted repeatedly, borderline violently, that I was the person who could help Cath, and I *had*.

Mari turned her head, probably feeling my stares. She smiled so brilliantly it made it hard to breathe. She took my hand and squeezed it.

"Thank you," she whispered.

I felt the words on my tongue, the declaration and truth, that everything was for her. They were right there. I would give her anything she ever asked of me.

Cath finished the song, and her eyes widened when they landed on Mari squeezing my hand briefly. The song ended, and Cath stood abruptly.

"We should probably wrap up," she said. "We are already over our time."

As she spoke, we both noticed movement in the sound booth.

We weren't the only people watching Cath.

There was a man with a look of surprised, impressed awe. He smiled as he looked from Cath to me, where he paused. His eyes widened fractionally, his smile fading from his face.

On the other side of the glass stood my former bandmate and best friend, Vander. All the exhilaration from a moment ago crashed to the floor.

CHAPTER 22
MARI

L eo had been looking at me with a quiet admiration more and more lately. How he looked at me now as I came to his side. His softened features and intense eyes told me a story I wasn't ready to read. I'd watched him play, and it was incredible, but I hadn't wanted him to know I was watching. There had been tension between Cath and him; they needed space to work through whatever was happening.

I squeezed his hand when I felt him stiffen.

Hands dropping to his side, he said, "I gotta go."

I followed his gaze to the mixing room and found a man I only recognized from pictures.

It was Vander from The Burnouts. His light-brown hair was almost to his shoulders and as thick and wild as his beard. He wore round, thin-wired glasses that evoked John Lennon and a gray blazer over a half-unbuttoned white collared shirt. His gaze was locked on Leo, features unreadable.

"Wait," I whispered to Leo. "Don't run away. You aren't alone."

His nostrils flared, and he glanced behind me again. "I'm not prepared for this conversation." Leo stooped his head, and the anxiety pinching his eyes tore at my chest.

"I won't let anything bad happen to you," I said. A protectiveness gripped me. As fiercely as I protected my students from Pin Dick, I would protect Leo. Just let this guy say something. He would see the full velocity of my wrath.

Leo held my stare like he was about to argue but stayed at my side. "He's coming in here."

"It's okay," I said. I grabbed his hand and squeezed it again but dropped it just as fast, not sure he wanted the visible protection.

Leo nodded and stepped closer to me, almost behind me.

Cath came to stand with us. She smiled, but through her teeth, she asked, "I'm trying not to freak out, but is that Vander Moore?" Her performance still glowed in her cheeks. "Because I might pass out if it is."

Leo mumbled something I couldn't hear.

"He's just a person," I said and lifted my chin.

"A rock star who is currently selling out stadiums, but sure," Cath said.

Leo's frown deepened. Cath finally seemed to notice his silent seething. "Oh. Sorry. This is probably so weird for you."

"No, it's great. I'm having the time of my life," he said flatly.

"You sounded incredible," I said to her, desperate to lift some of the tension.

"It's true," Leo added. "Did it feel better?" he asked.

"Yeah. That was fun." She glanced at me, guarded like I was about to say something else. "But better to stay focused on the audition."

I was about to tell her playing for fun was just as important as her audition, but Leo spoke first.

"We should probably get you home. It's later than I thought," he said, already shuffling back to the door.

"Actually, Ruby is coming to get me. I picked up a late shift tonight," Cath explained.

"You don't have to leave on my account," a voice said from behind me. Leo stiffened at my side.

We turned in tandem to the newcomer. Cath had already been facing him, but her eyes widened, and she stopped blinking.

"I just forgot my phone here from earlier," Vander added.

When none of us spoke, Vander extended a hand to Cath. "Hi, I'm Vander. You sounded great in there. Tell me you're the new drummer?"

Cath's jaw fell. "No. I'm Cath. I am drumming, a drummer. I play the drums."

"I saw that. And well." Vander gave a wide, charming smile. He'd always been the lead guitarist and vocalist in The Burnouts, and that energy was apparent in every quirk of his features and body movement. It was like he performed a character even now.

"Thank you. I'm a huge fan. I saw you three times on the *Vagabond* tour."

"Awesome. Love meeting the next gen of talent."

"I'm Mari Mitchell. I'm Cath's teacher down at Green Valley High." I extended my hand, and he shook it warmly. So far, he seemed nice enough. I pulled my claws in slightly.

Leo seemed to be stuck on what Cath had said. He had never looked so betrayed and shocked. "You said you'd never heard of The Burnouts," he said to her and then seemed to regret it.

"No, I didn't. You never actually asked me," Cath said with a sweet smile up at him. "You assumed, and you know what they say about assuming . . ."

Leo's jaw flexed, and his eyes narrowed. I was equal parts amused and worried by this interaction. It must have never come up that she idolized him. Probably because I was worried about it influencing how he treated her. But that was before I knew who he really was. And right now, he was on an uneven playing field and could use a hint of an ego boost.

"Cath is a huge fan of Leo's," I said to Vander. Then, to Leo, I said, "She has your poster on her wall. It's part of the reason we thought to reach out to you," I said.

Now, it was her turn to seem betrayed. Well, two could play at that game, missy.

"Very uncool, Miss M," she mumbled.

Leo, for his part, was slightly mollified but was still looking at Cath like she might change shapes at any moment.

I shrugged. "I didn't know it was a secret. I thought Leo knew you were one of his biggest fans. He's so incredibly talented. Nobody could blame you." Maybe I laid it on a little thick, so sue me.

Leo and Cath both looked at me in various stages of shock but refused to look at each other. Vander chuckled quietly and looked at the floor.

"Well, this has been super weird. My ride is here. Bye." Cath smiled shyly again to Vander. "Nice meeting you."

He waved goodbye, and the three of us stood there for what felt like roughly three years of heavy silence.

"So Green Valley High, huh?" Vander asked me. His gaze moved to Leo for a flash, but Leo was pointedly looking anywhere but at his former bandmate.

"Yep, I teach band. All the bands."

"Oh, you're who took over from Janice? Is that evil crossing guard still there? Christ, she hated me."

"To be fair, she hates everyone. And yes, she'll be blowing her whistle at drivers until they pry that thing from her cold, dead hands," I said.

Vander chuckled. "Did you go there when Leo and I were there? You look familiar."

Leo shifted at my side. Whether it was the mention of their shared past, I wasn't sure.

"I did. I was a few grades ahead. I was in the same year as your older sister," I explained.

Dammit, I was supposed to be getting rid of this guy, not playing small-town catch-up. I put an arm around Leo's shoulders. I'd meant for the action to display friendly camaraderie, but the second I moved close to Leo, his arm slunk around my waist, pulling me tight to his side.

"Leo is mentoring Cath. She's incredible, as you saw. She's applied to Berklee, and he's helping her prepare for her audition in spring," I said, pretending this was normal behavior for us.

Leo's ears burned red, but he still hadn't spoken to Vander.

"Fantastic. Well, she's obviously going places." Vander directed it to Leo but then looked back at me when he only got forehead.

"How's the album going? Devlin mentioned you were recording. Must be a lot of pressure, especially after how good your first three were," I said.

Leo glanced up at me. The first three albums were the only albums Leo had been on.

Ha. Suck it, Vander.

Vander scratched at the back of his neck but took my passive aggression well enough. "Ah, well. We're still finding our rhythm for this new LP. You know how it goes. Hit some bumps but we'll pull it out, yet. Hoping for some of that Smoky Mountain magic," he explained.

"Good album name," Leo mumbled at the same time I said it. He looked up to finally give me an authentic smile and some of the tension relaxed out of me.

Vander looked between us, brow furrowed, missing the punchline of our inside joke.

"Devlin was on his way out when I came in. He said you guys should have been wrapped up. I didn't mean to intrude," Vander said.

When neither of us spoke, he cleared his throat and nodded. "Right. Okay. Well, I'll get out of your hair. Devlin's gone into Knoxville with the family for the night. He just said to lock up the downstairs exit when you leave. Uh, see you." Vander glanced at Leo, but Leo was still focused on me.

Dang, I started to feel bad for the guy.

"Bye, nice meeting you," I said.

He gave a flat smile, glanced at Leo one more time, sighed, and went out.

Leo didn't move for a few minutes. He just stared at the floor as his cheeks grew more and more red. I tried to give him space, but when I moved, his arms locked me in place.

"Are you okay?" I asked softly. It had been so loud in here just a few minutes ago, and now the silence was deafening.

He made a sound that might have been a growl or a moan.

"Yeah. Stupid question," I said. I lowered my head to his chest and pulled him tight. He hugged me back. I should have done or said more.

I didn't want this to cause Leo to retreat. I wanted him to talk about what happened and process it, but my experience with men told me that now came the part where he got angry and shut down.

"I'm sorry—" I leaned back to meet his gaze, and he loosened his grip to release me.

"I've spent so much time thinking about what I'd say when I saw him." He spoke low and steady, still staring just past me into a void of memories I couldn't see. Leo wasn't like all the other men. Maybe it was being raised by a progressive single mother or just his nature. But he always shared with me. And it was a gift. "And then I just froze. I just—" He stopped and tugged at his hair, blinking himself back to the present. His gaze moved over me. "I'm just glad you were here. I-I don't know what I would have done."

I swallowed down the tightness in my throat. "I wish I'd done something more." I glanced at the stairs. "He might still be here. I could go slash his tires?" I asked hopefully.

He threw his head back and laughed. His Adam's apple bobbed before he turned to grip my shoulders. "God, I love you," he joked, pulling me into another hug. I froze at his words. My stupid heart went haywire at the sound of that confession. He hadn't meant it like that. I had wanted him to laugh. I had broken his trance, and that was what I meant to do, so why was I totally unable to move past what was just a common turn of phrase? "Nah. Then he'd be stuck here with us."

"Good point." My arms finally remembered how hugs worked, but he was already pulling back.

He let out a sigh and ran a hand over his face. "It was so weird to see him. I thought I would know what to say. I thought it would all come pouring out of me exactly as I meant it to after all my mental rehearsals in the shower." I smiled at his confession. "But . . ."

"What?" I prodded. He'd been about to say something, and I didn't want him to retreat into his head. I liked it so much when he shared with me. I loved being given the opportunity to make him smile. I wanted to help carry his mental load. I tugged him to the couch in the studio, quickly moving some paper so we could both sit. He didn't protest as I guided him to sit down.

"I wasn't mad." He swallowed, and again, his throat seemed to snag. "I just felt sad. I guess. And that is somehow worse." He scrunched his face and looked away.

"Worse?"

"I wanted to be mad. To somehow justify the past few months. But I just thought about how much fun we had. Maybe because I had just been drumming before seeing him. It was like I jumped through time. I wanted to tell him about Cath and you and Green Valley and how weird it was to be here without him and about all the changes too."

"You miss him," I whispered.

"Apparently." He nodded, again looking away to push down whatever was trying to come back.

"Have you thought about talking to him? I mean, really talking. Not the conversations in your head? I bet there are things he'd like to say too. It doesn't have to be a knock-down, drag-out thing. People can't read minds. We project whole narratives but don't know what they're thinking. Either way, it might be better to have closure. Sometimes you need to have the hard conversation, even if you've known them your whole life."

"Especially then."

"It might make you feel better."

"Or a whole lot worse."

"I don't think you feel very good now, Leo. Are you happy out here? Out in Green Valley? After reaching the heights you did, it can't be easy to be back here."

I was terrified to know his answer. It wasn't fair to expect that much of this new friendship, but I wanted him to be happy more than anything.

"It wasn't easy to come home. For a long time, I wondered why I did. Lately, I'm starting to think I might know what brought me back," he said.

The way his gaze moved over my face caused something in my stomach to flip and fill my chest with hope. My feelings for Leo had continued to plague me these past few weeks, no matter how I tried to rationalize them away.

I broke the eye contact first, glancing around the room. I saw the drum kit and suddenly remembered everything that had happened prior to the arrival of Vander.

"You sounded great too, by the way. I've never seen you play in person. It was . . ." Incredible. Amazing. Sweaty. Sexy. Riled me up faster than a GIF of

Pedro Pascal winking at the camera. None of these felt like appropriate things to say. "Really cool."

"You saw me?" he asked on a swallow.

When he played, he seemed entirely comfortable in his body. He played like he'd been taken over by a higher power. He wasn't doing anything for anybody else. He just existed, and he deserved to feel that way all the time.

"I may have peeked for a minute or two," I admitted.

He turned to me so that his knees nudged the leg I had tucked under me. "You liked it?" Something in the way he asked shifted the air in the room.

"Very much." I flushed and swallowed with effort. Maybe I hadn't been so subtle in my thoughts. "I wish I heard more."

"You want to watch me?" he asked, his words innocent enough but his gaze dark with intent.

I whimpered and nodded.

CHAPTER 23
LEO

Vander's unexpected arrival scrambled my brain but was not something I could process, not when Mari was so close and looking at me like that. She'd been here. She'd protected me.

Before that, I'd been pulsing with adrenaline from playing. To know she'd been watching . . . and liking it made me feel insane, primal pride.

Mari brought me back to the present. She always did. Because when I was with her, there was no other time or place I wanted to be.

I preened at being able to impress her.

I wanted to make Mari wet for me.

Maybe it was vain or crass, but I woke every morning as hard as a rock since our kiss all those weeks ago at the Rage Room, and I wanted to see her come undone.

I went back and adjusted the set, aware of her tracking my every move. I thought about what I told Cath—if I was playing to please her, it wouldn't work. I had to play for the sake of the music.

I closed my eyes and played my favorite song from The Burnouts. I knew it completely, listening to the recording in my head. It didn't make me sad like I thought it might. It felt right. It reminded me of the parts of playing with The Burnouts that I missed. I had a habit of only remembering the hardest parts of things. This was a good reminder of how much the music had meant to me.

I was sweating before long. The thin tee was creating too much uncomfortable friction on my skin. Mari watched me when I opened my eyes again to pull off my shirt. Her mouth was softly parted, her cheeks flushed. She squirmed in her seat, and I wondered if she knew what she was doing to me. I wondered if she knew how much she gave away. I wasn't one for random hookups on the road, but I'd been thrown enough looks from audience members biting their lips and rocking their hips to know what they were thinking.

Mari had that look now. She pulled her hair off her neck.

I played another song and only stopped when my hands began to throb. It had been too long, and my muscles may remember every beat, but the skin of my hands had grown thin again.

When I set the sticks down, my chest rose and collapsed like I'd just been on stage. I held up my palms. "I need to ease back in."

She frowned and disappeared into the bathroom. When she came back, determination set her shoulders. That was a look I knew all too well.

In a few strides, she came around the set to stand in front of me. I looked up at her and swallowed. My legs spread as I turned, and she came to stand between them without hesitation.

What was happening? I thought I could handle her looks, and maybe if it stopped there, I would have survived. I would not survive her physical attention.

She reached for my hands, and I lifted them to hers.

"You're incredible," she said.

I swallowed as I stared up at her. She gently examined my hands as though they had some secret magic she could discover if only she looked hard enough.

"Looks painful," she said. She pressed the damp washcloth to the fresh calluses forming over the decades-old ones.

"Nothing I haven't experienced before."

With smooth, careful ministrations, she cleansed me with the cool water and checked for injuries. My chest rose and fell as she cared for me. Whatever I had done in life to deserve this, please let me do it all the time. After she'd finished cleansing my hands, she gently set the washcloth aside. She gently lifted my fingers and brought my right palm up to place a kiss at the center, then did the same to my left. A breath whooshed out of me. She kissed each pad of my fingers. Hot desire rushed all over my body. I swallowed and tried to wrangle in my thoughts and racing heart.

"These fingers. So strong but soft," she said, still examining each one in turn.

"Can't hold on too tight. Have to let things flow as they need to," I said. Just as with the music, so with her.

"So . . . proficient. So good at what they do," she whispered.

"Is this really happening? Am I dreaming?" She grinned at my question.

She released my hands, and I reverently dropped them to her hips, tentatively at first, to see if she'd stop me. She stepped closer, and the warm scent of her flared my nostrils. Her hands went to my hair and pushed it off my face. If she was bothered by my sweat, she showed no signs of it. If anything, quite the opposite.

"Funny you should say that because I have dreamed about your fingers," she admitted softly, and heat bloomed on her cheeks. "Fantasized," she added. It was enough to make a man feel like a god. My hands on her hips tightened, digging into the soft flesh.

"You have?" My voice broke as I asked.

She nodded, releasing me. "Few things are sexier than a man who's really good with his hands."

My chest felt like it was collapsing with every breath. I wasn't sure what was happening right now, but it couldn't go on if she didn't mean it.

"Mari. I-I'm too worked up right now. The adrenaline—I don't have the—I can't be strong enough for both of us," I admitted.

She cupped my chin and lifted it until I met her gaze. "Good. You've been strong long enough," she said.

"I love when you look at me like that," I said.

"You're beautiful when you play," she countered.

"I make dumb faces. I always feel awkward."

"You make focused faces. Focus is sexy. It makes me wonder about what other expressions you make when concentrating."

I groaned. God, she was really just putting it all out there. Mari was never one to mince words. My head fell to her chest. I panted in and out, watching my exhalations harden her nipples through the fabric of her shirt. "I would be genuinely happy to show you."

I felt her soft laugh under my cheek. "Okay," she said on an exhale.

"Hmm?" My mouth brushed along her collarbone, inhaling her perfect scent. I was sweaty and couldn't smell fresh, but she didn't seem to mind. If anything, she was borderline feral as she ran her hands over me.

She pulled back to look at me in exactly the right way– pupils blown, mouth parted, and a thousand dirty thoughts passing through her mind. I would make all her darkest dreams come true. "Show me everything," she demanded.

I growled. Quickly, I stood, swooping her up with me. She wrapped her long legs around my waist and her arms around my shoulders until I pressed her against the far wall tucked away in the only corner not lined with thick, soundproofing insulation. Desire took over. I wasn't interested in anything but making her share more of these delicious confessions.

"Remember when you said that I should just feel what I feel and stop trying to push everything down, stop trying to control it?" she asked.

I nodded, watching closely as she licked her lips.

My mouth fell to her, licking or kissing or sucking any bit of exposed skin. She closed her eyes, head falling back. "I think you're right."

"Good." I kissed my way up her neck. I was rougher than I meant, and my short beard left the skin flushed where it rubbed against her.

"You're very wise. I've started to take that to heart."

"What do you feel right now?" I asked, heart hammering with hope.

"Like I might die if I don't touch you. Not to be dramatic."

I chuckled as I squeezed her hips. "I've *already* died and gone to heaven. Not to be dramatic," I mirrored. I let her feel she wasn't alone in these feelings of madness. She groaned as my length pressed firmly into her. "And will you let me touch you too?"

She whimpered.

"Say it," I demanded.

Her knees fell together, and I pressed my thigh between hers to balance her. "I want it all."

"Will you let me make you feel good?" I asked, my voice rough.

"Yes," she said.

I gathered her long hair and collected it to lift it off the warm skin of her back. I inhaled her sweet, perfect scent at the junction of her neck and shoulder. Something had changed in her. She said she was ready to give in to this tension between us, but it didn't mean I would accept her pushing me away the second this frenzy burned out.

"And after?" I asked, halting in my caresses and kisses.

She turned her head to meet my gaze. I blatantly studied how she licked her lips, memorizing every second.

"After?" I repeated. "I can't go back, Mari," I said.

"After . . . we will carry on until it doesn't work anymore." She swallowed with nerves.

It was just like the driving schedule. She gave herself to me in careful pieces. This was what I wanted. This was what I got.

"Until it doesn't work anymore," I repeated. I could play it cool. I could make her feel good. Part of me wanted it written down. *It* being the promise of us. If only I could have a sort of legally binding government document. Maybe with other people to witness us sign it. Maybe with gold bands involved and a party of all our closest friends and family. But one thing at a time. "I like that plan."

I dropped my head and tasted her, kissed her softly until she opened her mouth to me. I explored her tongue with my own, savoring the ecstasy of her taste. My hand reached for her, pushing up her shirt to get to her soft skin. I smoothed every inch of her side, and I spanned her middle, thumb grazing the bottom of her breasts as my pinky caught on the snap of her jeans. But the angle wasn't working like this. I needed more. I kissed her deeply. Pure, hot desire from my mouth to hers.

"I want to make you feel good," I said.

"Yes. Please, Leo."

My head dropped as I took a moment to collect myself. I felt an animalistic force trying to take over. I breathed in and out as she peppered my face and jaw and neck with kisses. Her hand went to the button of my jeans when I remembered what we were doing here.

"Wait," I said, gently grabbing her hand.

She whined. "No more waiting. I feel like I'm going to implode."

I chuckled. "Trust me, I know." I took her and gently turned her around to face the wall.

She did as I directed, shooting a curious but heavy-lidded glance over her shoulder. She had complimented my hands, and I was about to show her how right she was.

She gripped the wall for stability when I gently pushed her legs wider. I studied how beautiful she looked, waiting for me. My hands ran down her arms to her shoulders, back, and lower to her ass. Her legs trembled when I got to the top of her thighs.

I wished I could take off these damn jeans and lick her there, but that would have to be another time. Instead, I removed the space between us, pressing myself close to her back.

"Drummers are good at keeping several times at once," I said.

I lowered my head, gently pushing her hair off her shoulder to nuzzle the junction there. She exhaled softly.

My right hand smoothed over her stomach, slowly grazing her, feeling what areas elicited goose bumps. My left hand grasped her breast and toyed with her nipple at a slow, luxurious pace. "Four-four time."

Her head fell back onto my shoulder. "Leo," she gasped.

She turned her head, and our mouths clashed again. Keeping the beat of my left hand, the rhythm of my tongue exploring her mouth, my right hand went to the seam of her jeans. I traced the area softly with curious fingers, dragging just hard enough so she felt the pressure through the fabric. Heat emanated from her core, and she shivered.

"Three-fourths."

Her back arched, and she squirmed for me. I used one leg—another tempo —to lift her thigh onto mine. My other leg flexed, holding her wide and ready to be teased.

I pressed the heel of my palm more firmly against her core. She ground back, but it wasn't enough. I ground my hips, rock hard now against her ass.

"Six-eight."

"More. Please." She gasped.

I flicked open the snap of her jeans, the other hand now shoving her bra up to cup both breasts. My mouth tangled back with hers. Every part of my body was attuned to play the complicated melody of her pleasure.

I deftly pulled the jeans down over her gorgeous ass to give me more access. I leaned back far enough just to quickly examine my handiwork. She curled her fists against the wall, heels lifted with her greedy gasps. Her ass angled out, calves flexed, jeans half down, bra and shirt shoved up, she was writhing and ready for me. I'd never seen anything hotter in my life. I wanted to fall to my knees and worship her.

She looked over her shoulder, plump lips and chest heaving. "Leo, *please*."

I held her from behind, reassuring her, touching her everywhere. She dropped her forehead to her forearm as I found her center. I sucked in a breath at how hot, swollen, and wet she was for me. I used her desire to coat my fingers and tease her. I spread her and explored her. I pushed and retreated. She was wild and gasping. Every part of my body, set to a different beat, brought her closer to the edge. One of her arms came back to wrap around my head, and I watched her face closely. Studying how every different action of my fingers affected her. My finger found a spot just inside her that had her scream. My palm pressed against her clit as I rubbed the spot, her legs threatening to give out.

She climbed higher and higher but still held back. She was stopping herself from falling into her pleasure. Taking more and more air in without the relief of the exhale.

"Let it happen, Mari," I coaxed, my lips gasping against hers.

I felt tight as a wire, every single part of my body tense to deliver her pleasure.

"I don't know—"

"You can. Let it happen."

She was still holding on too tight, still trying to maintain control. I kissed her deeply as she held me. I tugged at her nipple at the same time I inserted another finger to tease that spot deep inside her, alternating between the taps and press of my palm. I was sweating and all coiled tense muscles, afraid to change any pattern that might keep her from her release.

She broke the kiss to throw her head back and call out. She was absolutely breathtaking as she freed herself to pleasure. Victory flooded me as she clenched and then pulsed against my fingers.

I relaxed my hand, careful to gently remove myself before it started to hurt. I kissed her flamed cheeks and whispered encouragement as her mind returned to her trembling body. While she was still blissed out, I returned her clothes to normal, discreetly wiping my fingers on the now conveniently located washcloth.

I scooped her up and brought her to the couch, boneless and mumbling.

"Was this the Smoky Mountain magic they refer to?" she asked after I set her back. She was beautiful and flushed and sated. Understanding came over me like a cool breeze. Not overwhelming or all at once, but a sort of quiet reassurance and peace of mind.

I loved this woman.

There was no remaining doubt. Giving her what she needed was all that mattered. I might never feel worthy of her, but I would damn well keep trying.

"No. That was all me."

"Drummers," she teased and rolled her eyes. "I don't think I'll be able to look Devlin in the eyes ever again."

"What happens in the studio, stays in the studio," I said.

CHAPTER 24
MARI

I returned to my physical self, breaths rasping, a sensation of swollen dizziness in my entire body. He had brought me to the couch. I was loose-limbed, warm, and satisfied.

I rubbed a hand up my neck into the damp hair at my nape. I lay with my body spread out on the couch, Leo looking down at me with that same look of awe that made me feel like the most incredible person on the planet.

"That was . . ." No words could possibly express how hard it was to get me to orgasm normally, let alone standing up. But there was no challenge when it was Leo doing the work. I had been correct in my assumption about his dexterity.

I flushed, the reality of the situation threatening to make it awkward. Except it wasn't. Leo looked at me with primal longing, making my body feel things it never had. He'd delivered on my internal hypothesis better than any of my fantasies. He'd played me expertly, found the tempo of my body like a musical virtuoso, but didn't leave me feeling like an object. He ran a hand over his face as he continued to watch me closely.

He was studying me for signs of regret, his features tortured with concern, not to mention the painful bulge nearly eye level, left ignored.

He wouldn't suffer a moment more. I reached for his jeans. He stepped back. "I'm okay. Are you?" he asked.

I nodded and sat up on the couch, legs tucked, back arched.

"This is . . . it will go down," he explained.

"Did you enjoy watching me come?" I asked bluntly.

He swallowed. "Yes." His voice rasped.

"I want to be able to see you now. There's no honor in keeping that from me," I said. I looked at where he subconsciously palmed his length. Just seeing the outline of the hardness pressing against the jeans sent a fresh wave of desire through me.

The last of his modesty groaned away as he carefully but quickly tugged himself free of his jeans.

"What do you want me to do?" I asked, licking my lips and sitting up more.

"You're doing it. Just look at me like that." His motions started smooth. I watched, mesmerized, as his thumb rounded over the tip to smear his precum. Slow and smooth at first, his hand roughly jerked himself. His beautiful cock was on full display as he abused it, his stomach muscles flexing with the exertion and focus. I felt beautiful as his gaze flicked over every part of me. I boldly caressed my body, thinking of the areas he touched me moments ago, remembering the pulse of pain and pleasure right before my orgasm, tweaking my tender nipple.

"Yes," he gasped.

His legs widened, and his strokes grew faster. He panted and made a sound of concern. I quickly grabbed a nearby tissue and handed it to him. The tips of my fingers dared to reach out and tease the area just under where he stroked without getting in the way. I lightly explored where his hand wasn't, cupping his balls and applying pressure just behind. Boldly, I leaned forward to barely tongue his leaking tip.

"Mari," he gasped and moved the tissue in time as I leaned out of the way, biting back my smile.

He stumbled forward, and I held on to his waist to help him balance.

I grinned up at him, and after a shake of his head, he blinked starstruck down at me. His smile rioted my heart.

We cleaned up and met back on the couch without speaking. He opened his arms, and I tucked myself against him as though we'd done it a hundred times. We had gotten more free with our touches these past few weeks, but nothing like this. Obviously.

"I was right," I said eventually. "I like your focused faces."

He chuckled with a groan, hiding his head in my hair. "Let's hope that Devlin doesn't have hidden cameras in here."

I sat up and looked wide-eyed at Leo. "You think he would?"

"Probably not after this."

I laughed, and it was my turn to hide my face.

"I'm kidding. In the tour, he mentioned that he always wanted to make sure the bands felt free to create without the pressure of being watched. And with zero risk of anything being leaked early. He's big on privacy."

"You know, I got that impression," I said.

We sat in silence for several minutes, neither of us ready to pop our bubble of contentment. The room seemed to soak sound up, and it was a new, restful type of quiet.

I looked back at the drum set, remembering how gorgeous he looked as he played, how in his element and in his body he'd seemed. He was far from the man who seemed to feel out of place everywhere he went. He was talented, wonderful, and sweet, and this growing sensation in my chest started to drown my lungs. I couldn't ruin this for myself. I wouldn't ruin it for him. I calmed my thoughts.

"Do you miss playing?" I asked softly.

"More than I thought I did," he admitted.

"Why did you stop?"

A long exhale escaped his chest, lifting and dropping my shoulders with it.

"You don't have to talk about it if you don't want to."

"I'm just trying to sort out my thoughts," he admitted.

I smiled to myself at his vulnerability. He was one of the most open people I'd ever met, and I could kick my former self for misinterpreting his care and deliberateness for lying or self-centeredness.

"I have nowhere else to be," I said and turned my head to kiss his still bare chest. I liked the little bumps that formed at the gesture.

"I think I associated the drumming with all the bad parts." He hesitated again, but I waited patiently. I would always be patient to hear his whispered confessions. "The fighting. The stress. The way it all ultimately ended." He cleared his throat. "I've been punishing myself on some level. I didn't feel like I deserved to play for how things ended."

My heart twisted for him and his pain. I knew this man so well now. I understood what an intensely giving person he was for those he cared about.

People like me. I closed my eyes and stayed focused on the now.

"How did it end?" I asked tentatively. "Since, you know, I've signed the NDA and all that."

His laughter rumbled through me. "They kicked me out. Like I said. I walked into rehearsal one day; we were halfway through the tour, and the moment I entered the room, the truth was on all their faces before I spoke." His swallow was audible behind me.

"How could they do that to you?" I shook my head.

"I deserved it," he admitted. I turned to study him as I pulled up my knees to tuck under my chin. There was no way this man who cared for me when I was sick, who had infinite patience for Cath and my antics, could ever be so bad that he got fired. It was incomprehensible.

He must have seen the confusion written all over my face.

"I was . . . I didn't like fame and touring. I didn't like anything about it except when we played music. But I hated how claustrophobic I felt as our fame grew. We got big pretty fast." He huffed a laugh. "It was all Vander and I dreamed about for so long, and then we got it. We were selling out shows, being featured in prestigious online music magazines, and being used in movie soundtracks. The faster we grew, the less *authentic* anything felt. The same mindless interviews. The screams of 'take off your shirt'—by the way, I only take off my shirt because I hate the way it feels when I'm sweating." I nodded. He would never do that to be some sort of sex icon. Now, at least, I understood. "The relentless schedule was the hardest. We never had a break. We never had downtime."

"Even doing what you love, what gives you life, you still need a break," I said.

"The record label didn't want us to be forgotten. We had a social media person tour with us, and we went viral."

I'd seen the short videos he was talking about, fan edits of him and Vander looking absolutely delicious. It didn't hurt that they were incredibly good-looking in addition to having legitimate talent.

"And after a couple of years, I realized I hated it. All of it. Even the touring because we didn't have the space or freedom to write new stuff. We were always on someone else's schedule. Even saying it out loud makes me sound like such an asshole. I should be grateful, but I was exhausted."

I wrapped his arms around me like a blanket. "I couldn't last as long as you did."

His sigh ruffled the top of my head. "Vander was never happier. He was living his dream. And that's what kept me going. I would think about being back in Green Valley and how badly we'd wanted to get out, and it would keep me focused. But then, I don't know. It started to catch up to me." He swallowed again. "I started having panic attacks before shows. I stopped going to the scheduled press stuff. I had this temper . . . You talk about having a temper, but it's nothing compared to my fits. I wasn't sleeping or eating. Everything felt like it was closing in on me. I just broke down. I threw my sticks in rehearsal one day and kicked over a set I was using. Thousands of dollars of damage. I was acting like a spoiled rock star. That part was true. That video of me walking off in the middle of a show." He groaned and rubbed his face. "Someone threw something at me. They don't show that in the clips, but I shouldn't have reacted that way. I should have just told security and had them escorted out. PR tried to downplay it, but the next day, I walked into the room and got fired."

"I'm so sorry," I said. I couldn't say anything to change what had happened, but I could be here now.

I felt him shake his head. "I'm just ungrateful."

"No, you're not. I think sometimes we *think* we want something, romanticize it so much, that when we get it, there's no way it won't disappoint. You had a bad moment. And unfortunately for you, it was caught and posted online. I'm trying to imagine a video montage of all the times I lost my cool. It is way worse than yours," I said. "No matter what you say."

His head was shaking, brow furrowed. "You're so wonderful, Mari. So determined and sure of what you want. It's inspiring. Drumming was my life for so long." His voice shook. "Sometimes . . . sometimes I don't know who I am anymore without it." He wouldn't meet my gaze.

I grabbed his face until he looked at me. "You are many wonderful things. You also happen to be a great drummer. It's part of you, but it doesn't define you."

His gaze moved over my face. "I never understood why you wanted me to help Cath. I knew my reputation preceded me. Especially out here. You had to have seen the footage."

I swallowed and looked up at him. A growing realization about Leo settled the anxiety in my bones, growing like a cold mist. I reimagined every interaction we'd shared since the beginning. His mom mentioned his sensitivity when she asked me to reach out to him. Now, it might feel like some sort of betrayal. He couldn't understand his inherent value. Leo had lost his self-worth along with his band. If Leo found out this arrangement was all due to his mother's suggestion, would it hurt him unnecessarily?

I chose my words carefully.

"I saw your skills. Cath idolized you. Devlin and your mom highly recommended you. I wanted to do what was best for Cath. There were so many reasons. And today proved that you brought out something in her that none of us could."

He searched my eyes as I spoke, his shoulders relaxing as he nodded against my hands. "It did feel good hearing her play like that today. I wonder why she holds back so much," he said.

"I'd wondered that too."

171

We were silent for a few minutes as he watched our hands toying with each other.

"Okay, I'm just going to say one last thing, and I promise I'll drop it," I said eventually.

"Don't make promises you can't keep," he said teasingly.

"Fair." I poked him. "Sorry. I just . . . can't stand people not talking about stuff. Vander should know all this stuff you told me about the anxiety and fame. I think, as someone who cares about you, that I would want to know." He sighed, but in a dreamy way, when I admitted that I cared about him. Of course, I did. "It might not change what happened, but it might help you both at least start to restore your friendship. I think you miss him more than you want to admit."

He nodded, mouth tight and eyes squinting. I put a hand on his cheek.

"It's your decision. But it might help you."

"Yeah. You might be right."

I fell into his arms. God bless men who listen to women.

"But let's circle back to you caring about me."

I rolled my eyes as he stopped to kiss me before losing myself to him once again.

CHAPTER 25
LEO

Wrapped in my arms, Mari whispered secrets long into the night. A type of adolescent hope and hormones drove me, overpowering any desire to sleep or miss a moment. Her eyes shone with hope as she detailed her family's possible visit over the holidays. Her throat grew tight and her eyes gleamed as she shared how when her brothers went off to college, she would sometimes stay in their room just to feel close to them. She talked about many lonely afternoons after school, and I wished I could have known her then, just to be a person she could count on.

"It never occurred to me that my parents would move after we all went off to college. I assumed we would be one of those families that all came together for the holidays to the same loud house I grew up in, filled with children running around and too much food." Her voice cracked, and I held her tighter, brushing my lips against her temple. My heart ached for the hurt of young, lonely Mari, and I vowed she would never feel alone so long as she let me be around.

"I know all families are different, but did you ever want that?" she asked.

"Maybe. Sometimes I wondered about my birth family. But growing up, Janice and I were one of the most stable family units I knew. I thought we had the best arrangement because it would break the peace once too many people got involved. Only recently have I started to wonder if it was enough for Janice."

If *I* had been enough for Janice. Breathing became difficult, and my palms itched, so I changed the topic to Mari's family. We drifted in and out of sleep until around midnight, when we decided we should probably leave. I drove her to her apartment. She dragged me upstairs and into her bed. She tucked herself into my open arms, and we slept until the alarm went off all too soon.

I woke up to her warmth and sleepy smile. It was enough to make me break out in song on Main Street.

The day continued like all the others had, except I got to be the first person she saw and shared her smile with. We went to Daisy's as normal. It wasn't weird or awkward. She was Mari, except now it was Mari with bonus hand-holding. And when we got to school, she leaned over and kissed me goodbye. Even if Pin Dick gave us the side-eye as he walked past, I couldn't be bothered. I was floating on air, as the taste and smell of her lingered on my skin.

I wasn't sure what this development meant for our future, and the desire for clarification was on the tip of my tongue all morning, but I wouldn't rush her. I wasn't going anywhere. We had time.

When she walked away, the car was too quiet. She took the joy with her. The conversation from the night before settled into my shoulders. Seeing Vander had been such a jolt, and now I was alone with my thoughts. Vander had been the one person I saw almost every day, completely intertwined with my life, only to be gone in a moment.

Imagine my surprise when I pulled up to the house to find Vander sitting on the front porch laughing with Janice. My palms went sweaty instantly. They saw me pull into the driveway. Otherwise, I might have been tempted to keep driving and pretend I never saw him. There was no avoiding it. No Mari to keep me safe. Only Janice waving all too eagerly.

Then I thought of Mari's tenacity, the full force with which she approached problems. She wouldn't avoid this any longer, and neither would I.

I parked the car, took a steadying breath, and walked to the front porch.

"Look who's doing the walk of shame," Janice called.

"Super inappropriate, Janice." I squinted in the early morning sun as I came around the corner.

She shrugged, looking all too pleased with herself. Vander ran a hand over his long beard to hide a creeping smile.

"Unless you would like to start delving into both of our free time activities?" I taunted.

Janice stood and stretched. "I have places to be. I'll bring the car back before you need to get Mari later."

Vander stood too, hugging her goodbye. "Nice to see you," he said.

"Nice to see you too, love." She patted his cheek fondly.

It wasn't the first time I wondered how the loss of our friendship impacted my mom. The maternal smile on her face told me that she had missed the man who was like my brother.

I hugged my mom and kissed her cheek. "Just listen to him," she whispered in my ear.

I glanced up to see Vander staring at his shoes, now seated again, forearms on his knees.

"Have a good day. Care to tell me where you're going?" I asked.

"Nope." She waved her fingers as she rounded to the side of the house.

After she backed out and waved goodbye again, I moved to sit across from Vander.

The air was thick with silence. How does one start a conversation with their former best friend after months of silence?

Vander didn't lift his head, but said, "I think your neighbor is watching us."

"Yeah. She's a little creeper, but she's cool." I lifted a hand and waved it at Clara, who pretended to water her potted perennials. She waved back, not even trying to hide her eavesdropping.

"Seems like a lot has changed around here, huh?" he asked.

I thought of my past few months in Green Valley. How wrong I'd been when I returned. How Mari had shown me all the ways this town had grown. There were still small minds and those clinging to old ways, but there had also been so much growth and a sense of pride woven into so many things. I found myself looking forward to things like the Christmas Market in a few weeks and her band's winter solstice performance. The concert band had been practicing Tchaikovsky so much that I found myself humming it as I prepared the garden for winter or cooked a new recipe.

"Yeah," I said, ever the great conversationalist. He cleared his throat. I had so much I wanted to say, but my worst-case-scenario brain was hard at work, muddling the words before they could make it out of my mouth.

I thought of Mari last night in my arms and the look on her face. She had been right. I'd been holding on to this pain for too long. It was time to clear the air, regardless of the fear.

"I'm sorry," I said, throat tight.

When I mustered the courage to meet Vander's gaze, he stared at me, mouth parted.

"The way things ended was so fucked," I said.

He started to speak, but I held up a hand. "I think I just need to get this all out." He swallowed with a nod, and I went on. "I was *not* happy. I should have been happy, though, you know? And grateful. But I wasn't. And the more unhappy I was, the more I beat myself up for not being thankful for all we had. I should have wanted the success, fans, and attention, but it was like I-I couldn't breathe. It was like I was playing a character of a rock star. I didn't know who I was."

The words, stuck at first, poured out of me. Vander listened without interrupting, his brows pinched with focus.

"The worst part is that toward the end, when I started to lash out"—I took a bracing swallow—"I think on some level I did it all subconsciously just so you would fire me." I let out a long breath. My foot bounced, shaking the whole porch. Saying this out loud made me feel even more like a failure. This was exactly why we didn't have hard conversations. This was why it was easier to sweep things under the rug . . . Until they reached a boiling point, and I exploded on stage.

Okay, I saw Mari's point.

Vander swallowed, his thick beard moving with the action. "I know," he said.

I blinked at him. "What?"

"I knew you were miserable, man. And I hated seeing you like that. *I'm* so sorry." He sucked in his lips and rubbed at his mouth. The action was so familiar to me. Even with the rock star look, he was still the kid I knew.

"It's not your fault I couldn't handle the pressure," I said.

"But it is." He rubbed his lips in thought before he spoke. "I have shit to get off my chest too. The whole reason we even started the band was because of me. I was the reason we went on tour and signed to the big label. It was *my* dream, my desperate need to prove something to this town and to the people here. You only ever supported me and my dreams. You made them your own. But I think I knew, even as a dumbass kid, that it wasn't what you wanted."

"I—" I tried to swallow, but my throat was too tight. My heart raced with relief but also more fear. I struggled to keep up with this revelation that we'd both been beating ourselves up. "I was just as desperate to leave."

He nodded. "True, but more than that, you wanted to support me. You always went along with any wild idea I had. I got you in trouble all the time."

"You protected me from guys who wanted to hurt me," I defended.

He nodded, but it morphed into a headshake. "But still. I just pushed and pushed you. When our success started coming so fast, I said yes to everything. I saw that it was taking its toll on you, but I couldn't stop."

I sat still and absorbed.

"You never liked the limelight. I was always speaking for you and telling us both what we wanted, and *man*, I had something to prove. But you know, if you aren't happy, all the money and fame won't suddenly make that better. That's a tough realization to have at this point." He scoffed.

"I had no idea," I said.

"You wouldn't because . . ." He gnawed at his thumb before tucking it away. "I knew you would stay for me. No matter how bad it was, I knew you would never quit." His eyes closed and his nostrils flared. "Because you were just that loyal. And I was so stupid and selfish. I should have just said something, but I thought maybe if it seemed like you didn't have a choice in leaving, it would be easier for you somehow. If you were angry . . . then maybe it wouldn't hurt so bad. That you weren't letting me down."

I leaned forward, hand over my mouth. This was insane. I thought I had cursed myself to a lifetime of loneliness. That I was somehow a bad friend or person.

But so did he. He'd been beating himself up and tormenting himself just as much as I had. Maybe even missing me as much as I had missed him.

"I've wanted to apologize for everything for so long." My voice cracked.

"You have never let me down," he said, holding my gaze with ferocity. "Not once in our whole lives. Just so we're clear."

Heat burned the back of my eyes as I nodded at him. "Okay." I broke his gaze to clear my throat. "We probably should have talked about this a long time ago."

He laughed. "Probably. Being a guy doesn't exactly come with an instruction manual on communication. Especially if you were never taught how," he said with a hint of bitterness.

"What are you talking about? Us men love being vulnerable," I said flatly. I leaned back and groaned. "I wish I'd known all this before my dramatic exit," I admitted.

He chuckled without humor. "When I saw you last night, and met Cath and Mari, I thought maybe, even though I went about it a total shit way, that you were finding something like . . . happiness here?"

"Yes." I didn't have to think about it. "I admit that I haven't been doing good the past year, but recently, I'm starting to live again."

Vander smiled in genuine relief. "Good. Mari seems great," he said.

"She is." I didn't elaborate that things were tenuous and new. I didn't want to try to label it and risk jinxing it, but no doubt her arrival on my lawn was when my life started to change for the better. This conversation with Vander was because of her. "I didn't think we would ever be back here in Green Valley." I laughed.

"And here we sit," Vander said.

"Why did you come back?" I asked.

"I think when I saw you, it really made me understand the guilt I was holding on to. I've been . . . struggling lately. Creatively. Emotionally. Someone told me recently that I need to 'sort my shit,' and I think she may be right."

"Women," I said.

"Exactly. But I have all this guilt for the way things ended. Maybe on some level, I came back here to try to fix some things."

"You don't have to worry about me, man. You can let yourself off the hook."

"It's not just that," he said.

His gaze went cloudy as he looked into the distance, but he didn't go on. More than once, Vander stayed with us after showing up in the middle of the night. He never let me know the extent of what was happening or tell Janice because our place was his safe space.

"The record isn't going well?" I ventured.

"I'm just tired," he said. And with that confession, the bags under his eyes seemed more pronounced, his shoulders hunched with weariness.

"Take a damn break," I said, hating to see him like this. "You've been going nonstop for over ten years. You're getting old. Your body and soul need to rest," I suggested, and he narrowed his eyes. "I know a ton about gardening now if you're looking for a new hobby."

His pretend hurt melted into a grin as he admired the yard.

"Come back in the spring or summer and see it in all its glory."

His head shot to me. "Really?"

I hadn't thought about what the invitation would mean after all this time. It had just slipped out. Because I wanted it and meant it. "Green Valley would be a great place for a tour stop."

He laughed. "The Burnouts and Mrs. McIntyre's famous coleslaw. What's not to love?" He let out a sigh and relaxed back. "Well, at this rate, we may never leave. This album seems to be cursed. I won't go into the details, and our social media director has been doing her best to keep the fans at bay. I don't suppose you're following any of The Burnouts news?"

He looked up at me, and whatever he saw on my face confirmed that I was definitely not. "Right. Understandable. But among a series of unfortunate events, now we are down a drummer."

I stiffened. A sudden panic clawed at my throat. If he asked me to go back on the road, would I be able to tell him no? Just these few minutes of conversation had brought something back into my life I didn't even know I'd been missing. Or, at the very least, was unwilling to admit. And I felt myself wanting to please him.

But then I pictured Mari and Cath and Janice and bunco and my garden and this town.

"I can't go back," I said flatly. I couldn't do that to Mari or to Cath . . . but especially not to myself. I'd just started to build something like a life here. Mari would be proud that I said what I wanted at the moment.

"Fuck no, man!" I sat up at his exclamation. Clara made a sound across the street. He lowered his voice and leaned in to hold my gaze. "You think I would ask you after the conversation we *just* had? Listen, I know I'm an egotistical singer-songwriter, but I have changed some."

"Sorry," I said.

"Don't be. We said our sorries. Let's just, I dunno, promise to talk more?" he asked hopefully.

"Good plan."

"And I wasn't expecting you to tour or anything. Maybe just laying some tracks until our drummer is back. Or even Cath? It wouldn't hurt for us to have some fresh blood in there. She was rad, man."

"She's not eighteen yet. But I can't wait to tell her you said that and watch her freak out." *Maybe I shouldn't tell her.*

"Think about it," he said. "We want to be done so we can go home to our families for Christmas. Or at least, that's what everyone else will be doing." He said it jokingly but didn't meet my eyes.

"I'll think about it. Slow gardening season after all. But, uh, if you're still here for Christmas and stuff, Janice would have my head if I didn't invite you for dinner. You know how she is."

Vander's eyes lit up. "Does she still make those little cheese-stuffed mushroom things?"

"She does. But I do most of the cooking now."

His eyebrows shot up, impressed. "You always were a good cook."

"Uh, thanks." I scratched the back of my neck. "But yeah, just go ahead and assume you're always welcome here. For any holiday," I said, and inexplicably, my throat tightened.

I stood quickly. "I better go." I thumbed toward the house.

At the same time, he stood and brushed his hands on his jeans. "I better get back to the studio."

We looked at each other and then burst out laughing. "Not at all awkward."

"Toxic masculinity, my ass. Come here," Vander said as he pulled me into a hug.

It wasn't even lunch, and this was one of the best days I'd had in a long time.

CHAPTER 26
MARI

Leo's prepared lunch wafted up appealingly, but my stomach wasn't having it. There was an ever-present tension in my shoulders that had recently shifted to my gut, giving me an almost constant stomachache. Did the timing correlate to Leo and Vander's reuniting? Yes. Did that make me an awful person? Maybe.

I sighed and pushed my lunch away.

It wasn't that. I was glad that the two best friends had made up. Leo's face lit up with joy when he'd replayed their conversation with me several weeks back. The fact that he was drumming with his former band was a bonus. He loved music, and it filled his soul. How could I be anything but thrilled for him?

Leo was as busy as me now. Coordinating my packed winter schedule with his band rehearsals and lessons with Cath meant I had to break down and finally get a new car. No more car rides or late nights at the recording studios. That independence I'd always said I wanted was returned to me but now it felt like loneliness.

All of us were getting what we had wanted when Janice approached me back at the start of the school year. Leo was out of the house. Cath was more prepared every day. Everything was going according to plan.

Eventually, my stomach would stop hurting.

"What's that face about?" Clara asked as she slumped into the seat next to me in the teachers' lounge.

"You'd think by now you'd realize this is just my face."

"No. This is you pouting. Perhaps something you'd like to share with the class about a certain someone who's almost never home these days?"

"Not anything I can share about *why* he's not home." I wasn't sure if him helping The Burnouts was a secret, but it was safer to be vague on that subject. "We're spending less time together. I was thinking about that."

This subtle nagging sensation would go away as I got used to being without him as much. That was always the plan. It was never meant to last, but I thought we'd have more time. It wasn't so bad. I only missed Leo in the mornings. Or in the evenings when the band practice went late. Or when I was so busy throughout the day, I could only respond to his corny dad jokes with that constipated-looking emoji. We still saw each other when I brought Cath up for their sessions. But we almost never had time together, especially not *alone* time. While superhot, our rushed make-outs in one of our cars made our relationship seem cheap, a poor substitution for the real thing.

If the change in our schedules was any indication of what would happen when Cath went off to college, it meant this time with Leo had an expiration date.

My slight stomachache turned into a hard cramp at the sudden understanding. Time was running out. I felt the color drain from my face.

"Is everything okay?" Clara asked earnestly.

"I'm freaking out," I admitted. "I feel so unsure." I shook my head, hunching in on myself.

"This isn't the Mari I know," Clara said. I frowned up at her. "The Mari I know attacks a problem full-on. She doesn't wait for someone else to fix things. I admire that about you."

I sat up straighter. She was right. Who was this passive person moping around?

I didn't like this new schedule, and that was okay. I could be happy for Leo and still want to see him. I wanted to make an effort when we had time together. I sat up and felt a comforting sense of determination begin to grow. "You know how I can be aggressive at getting what I want?" I asked, an idea forming.

"Of course. It's one of the many wonderful things in our shared DNA."

"There is one area I feel is decidedly lacking that I wish I could, um, expedite a little." A blush burned my cheeks. I was too old to be embarrassed to talk about this.

I'd had a taste of Leo's talents and wanted more. His desire for me was evident as our kisses grew more and more intense, but this change to our schedule had somewhat stalled any forward progression. Maybe it was a setting issue. We were only at his mom's house, in my car, or at Devlin's.

"Go on," Clara insisted.

I groaned. "You're just better at being seductive than me," I admitted.

"Thank you," she said with a knowing dip of her chin.

Clara naturally caught eyes with the way she moved. Her years as a dancer gave her the added element of knowing how to drive a man wild. I wanted Leo to lose control. I'd seen a glimpse of it in the studio and needed more.

"I just want to be bold and clear in what I want." *With the time we have.*

"Well, aside from the obvious . . ." she started.

"What?"

"Just talking to him. But I'm sure you already did that." She side-eyed me, and I gave a non-confirming shrug. "Body language is everything. Little touches. Accidental boob grazes and booty bumps," she said right as Mr. Geoffrey Neal walked in. He shot a disapproving glare toward Clara, who just waved back with a twinkle of her fingers.

"Hmm, I could do that. But I still think that's too subtle." I sighed. "I think we need a new location. There are too many damn people in our lives," I snarked.

She snorted. "You really are hard up," she said.

"It's been a while," I grumbled. "Either I'm exhausted, or we're at Janice's, which . . . I mean, she gives us our space and is gone a lot, but I don't know. I want privacy."

"What about your place? You might be overthinking this, babe. He's a dude. It's not like he needs champagne and roses."

But Leo deserved it. It might sound corny, but Leo was a sensitive soul. Why shouldn't men get to have a little romance during sex? Lord knew he always took care of my needs.

"My apartment is just so blah. I'm never there. When I am, I just wish I was somewhere else."

"I think that's worth investigating. But okay, I get your point." She pursed her lips and tapped her fingers in thought. She took a deep breath in and started to count off her fingers. "Back of a truck. On a blanket near Bandit Lake. Donner Lodge. The backseat of a car. In a barn. Next to a bonfire." I reached forward to cover her mouth as she mumbled against my hand.

"Okay, okay, thank you. God, you're like a deviant Dr. Seuss."

Mr. Neal was now fully glaring at both of us. I dropped my arms.

"Thank you," she said. "Needs must, and all that," she added flippantly.

"My point is, the key is not to overthink it or put too much pressure on it. It'll happen when the time is right."

I worried my lip. "We don't have time."

"Says who?"

I waved away her question. "It's more complicated than that. There are things you don't know about."

There wasn't even time to go into explaining it. I could see the writing on the wall. Leo wasn't happy in Green Valley. He had made up with his best friend and his band. He may have had issues playing and touring before, but now that he could communicate his feelings with Vander, they could work around it. Aside from his obligation to Cath, which was over in just a few short months, nothing kept Leo in Green Valley.

"Mari, I don't think Leo is going anywhere any time soon. Look at all he's—"

"I have a plan," I snapped loudly. "Operation Seduce Leo begins." I smacked the table loudly.

She sighed. "Then I guess the only thing you can do is take an everything shower, wear some sexy underthings, and jump the man," Clara said. "Oh, get laid, Neal," she called when he gasped.

I wanted Leo. He wanted me. The time was nigh.

CHAPTER 27
LEO

The week before the holiday, I took Mari to help set up the performance band inside the gazebo wrapped in twinkling lights. She never specifically asked for my help, but since I woke up in her bed and followed her here to the Christmas Market, it was assumed. So long as she let me, I'd always be a given in her life.

The first hour blurred by as together we found missing sheet music and extra reeds and fixed any last-minute wardrobe malfunctions. When the band performed, I studied Mari from the sidelines with a proud smile on my face. They went on early so that the local choir could go on by the time the sun set.

Now, as we strolled through the stalls of local vendors selling goods, the Christmas Market glowed with holiday magic.

Cath came and hung out for a minute after they played but quickly went off to meet some of her friends.

If pressed, I could name every student in all of Mari's classes and what instruments they played. And not only that, but I could also say the name of almost every Green Valley resident we passed and recall at least one detail about them. There was Devlin's wife, Kim, arm in arm with three other women, walking past as they talked and laughed animatedly. I wouldn't recognize myself only a few short months ago. I was filled with content warmth just walking side by side with Mari, even if I wished she'd reach out and hold my hand. Various members of the Bunco Broads were out and about with their families, and they all stopped to chat and not so subtly pry into my relationship status with Mari.

I'd like to know that too.

"You two make a fine couple," Belle Cooper said.

I glanced at Mari, but she just smiled and shifted the conversation to donations for next year's band trip to Knoxville. She'd managed to gather quite a few donations this evening because of the show they'd put on. I wasn't surprised. Just in awe.

Mari had given no indication of our relationship status. We hadn't discussed labels. Anytime we got close to it, she shifted the topic. It was hard not to feel like that was my sign that she didn't want to be seen as dating me.

I gestured to a display of snow globes, thinking of the one at her apartment, when her features pulled into a frown. She pulled me behind a stall, out of the flow of traffic.

"What's all this?" she asked.

My hand was tugged up to her face as she examined all the pieces of fabric covering my palm and parts of my finger.

"It looks worse than it is. It's just an added layer of protection."

She pressed one of the hands to her chest. "Poor thing." Maybe I should have played it up more than this. The attention and pampering were nice. In fact, she'd been touchy-feely all afternoon. I couldn't be sure, but she seemed to have less control of her body as parts of her continued to accidentally graze me. If her ass brushed my crotch one more time . . .

"Does it hurt?" she asked.

"Not too bad. I'm just getting some calluses back but mostly it's for grip and to prevent worse pain."

"It looks metal," she said, not releasing me.

"All for that rock star aesthetic," I joked.

"Are you doing okay?" she asked.

"Yep." I smiled.

"This isn't too much? Being here around the masses of Green Valley?" She studied me carefully from under her winter hat.

"I'm having a good time." My gaze moved over her cheeks, rosy from the cold. If I leaned forward to kiss her, in front of everybody, would she let me? I leaned closer to whisper, "Don't tell anybody."

She swallowed and licked her lips. "I like being here with you," she said.

Warmth spread through me. She had no idea. "Me too," I said.

"Can I?" She reached for my hand, and I squeezed her hand tight.

"Much better." I smiled at her, and she grinned back up.

We continued to walk hand in hand. Adrenaline surged through me at the small gesture. She wasn't ashamed to be seen with me. I tried to calm down my internal celebration. Mari was here, in the middle of her town, essentially shouting for all to see that we were *something*. I felt important and good and special.

"You never finished telling me about how the rest of the album went," Mari said.

"It's been really great," I said nonchalantly. I didn't want her to think I wasn't grateful for her support. She and Janice had been incredibly encouraging when I'd hemmed and hawed about playing with the band again.

I was grateful to be drumming, and glad to be on good terms with the band, but my heart wasn't in it anymore. I gave The Burnouts a shot. Just a few sessions. The Burnouts had made progress, and it was nice to be playing with them, but I was able to leave at the end of the day feeling like I'd done a day's work with a healthy level of detachment. The record wasn't done, but most of the guys were back home to be with their families. Except Vander, who opted to keep his place at the Lodge and hang out here rather than somewhere else. He was coming for Christmas, but I still felt bad that he'd be alone for so much of the holidays.

"And things are good with Vander?"

"It's nice to be talking again," I said lightly, but in reality, it was so much more than that. Thanks to Mari, a piece of myself had been returned to me. Thanks to Mari, so many missing parts of my shaken-up soul were coming back together like the perfectly constructed climax of a song.

"I'm jealous, I'm being usurped," she said it lightly as she brushed her coat against mine.

"No way. You are still bestie number one. Tied with Janice," I said with a shrug.

She stopped and looked at me with such wide and open eyes I thought I missed something and glanced around. "What?"

"I'm up there with Janice?" she asked in wonder.

I tugged at the scarf she'd made me wear. "Yeah. I talk to you every day. I spend the most time thinking about you and what you're doing. You know me better than anyone."

Abort, abort. You're saying too much. I cleared my throat.

"You're my numero uno bestie too," she said as we kept walking.

"Last performance for the season. How do you feel?" I asked.

"Good. They sounded great. Even though they were all jacked up on the prospect of winter break starting. They're good kids," she said with a hint of wistfulness.

"What's on your mind?" I asked gently.

She squeezed my arm and rested her head on my shoulder briefly. "The school year goes so fast. Soon, the seniors will be gone, and I don't know. I guess I'm feeling sentimental with all the holiday stuff."

"And what about Christmas? Did you ever reach out to your brothers?" I asked, wondering why she seemed sad. Normally, after a performance, she beamed with pride.

"Oh, um, yeah." She fidgeted with her winter hat. "It's Alice's year with her family in North Carolina. She has a bunch of nieces and nephews, so the kids will have a great time. And since Mom and Dad are on a holiday cruise, Noah and Asim decided to use their miles to book a last-minute holiday in Switzerland. Very posh," she said lightly.

But that meant she would be alone. My heart stuttered. She'd brushed it off, but this was a blow for Mari. It would be for anyone, but especially for her. She'd spoken so much of her distant family and her hopes for future plans. My heart absolutely broke.

There was no way she would be alone for even a moment if she didn't want to be.

I stopped and grabbed her hands. "Stay with us. Over break." I almost begged.

She blinked rapidly, lashes fluttering. "You don't have to do that. It's fine. I'm actually usually alone for the holidays. I don't mind. I get a lot done."

I absolutely couldn't handle the thought of her alone at her apartment, combing through sheet music or entering grades, while forking a disgusting frozen microwave meal.

"I want you to. I'm asking you to."

She chewed her cheek. "You don't think Janice would mind?" Her voice shook as she asked, eyes damp.

I gave her a look. We both knew Janice would never mind. "I can check with her first, if you prefer."

She deliberated as I made my case. "We have a fireplace. Plenty of books and puzzles. An at-home gourmet chef. You can treat it like a mini vacation. We have two extra bedrooms that are just sitting there."

She stepped closer. "I don't want to use the extra bedrooms."

"Oh. Okay. No problem." I'd been giving her space, but maybe I'd given her too much space. Maybe the spark that ignited a forest fire in me had burned out with the distance and time apart.

"I would want to stay in your room," she added and swallowed. "Would that be okay?"

Electricity passed from my toes to my fingertips. "I would very much like that." My voice shook.

She beamed up at me, and I bent to kiss her lightly on the mouth.

"Get a room!" Clara called as she passed arm in arm with who I thought was the football coach.

"I tried, but the Lodge is booked!" Mari called back.

I didn't get their inside joke, but then again, I rarely did.

Clara threw her head back and laughed before whispering to the man on her arm.

Mari's gaze returned to mine and never left, but I'm pretty sure she performed a gesture behind her back that I couldn't see.

We shopped a little longer, getting gifts for Janice, Cath, Vander, Clara, and a few other people. That night, we packed up her bags—after a quick call to Janice in which I could feel her rolling her eyes at me for even asking—and I brought her to our house.

It felt so right and natural that I didn't want her to ever leave. Yet I kept the words locked in, trying to be grateful for the week she'd stay with us.

We sat quietly in front of the fire that night, her reading and me trying not to stare at her as she did so. Occasionally, I'd get caught in my staring, and she'd narrow her eyes and tilt her head. She'd been quiet since we arrived, and I worried she was having regret. But the look in her eyes now was more thoughtful and curious.

That was Mari's scheming face. I recognized it just as I heard Janice come downstairs. I swallowed, wondering what Mari had in mind.

Janice came into the room and cleared her throat. We both looked at her, and she stood, coat on and an overnight bag on her shoulder. "I'm going to the Lodge for a few nights. I'll be back by Christmas Eve." She lifted her chin as she spoke.

I shot a look at Mari, who was biting back a smile.

"By yourself?" I asked.

"No," she said, elaborating no further. "Once I'm gone, you can pull into the garage if you want, Mari."

Mari nodded, a blush on her cheeks.

"Did you know about this?" I asked Mari.

She flipped a page in her book, avoiding me. "I did not." But was this the same as that inside joke with Clara?

"You two are very schemey. I don't know how I feel about that. If I hear a marching band, I'm leaving."

"Mari had nothing to do with this. The Lodge is all decorated for the holidays, and I need a change of scenery. Unlike you, I need time outside these four walls."

I held back, pointing out I was out of the house most days. I wasn't looking to argue or make her stay. In fact, my heart began to hammer.

"Have fun, I guess?" I said, but felt weird, considering where she was headed.

"You two have fun too. Be mindful of shared spaces," she said on a turn and walked out.

Mari's face was bright red. Four whole days with Mari. No plans. Just Mari.

My heart went wild. I smoothed my hands on the couch and studied her where she was sprawled on the floor. The fire caused her features to glow, and her long hair flowed over her shoulder. She looked at me with a soft curve to her lips.

"Janice and I are weird, aren't we?" I asked Mari.

She shrugged. "I'd prefer that sort of relationship to none at all."

I frowned, desperate to reach for her. "Mari. I'm so sorry about your—"

Mari launched herself at me.

CHAPTER 28
MARI

The time for subtlety had passed.

I straddled Leo and grabbed his cheeks. "I want you."

His gaze moved over my face. "In any particular way? Just want to make sure—"

"All the ways," I said.

Four days. Four days of just Leo and me. No plans, no distractions or accidents. Nothing to get in our way.

"Merry Christmas to me." He breathed.

"I'll be right back," I said as I shimmied to move off his lap.

He made a whimper of confusion and held on to my hips. "What? Where are you going?"

"I just need to grab something." I hopped off his lap. "Meet me upstairs in ten minutes."

"O-okay. I'll just wait here for now." He wiped his palms on his jeans and watched me leave like I'd dropped him off at puppy day care.

I ran upstairs and straight to the suitcase I'd packed. I dumped out the contents to begin Operation Seduce Leo. Candles, a bottle of massage oil, and condoms sprawled everywhere. I would clean those up after as I got myself ready. Any lingering sadness I'd felt about my family being gone for another holiday had been erased by Leo's invitation to stay with him. With Janice gone, there was no more time to waste. The Christmas Market practically marked the end of the year, so from here on out, time would fly even faster

191

than it already had. I wouldn't lose another precious moment with Leo while I had him.

The black lace and stringy negligee looked even more scandalous in his bedroom and outside the fancy lingerie store. I chewed my lip and debated how to go about the process of putting it on. The sales associate had instilled me with false confidence, insisting that my long limbs and slim waist (and modest bust) would be perfectly emphasized in this getup. She'd patiently instructed me on how to put it on, detailing what piece went where. But now, as I stared down at what was laughably described as clothing and priced higher than my water and electric bill combined, I couldn't figure out where to even start.

"In for a penny," I mumbled to myself.

It was important that I made this night special for Leo. Maybe it was corny, and perhaps it shouldn't be something I thought about so much. Leo deserved romance and tenderness. He gave so much to Cath and his mom and now even to Vander. But especially to me. Not a day had gone by since our lives intertwined that he hadn't made some sweet, thoughtful gesture, whether it was a home-cooked meal, a stupid joke texted on a stressful day just to make me smile, or helping out in big ways that pushed him way outside his comfort zone. I could also get outside my comfort zone for him.

If only I could get *in* to this.

Things went downhill quickly. After I'd pulled the negligee up my legs, the action of trying to get my head and arms through created some sort of Gordian knot. The harder I pulled, the more tangled I became. I cursed as my hips slammed into a dresser, causing me to almost fall over, and getting my long hair snagged around, oh yes, *a new knot*, at my neck.

"Ow, ow, ow."

The few bits of strategically placed lace were so far from their intended areas I couldn't even fathom what scrappy triangle went where. Panic soon set in. And then the rage.

"If you would just cooperate," I yelled at the fabric, and it retaliated by pinning my arm up next to my head.

My anger made my actions more violent and abrupt, which only encouraged the little Horny Lady Trap.

Ten minutes must have passed as I felt Leo enter the room behind me.

"Everything okay? I heard some bangs and—"

I penguin stepped to turn and reveal myself in all my glory.

I slumped onto the bed and looked up from where I'd given up. I could only imagine, in my wildest nightmares, what he saw right now.

Mostly naked, crisscrossed by black straps like I'd fallen through a hammock, and just as visually appealing, sweating and red-faced. One arm stuck lifted above my head and my other arm pinched tight to my body, at least covering *some* of my more delicate areas.

Wow. Who could resist me now?

Leo laughed and tried to cover it with a sympathetic, "Oh no."

I looked up, my mouth turned down in an exaggerated frown, my chin trembling slightly. "Help."

He laughed again and covered it with his hand. He stepped to me, humor and pity written all over his features. "What happened up here?"

The rest of the room was forgotten in the madness of trying to get unstuck. My suitcase and its contents littered the room still. I didn't have any time to light candles or get out the massage oil.

"My attempt at seduction," I said with all the enthusiasm that I felt.

"Mari," he said gently, coming to help me escape.

He stood me up, and to his credit, his gaze stayed mostly focused on my moping face as he began detangling me from my medieval torture device.

"You really didn't need to do all this for me. It's incredibly thoughtful, but it's just me," he said.

"All I did was make a mess and massive fool out of myself." I sniffed and rubbed my tingling nose with the arm currently trapped above my head.

My cheeks burned red, and I'm sure my flush matched the rest of my body. Who would want to stay with this lonely, gangly wreck who literally could not even get dressed?

"You don't have to do all this," he whispered as his arms wrapped around behind me.

I let out a long breath, dropping my head to his shoulder as he worked.

"I've got you. Don't worry," he said.

I was so used to being alone, doing things alone. The only thing that worried me was how much I already relied on him and how necessary his presence was in my life. Not just when he was saving me from myself—which was a lot of the time—but when he was driving me or watching me at dinner or waiting for my reaction to a dry joke he'd set up. My body craved his nearness, his company, his thoughts, and his attention.

I wanted it all from him, and it made me feel greedy and out of control.

My stuck arm was freed, and he slowly brought it down, my fingers tingling as the blood rushed to the tips.

I turned my face away, muscles limp and pliable as he worked on the rest of the lingerie.

"This is humiliating." I pouted. "All I wanted to do was try to be sexy for you. I wanted to get a room at the Lodge, and it was booked. I ordered chocolate-covered strawberries from Donner Bakery, but they looked like little Santa hats. Not sexy." He chuckled as I went on. "I wanted to dress up provocatively, and here I am stuck like a mummy who just woke up from a curse."

He paused in his work to kiss my temple. "Are we taking this off or . . . ?"

"Cut it off me for all I care. I just wanted to be sexy for you." I tried to get angry but just felt sad.

Sad, horny Mari.

"Oh. There's a hook." Something loosened, and the whole contraption slid to my ankles. "There we go."

I stood completely naked, arms crossed strategically, humiliation making me glow. "Taken down by a negligee," I said. Then I sniffled as I added, "Good album name."

He chuckled and grabbed the throw on the edge of the bed to wrap me up.

"Mari, look at me." I met his awaiting gaze with reluctance. "You are the sexiest woman I've ever met. You have been driving me wild since you brought a marching band to my lawn."

"I think that emotion is anger."

"No." He cupped my face. "I have wanted you for so long. You're incredible. You're sexy. You're talented and passionate. Trust me, none of this is necessary." He gestured around the room. "Appreciated, but not needed."

"Then . . . why?" I trailed off, kicking the last of the fabric off my feet. This wasn't on him. I'd been pushing and pulling from the beginning. Maybe I'd been sending mixed signals.

"I'm in no rush. I was waiting until it was right for you. I'd wait forever." He shrugged, and a hand tugged his hair. Why was that action so damn sweet to me?

But we didn't have time. Didn't he feel that same ticking clock?

There was a flush to his cheeks that hadn't been there before, and his eyes were dilated as they darted quickly back and forth between mine. Maybe destringing me had affected him more than I thought.

"You're too much. You say these things . . . and it's like." I grabbed his hand to rub at the area around my heart under the blanket. His hand felt cool compared to the burning skin. "I feel everything so much. It's changing me. You're changing me."

He swallowed, tearing his gaze to where the blanket began to slip. "Is that good?"

"It's more than that. It's . . . ." I struggled for the right word. "Real. It's the

most alive I've ever felt. It scares me a little, though. I've never felt like this."
I've never wanted to.

I expected the worry to set in, the understanding that this too shall end, but when I looked into Leo's eyes, I didn't feel anything but that familiar peace of his presence. I held on to it.

"It scares me too. You make me feel alive," he said. "You make me feel like I've been sleeping or something. Like I've somehow wasted so much time already. You've turned my world upside down." He cupped my hands, his bandaged knuckles wrapped around mine. "Let's be scared together."

I nodded and dropped my cheek to where we connected, rubbing against his abused knuckles.

He nudged me with his nose until I lifted my chin. His mouth dropped down to mine, and I opened for him. When I lifted to wrap my arms around his shoulders, the swoosh of the blanket, as it fell to the ground, was audible between our gasps for each other. He groaned against my mouth, deepening the kiss.

I loved the way his callused and wrapped hands scraped against my skin as they explored down my back. It was already so overstimulating, and it drove me wild to know how hard he worked. The soft caresses soon turned to greedy grabs as neither of us seemed to get enough of the other.

He stepped back to pull off the sweatshirt he wore over a tee as I tugged at the buttons of his jeans. He already strained hard against his briefs.

He looked down to catch me staring. "I want to be clear that I, uh, have been living somewhat of a monk-like existence these past few years." He licked his lips and winced a little as he adjusted himself.

"I recently had a test and am good to go," I offered so he wouldn't feel weird discussing our health.

"Good. Same. I was tested before I came back, and there hasn't been anyone else." He stepped out of his jeans and pulled me to his hot, hard body. "But, uh, what I meant is that this first round might be a little quick and intense."

"First round?" My eyebrows shot up as I understood his meaning.

"Of many. But I'm stating for the record that this first time may not be an accurate representation of what's to come. Heh. No pun intended."

I kissed up his neck to his mouth, letting my lips get scraped by the coarse hair. Every part of his body was designed to make me feel more electric. "I'm really not worried about it. You've been getting me off every night since the Rage Room, so I figure I owe you . . ."

His head dropped to my shoulder, impatient hands still roaming me.

"Mari," he groaned. "I wish I had really been there. I would make you feel so good."

"You do." I gasped.

He pushed off his briefs as I fell back onto the bed. I crawled back, propped on my elbows, and watched as he walked on his knees to get between my now spread legs.

His gaze roamed the view of me, and I let him take his fill, not even an ounce of modesty to be found. I couldn't feel anything but magnificent in the way his dark gaze devoured me. It was as tangible as his finger that traced a pattern up the inside of my thigh. My legs shook as he leaned down to kiss my thigh, hand gripping it tight, his mouth sucked at the sensitive skin. Those strong, talented fingers gripped the smooth skin, making me feel cradled.

I gasped out his name. "I'm going to devour you later. Do you under-stand?" he asked.

I nodded, unable to speak after the control in his tone. I bit my lip, and he bent once more to lick up my seam. He toyed and teased me until I was wet and swollen and needy to be filled.

"Absolutely. Devour." He spoke to the core of me, his hot exhalations causing a quake.

He took a steadying breath before leaning to grab a condom off the floor. He grabbed the hem of his shirt and put it in his mouth. His teeth held the fabric as both hands worked to roll on the condom. His chest rose and fell, his abs flexing as he focused. When he looked back at me with dark, greedy eyes, I was panting just as hard. His singular focus on getting inside me was the hottest thing I'd ever seen.

I thought he would drop the shirt from his mouth or rip it off entirely, but he didn't seem to even notice he still gripped it in his teeth. His hands hooked behind my knees, draping my ankles on his shoulders. His hot gaze was focused intently on my body as he brought himself to me. He groaned as he swirled me with his tip, and my muscles began to shake since I'd been tense, sitting up to watch his every action. I was desperate to pull him as far into me as possible.

He pressed in with a tight suck of air before he began to rock slowly, deeply. The shirt was still in his mouth, so I could see every muscle in his body working to keep the steady rhythm. I clenched around him, and his nostrils flared. He was so distracted by looking at where we met that he didn't seem to realize what he was doing somehow was making me even more wild. He was usually so careful. So thoughtful. But I wanted him to take and be selfish with my body. My pleasure was so rooted in his that both were inevitable. I couldn't lose.

He looked up at me briefly, almost pained and apologetic.

"It's so good," I reassured him.

As he undulated into me. I pushed back, grinding into him, finding a sweet spot. His hand lifted my hip as he bent to kiss me, finally releasing the shirt from his mouth, his arm catching him before we crashed.

"You're incredible," he said. He kissed me, and I arched up. I tightened around him to make him feel good. A wildness started to take over. I pushed up his shirt to scratch my nails down his back. I hooked my legs to lift more firmly to him. I grabbed whatever I could to bring him as close as possible.

That initial spark—that previously could only come through careful attention and the right conditions—began to catch, but Leo was so hot, so wild for me. I'd wanted this, *him,* for so long; the foreplay had been building up to this for weeks. The spark caught, heat rolling through me. It built and built so that the excitement of knowing I would come like this launched the act itself. I came without warning, hard and fast, and unexpectedly.

I screamed out his name as I broke, and that shattered any remaining self-control he had. He pumped into me without his normal, careful rhythm, a freestyle of overwhelming desire.

His neck muscles flexed as his head lifted on a final deep thrust.

He stayed hovered above me, braced on his forearms, trembling slightly. His curls were even more extraordinary when damp with sweat, and I couldn't help tugging my hand through them just as he did.

"Rest. Hydrate. Protein."

"What?" I laughed at his mumbled nonsense.

"That's the plan. Then we are coming right back here to set a world record."

"For what? Most sexual positions in four days?" I asked.

He flopped over and onto his back, still panting. "You really get me."

197

CHAPTER 29
LEO

"I have your balls!" The announcement came from the living room.

"Not mine," I said, holding up my hands. Mari looked at me at the pronouncement before the new guest made themselves known. "You know exactly where they've been . . ." I whispered in her ear.

She elbowed me, but not before a blush burned her cheeks, and she looked at Janice, who was already headed to greet the guest, not paying attention to us.

After almost a week of pure bliss, it was Christmas Day, and Janice was back. I had been enjoying playing with the band and tutoring Cath, but having so much uninterrupted time to be greedy with Mari was the only gift I needed.

Vander rounded the corner as my mom came to meet him. "You always bring so much class to my house, Vander." She playfully swatted at him but kissed his cheeks as she grabbed his Crock-Pot. Dinner was open for anybody who didn't want to be alone. Janice and Mari sang along to festive songs as they set the table and cleaned while I prepped for the meal.

"Cocktail meatballs, made with my special recipe," Vander explained.

"It's just jelly and barbecue sauce. He uses frozen meatballs," I said to the room.

The two women shot me disappointed looks.

"What? I'm not saying they're bad. But it's not some treasured secret recipe."

"Thanks for bringing a dish," Janice said.

"Thanks for having me, Janice. The house smells great."

"That's all Leo. He made braised pork belly with a cherry glaze."

"Among other things," I added. I had at least five exquisitely perfected side dishes. Shopping and preparing for this meal was the only thing that finally got me out of Mari's arms. And even still, we drove into town to the Piggly Wiggly, unable to detach completely. Hands around waists when pushing the cart. Her accidentally brushing her breasts against me when she reached for something. More than once, I had to take a minute to kiss her senseless on a deserted aisle until somebody strolled through. It was a miracle we ever got out of there and with everything we needed.

"Sounds amazing," Vander said.

We hugged, and I quickly tugged Mari back under my arm. He chuckled at my protective action, but then stage-whispered to Mari, "He's just jealous of my balls. Always has been."

"Hi, Vander," she said as he bent to kiss her cheek. He lingered just for my benefit.

When he straightened, stance akimbo, he looked back and forth between us. "Aren't you two cozy?"

"Yep," I said with no further explanation. I squeezed her tighter, and she looped her arms around my waist.

We were cozy. We were so much more than that. The past week had been a delirious carbs-driven sex-a-thon where Mari and I drove each other to the brink of madness with our bodies. Mari's desperation for me could only be matched by my own for her. I felt like I'd known her forever, our spirits reacquainted. There was no doubt in my mind that Mari and I were meant to meet. That everything had led me to her, good and bad. It was this assuredness that told me not to worry about the bits she still kept to herself. She didn't care to talk about her family. She spoke about Cath's audition as if it were a looming deadline. Maybe after that, she would be ready to define our relationship. Until then, I was content.

We'd been just about to sit down to eat when another knock came at the side door. As only strangers used the front door, it had to be somebody familiar.

But when I looked around, everybody I knew was there.

I counted on my fingers, just in case. I noticed then the extra plate I had missed.

My mother fluffed out her sleeves, clanking her wooden bracelets in the process. She took a breath and patted her short curls. Mari raised her eyebrows in my direction as Janice left to answer the door. We shared a look that said, *Are we about to get the big reveal?*

Sure enough, when my mom returned, she had a person in tow. A person I knew.

Pin Dick stood, ruffled and scowling.

My insides felt like they were turned inside out. All the color drained out of Mari's face. Whatever her worst fears were, they could only be matched by mine. This wasn't happening. My mother was a wise, kind, gentle woman of the contemporary world. She raised me to love and accept all.

Pin Dick was her complete opposite. Aside from the most obvious, there were so, *so* many reasons this didn't make sense.

I stood on instinct. I wasn't sure what I would do. Maybe I should punch him in the face. Yes, punching him in the face felt right. Screw toxic masculinity. Sometimes, you fought fire with fire. Vander, likely sensing the tension in the room and seeing my sudden rise, stood at my side. He looked among all of us, clueless but ready to fight.

It was like being fourteen again, walking home to be cornered by the football team. He had my back, no matter what.

Mari stood then too, her hand gently resting on mine. When I looked at her again, she glanced subtly at Janice. A reminder. This wasn't about me.

The past few months, Janice had an ever-present smile and a lightness to her step. But *how*? Not that I liked to think about these things, but I was confident this man knew less about a woman's needs than the types of musical instruments in his own school.

The math wasn't mathing.

Principal Pin Dick looked down his nose at Vander and me, standing shoulder to shoulder. "Well, looks like your boyfriend is back. Am I gonna be in trouble?" He snorted at his own "joke." "Sorry. That's probably not PC or whatever you're sensitive to these days."

Vander tensed at my side. He would totally be on board with the face punching. It had been weeks since I felt this way. Most of the town accepted my return, and I'd grown comfortable around town, especially when flanked by Mari. One comment from Pin Dick and old insecurities burned down my esophagus.

Failure. Loser. Loner.

No. I wasn't a loner. I was in a room filled with the people I cared about. People whose opinions actually mattered.

My nostrils flared, and my head turned slowly, wide-eyed, to Janice as if to say, *THIS GUY?*

She crossed her arms, a slight smile to her lips. Turning to the new guest, she said, "All are welcome on Christmas, Curt, but was there something you needed?"

Even hearing her use his first name made me queasy—

Wait, what had she said?

Pin Dick was still glaring at Vander. "I suppose it's your foreign piece of trash blocking my driveway."

Mari squeezed my hand as a sense of absolute nirvana flooded me. He wasn't here as my mother's date. He was just here to complain as normal. Confetti cannons went off in my mind.

"I didn't think I was blocking it," Vander said, tone flat.

"Two inches into my driveway," Pin Dick said.

"Right. I can move my car," Vander said, but not before looking back to check with us.

"Two inches is a lot to some people," Mari said to Vander with doe-eyed innocence. I almost choked on my tongue, trying not to laugh. She said it so sweetly that Pin Dick just narrowed his eyes like he was looking for her to crack.

"Miss Mitchell. You've been spending a lot of time in my neck of the woods lately," Pin Dick said. I *really* didn't care for the way his gaze tracked her figure when he spoke.

Mari, holding far more restraint than she ever gave herself credit for, didn't reply to his non-question. Except I did just now notice the fork she had a white-knuckled grip on.

Will. Not. Punch. On. Jesus's. Birthday.

The principal shifted on his feet. "Better make sure that student of yours is in tip-top shape. Just a few weeks away now. It's bad enough that—"

"Thanks, Vander," Janice said loudly and interrupting whatever garbage he was about to spew. "We'll be out of the way now. Anything else we can do, Curt?" My mother's calming voice, when using somebody's name, still had the same power as it did when she'd been a teacher.

"Just don't let it happen again." He turned on his heel and stomped away.

Vander jogged to get his keys and went out the door, following *Curt.* "Merry Christmas," Janice said. "Thanks again for finally taking care of the tree."

Pin Dick grumbled, shoulders up to his ears as he left the house.

The second he was gone, I slumped into the chair, hand on my slamming heart. It was that feeling of skipping the last step times a million.

Janice came up and flicked my ear.

"Ow!" I turned to her. "Why?"

"You really thought that was my guest?" She stood with her arms crossed, head tilted and shaking.

"I-I didn't know. I certainly didn't want it to be. Or understand it."

"You are something else," she said.

"Sorry." I slouched. "But Mari did too," I mumbled.

Mari held up her hands. "Only for a second."

"Lies!" I shouted.

She looked at me and glared but was also sort of laughing around her eyes. "Mostly, I was just shocked to see him here, threatening to ruin Christmas. But it couldn't be him because he was at school that day we came here, and, uh—" She flushed.

"Oh yeah," I said, remembering the day we got my drum kit.

"You both owe me an apology," Janice said.

"Sorry," we mumbled in unison, heads down like scorned children.

Vander jogged back into the room, tossing his keys to the side table. "Who was that toolbag?"

"My boss," Mari said as Janice said, "My neighbor."

"He seems like the guy who brings up old football plays to any woman he talks to," Vander said.

"He tells women they'd look prettier if they smiled," I said.

"He pop quizzes any person wearing a band shirt and says, 'Oh yeah, you like Nirvana. Name five songs?'" Vander returned.

"He asks the beverage cart woman on the golf course for a hug."

"He thinks the vulva hangs at the back of your throat."

"He's gestured at countless women to take off their headphones at the gym, just to talk."

"A pair of brass balls hangs from his lifted truck."

"He actually does have that," Mari cut in before our back-and-forth went on too long.

We were all laughing when a new person entered the room.

It was Faye Brentmore, one of the newest women to join the Bunco Broads, a transplant from New Jersey who had moved here after she retired . . . *oh*.

"Is there a reason that awful man is out on the front lawn with a tape measure?" she asked by way of greeting. We all turned to the new arrival, and Janice made a sound of happy surprise. Faye carried a holiday tin with a big red bow on it. Her long, straight black hair was streaked with gray and pinned over her left ear with a sparkling clip.

All at once, I was filled with warmth.

Faye was funny and kind, and I genuinely liked her. Not that my opinion mattered if she made Janice happy, but compared to having just assumed the worst, I wanted to scoop Faye up like a trophy.

Instead, I went to her and gestured for a hug. "Nice to see you again, Mrs. Brentmore."

"Faye is fine." She returned my hug. "Hi, Leo. Nice to see you again."

"Excuse me, son," Janice said, gently knocking me out of the way. "Hi, dear," she said and embraced Faye.

The two women shared a look that had me going to Mari to hold her.

Introductions were made all around, and we finally sat down to eat.

Much later, full of food, cheeks sore from laughter, I looked around the table as peace spread through me.

These were my people, and I was happy here in Green Valley. Maybe if I wasn't so content, the realization would have surprised me, but I'd felt it for a while now.

Mari had her head on my shoulder, and I kissed her hair.

She sighed contentedly. "I wish this could last forever."

Her voice was tight with a whispered sentimentality for the moment she was currently in.

It could last forever, though. Or at least, this—*us*—could last. I sat up and turned to her, hoping for clarification. Her smile was genuine but tinged with sadness. Why did she say it like this was the beginning of the end instead of just a great moment of many to be had?

I was about to pull her to the side when the doorbell rang. This time, all of us looked at one another in confusion.

"I don't think my heart can take any more surprises," I said as I got up.

I opened the front door with a blast of cool air to find Cath in a black beanie and only a hoodie despite the winter night.

"Hey." I smiled.

She waved back, sleeves pulled down over her hands. "Hi. Sorry to show up unannounced like a weirdo."

"More like a Christmas miracle," I said with the over-the-top enthusiasm that she pretended annoyed her.

"Don't make this any weirder than it is," she said in her usual deadpan tone.

"Come in?" I thumbed behind me to the warm house, where laughter rang out.

"Nah. We gotta head up to my grandparents' in Merryville," she said. I bent forward to wave at her parents parked in the street, and they waved back.

"I just wanted to give you this. And say Merry Christmas and thanks and all that." She rushed and mumbled the words.

My heart felt like it might explode out of my chest with glitter and rainbows. But expressing any of that would definitely make it weird.

"Aw." I reached for the gift excitedly, not making eye contact with her to ensure she didn't crawl out of her skin. "It's almost like you like me or something."

She scoffed. "Just stop talking."

"You like me," I said in a singsong. "You're glad I teach you."

"I regret all of this."

I ripped open the packaging and stared down at a cheap pair of drumsticks with writing on them.

"I know you have like a million," Cath explained, "but I signed these ones. So you know, when I'm super famous and stuff, you can be like 'I knew her when . . .'" She affected an old-timey grandpa voice for the last bit. "I just thought, since I was your first student, or whatever, it'll make you seem legit to the next kids you tutor."

I sniffled a laugh, but the truth was the emotion had made my throat too tight to speak or even swallow. My next student? It hadn't even occurred to me.

"Man, you're making it weird," she said. She tugged her hat down with both hands, almost covering her eyes as she groaned.

I cleared my throat. "You think I should tutor more drummers?"

"I guess I just assumed you'd want to keep going since you're actually pretty good at it."

"I thought I sucked."

"You're all right. Just don't let it go to your head."

We stood a moment in silence before I held up my fist for her to bump. "Thanks, Cath. I will treasure this forever," I said sincerely as she bumped my knuckles.

"Yup. No biggie." She flushed and kicked at the ground.

"Actually, I have something for you too," I said with excitement.

Her eyebrows shot up. I turned around to yell into the house. "Yo, Vander. Come here."

When I looked back, Cath's eyes were wide, and she was completely still. "Don't mess with me."

I chuckled as, a second later, Vander came to the door.

"Cath," he said and high-fived her.

She lifted her hands with robotic jerks to hit him back.

"Cath's gotta head out soon, but wasn't there something you wanted to ask her?" I asked Vander.

"Yeah?" He looked at me, and I nodded. "Cool. Yeah. The Burnouts are still working on our album after the break, but would you want to maybe jam sometime?" Vander asked.

"She's gone Cath-atonic," I said, grinning at my own joke.

Cath had just enough wherewithal to roll her eyes at me before she jerkily nodded at Vander.

"Yes. Sure," she said. "Cool."

"Rad," he said. "We'll work out the details. Merry Christmas." He fist-bumped her this time before going back inside.

"Did that really just happen?" she asked, staring at the shut front door.

"It surely did." I put my hands in my pocket, rocking back on my heels with a contented grin.

What a weird and wonderful and awesome day.

Cath's parents shouted her name out the window. She blinked back to herself with a headshake.

A flash of worry crossed her brows. "You don't think Miss Mitchell will mind?"

I frowned, wondering why that would be an issue. "As long as you're not skipping school or anything, I don't see why she would."

She worried her lip. "It's just not, you know, the plan."

"It won't get in the way. But want me to go get her?" I asked.

"No," she said quickly, flicking a look behind me. "I really should go. Merry Christmas. And thank you. This is—" She widened her eyes with a shake of her head. "Thank you."

"Merry Christmas, Cath." She skipped down the steps and toward her waiting parents. "See you next year," I teased.

She groaned loud enough for me to hear as she got in the car and waved goodbye.

Only after she was out of sight did I wonder if I should have checked with Mari first. But Mari wanted Cath to be happy, and this was an awesome opportunity. Plus, it would mean more time for Mari and me to spend together. Two birds, one scone.

CHAPTER 30
MARI

I understood the balance of the universe. Good and bad, ups and downs. People come and go. That was the natural order of things.

Even in the biggest moments of joy, I'd felt that ennui of knowing that this too would end. It had felt too good being at Janice's with this temporary family, pretending it could be my life. Everything was fleeting, and I had to protect myself against the future pain.

I ended up staying with Leo until after the new year. I would half-heartedly mention leaving, but I didn't put up much of a fight when he insisted I stay. We checked on my apartment once or twice but returning made me feel like a visitor to a cold place. And since Janice and Faye had officially announced their relationship, his mother spent a lot more time at the other woman's house, presumably to give us more space so they could have alone time.

It made sense that after the holidays, everyday life would feel lackluster and dull. Everything in the "real world" felt less exciting without Leo. Being around him was like watching things in hi-def, only to go back to analog.

I told myself it was the doldrums of January that caused this general malaise. Though now, it was nearing spring break, and the mid-March weather remained dreary, the final days of winter clinging on like a lingering cough after a cold. With each passing week, though things remained great with Leo, the ticking clock in the back of my brain grew louder. We never meant to get this close, but now were so intertwined I didn't know how to be on my own without him. I didn't want to be. I couldn't even feed myself regularly without his reminders to eat or prepare meals. But when it was no longer easy or convenient for him, I'd fade away from the forefront of his mind, like every-body else.

The only minor hiccup had been when he'd told me about Vander's offer to have Cath play with The Burnouts. He'd told me after she'd already accepted. It wasn't that I was mad about the amazing opportunity; it was only that it made me feel like an outsider to their relationship. I had been an afterthought. I wouldn't have expected it from them, but this was the way of things. It was like introducing two friends only to watch them hit it off and make plans without you.

It wasn't like Cath and Leo even needed me, really. They were their own people who had formed a strong connection. Their tutoring and jam sessions would run smoothly regardless of whether I was there. I *was* happy for them. This adolescent yearning to be included was my own issue, and there was no way to express it without sounding needy and petulant. I couldn't risk pushing Leo away, coming on too strong as I so typically did. I wouldn't ruin what we had.

"Hey, Cath," I said as the bell rang to end class. "Hang back for a sec?"

She glanced at the hallway but lingered as everybody else bolted out for the day. "What's up?"

During today's performance band rehearsal, her fellow musicians surprised Cath with a party to celebrate her early graduation and audition. Despite the friendly gesture, Cath's jaw clenched, and the tension she'd been carrying in her shoulders seemed to worsen. She'd been more distant than I'd ever seen her, and I worried her nerves were getting the best of her. She needed a last-minute pep talk and reassurance that she had this audition in the bag.

"Tomorrow's the big day. How are you feeling?" I asked.

"I wish everybody would stop calling it that. It's not like I'm getting married."

I blinked back, hurt at her sharp tone. I told myself the jitters made her lash out, and it wasn't because she wanted nothing to do with me now that she'd bonded with Leo. "You're right. It's just another day. No pressure."

"Right." She scoffed.

I scratched at my brow, wondering how I kept getting it wrong with her. Maybe playing with The Burnouts in addition to everything else on her plate was too much. Perhaps she was spread too thin. "I just wanted to check in. Make sure you're okay. It's probably a lot of pressure to be preparing for college and playing with an actual rock band. If you need to talk—"

"I'm fine."

Right. Why would she want to talk to her teacher?

"Leo mention they finished their record? That you're even going to be credited on a couple of tracks. That's pretty cool, right?" I reached for anything to get her to connect with me, but she grew further away. I could almost see the shell coming up around her.

She nodded, studying her shoes. The more she retreated, the more desperate I grew. My time as her teacher was coming to an end, and I would never see her again. Except for the few kids who stayed in town after graduation, I rarely heard from former students. I wanted it to be different with Cath.

"Aren't they going back on the road soon?" I asked, and my voice felt too high.

Cath gripped her backpack and glanced to the side. "Yeah. Problem solved, right? I have to go. I'll see you at dinner or whatever."

She left before I could understand what problem she referred to. I had only meant that if she was feeling stressed out, she could talk to me. My impulse was to chase after her and demand we talk things out, but I thought about Leo and what he would suggest.

She needed space and probably a friend to talk to. That wasn't me.

That evening, Leo and I were going to Cath's house for dinner. Her parents wanted to thank us for all the help with her audition. Maybe she'd calm down by then. I just wanted to leave campus for the day and try to get out of this funk. I packed up all my belongings and was just about to leave, anxious to sit, even if it was just to drive back to my apartment.

"Miss Mitchell, a word in my office, please." Principal Pindich stood at the doorway, arms crossed, waiting for me to notice him. At least he'd gotten my name right.

"Right now?" I asked. "I was just on my way out."

His nostrils flared. "This won't take long."

The trepidation I'd felt all morning made my feet leaden as I trailed behind him to his office.

"Have a seat," he said, already waiting behind his desk.

There was a picture of him from a GVHS game of old, clutching a football and giving that same arrogant grin at the camera. The remembered conversation between Vander and Leo at Christmas had me biting back a smile. Just thinking of Leo allowed me to take a deep breath. There was no reason to assume the worst.

"Tomorrow is all set?" Pin Dick asked as I sat.

"Yep. Miss Hill is subbing my classes. Cath and her parents will meet me up in Knoxville."

He made a sound of disapproval.

"Is that burnout coming?"

If I called out the insult, he would claim it was a reference to Leo's former band and not a dig. "Yes. Leo will be going to support his student."

Not that it was any of his damn business.

I bristled at him questioning me like I hadn't been planning this for months, like I was just some flighty idiot who was going to wing it on my student's most important day. Instead of frothing myself up more, I calmly explained how Leo was driving up separately. I didn't tell him that Leo was taking a van from the charity Triple F to bring his drum kit as a surprise for Cath after her audition. I had several students who had been part of the local charity program started by Ford Rutledge to help teens and were happy to help. Leo had been so excited when he told me about his secret plans, and I couldn't wait to see Cath's face when Beatrice and the kids were officially gifted to her.

"She's been spending a lot of time with that band," he said with an undercurrent that had my just-smoothed hackles instantly prickling back up.

"Yes. They're very good to her. And I'm always there," I added to be safe. "My students are the most important thing to me," I said honestly, staying focused. It was a sentiment he probably couldn't relate to: caring about his students.

"I'm just warning you to keep an eye on her. Men like that are born trash and stay that way. Even with their money and fame. You better hope she doesn't get seduced by the lifestyle and throw her future away like your boyfriend."

I could talk about how Leo is financially secure for the rest of his life. Leo shyly admitted to me one night that he'd invested much of his money, and he still received royalties to cover the day-to-day expenses. The Burnouts' continued success guaranteed that he would always be okay. I could also mention that Leo laid tracks with the band and got paid for it or about how much he'd done for the GVHS band and its community. But I didn't need to justify Leo to a man like Pin Dick. The sun doesn't justify its brightness to a desk lamp.

Pin Dick just needed to stroke his own ego to make himself feel better about the choices he'd made in his life. A classic case of insecurity coming out as cruelty.

"If we aren't going to discuss my students, I'm leaving." I stood.

A flush rose under his collar, and he jabbed a finger in the air. "Just make sure that kid doesn't screw up tomorrow. Otherwise, I have to reconsider any funding for the band next year."

The thrumming in my brain grew, almost causing me to tilt over.

"Are you serious? You'd cut band? After all I've done?" I asked, voice rising.

"It's not a moneymaker for the school. You work hard, but this is never going to be a profitable program."

"It's a high school. Not a corporation."

"Exactly. Our funds are limited. Before you get yourself all worked up in a tizzy, I'm just saying I might have to reconsider the budget next year. If we have an alum going to the prestigious Berklee College of Music, I could understand the value."

The world spun around me. What was the point of all this? To work me up? To get under my skin? It was clearly working. Did he even have that sort of power? He was buddies with someone on the school board. How else would he have gotten this position in the first place? It wasn't like he'd earned it.

"Thankfully, Cath is brilliant. So there's nothing to worry about," I said.

Pin Dick gave a shrug of *we'll see*, hands clasped at his chin.

I left his office in a haze of anger and fear. He'd always been a jerk, the kind of guy who delighted in the little bit of power he'd been given, but he'd never threatened to do anything like this before.

The rest of my life spread out before me. Year after year, as I alone fought tooth and nail to keep these music programs going. Soon, the residents of Green Valley would stop turning out their pockets, and then where would I be? All alone and not even a job to occupy me. I suddenly felt so weary and exhausted, I had no idea how I would make it through dinner with Cath and her parents.

As I drove up to Cath's parents' house, I yelled out loud in the car all the things that I wished I'd been able to say to Pin Dick.

"You are just a sad little man with nothing but a pathetic high school football career to cling to!" I shouted at the windshield.

By the time I pulled up to Cath's house, I must have looked slightly unhinged.

Leo had already arrived and was waiting for me. "Are you okay?" he asked as soon as he helped me out of my car.

I shook my head. "I'm so pissed off."

He pulled me in for a hug and some of my tension dissipated. "What happened?"

"Pin Dick."

"Of course. What did he do?" He rubbed my arms as he studied me.

But I didn't get a chance to vent the frustrations out of my system because, at that moment, his cell rang. He looked at the screen and quieted it. "It's just Vander. Probably just wants to meet up before they leave."

I shook my head. "Go ahead and answer it."

"Sure? It can wait if you need to vent about your day."

"Trust me, my anger will keep." I smiled.

He chuckled as he slid out his phone and said, "Hey, what's up?"

His gaze never left mine as Vander spoke. I couldn't hear what the other man said, only his deep, muffled rumble, but Leo's features cleared. Not happy or sad, just neutral, and that was worse. It was as though he didn't want me to read anything from his face. Any relief I'd felt seeing Leo at the end of this awful day was quickly swallowed back up by trepidation.

"When do you need an answer?" Leo asked.

His eye contact broke, and he turned away slightly, lowering his voice.

"So soon? Okay. Wow. I'll talk with her."

I'd become well-equipped to handle bad news over the phone, probably more so than most. So it surprised me just how sick I felt and so suddenly. It was like my knees were about to go out. This had to be about the tour. This was why I never made any future plans after Cath's audition, because I knew Leo would never want to stay here. Not after everything got better with Vander, and he no longer felt obligated to me. Even if he didn't like touring, he still hated living in Green Valley. And here was an easy way out.

I had planned for this exact scenario so it wouldn't hurt. Yet the air felt knocked out of me all the same.

I didn't want Leo to go. I think I'd gone and fallen in love with the man and this was a really, *really* shitty time to figure that out.

Leo ended the call, tension in his features as he found me watching and waiting.

"Everything okay?" I asked, trying to keep my tone light.

Leo deliberated a second too long. A moment to find an answer that wasn't the truth.

This couldn't be happening again. Not when I'd been so careful to protect myself.

Cath and her parents came outside to greet us.

"Let's talk about it later," he said.

I nodded and plastered on a smile, as inside the last vestiges of self-sufficiency crumbled to pieces. This time, there would be no picking me up and putting myself back together.

CHAPTER 31
LEO

Throughout dinner, though she managed to be perfectly polite, Mari carried a tightness around her eyes that told me if she didn't vent soon, she would burst at the seams. The stilted conversations with forced smiles were not made easier by Cath's short, evasive responses to everybody's questions. The student carried a heaviness like a secret burden. Having just spoken to Vander, I understood why.

The Burnouts had asked Cath to tour with them over the summer. Vander tried to wait until after her audition, but they needed her decision as soon as possible.

Instead of going the collegiate route, Cath would tour the country with one of her favorite bands, living out her wildest dreams—or rather, *somebody's* wildest dreams. She was impossible to read, and talking to nobody.

With that amount of talent, the expectations were high. That put a lot of pressure on her young shoulders. How could she make such a choice? How was Mari going to react to the news? College had always been the plan, but there was no doubt this was an incredible opportunity. Mari needed to know as soon as the time was right. And this wasn't it.

With every passing minute, Cath retreated more into herself. I wished I could pull her aside and talk to her, but she hadn't mentioned the offer, and I wasn't sure if she had spoken to her parents yet. Her parents, for their part, tried to encourage and reassure her about the audition at dinner, but it only caused her shoulders to move higher as she sank farther into her sweatshirt.

The whole meal couldn't have been more than a couple of hours, but time had crawled with painful awkwardness. By the time we left that night, I felt exhausted from trying to carry the conversation. I wasn't a big talker, but everybody else was so introspective that I didn't want Cath's parents to think we weren't grateful or give potentially unnecessary implications that something might be wrong. I felt put in the middle of everything, and it wasn't a place I was comfortable sitting.

We agreed to head back to my house for the night. As soon as I parked, I went to Mari's car to lift her out of her driver's seat to hug her.

She squeezed me back, and I inhaled her. I didn't want to have a hard conversation, but I knew that she would want the truth more than keeping the peace.

When she pulled back, she smiled up at me. "Hi," she said.

"Hi." I brushed my thumb along her cheek. We'd been sitting next to each other all night, but it felt like this was the first time I'd seen her all day. I wished she'd just move in with us. I planned to ask her after the audition. I'd been patiently waiting for her to catch the hints, but again, best to be direct with her. Things might seem fast, but to me, every moment we weren't together was a moment wasted.

"Better?" I asked.

"Getting there." She looped her arms around me and squeezed until I made a groan from the pressure. "My thoughts are spinning out. I'm jumping to conclusions."

"Tell me about your day." I used my thumb to tilt up her chin and meet her gaze.

She shook her head lightly. "No. I just want to put it behind me. Focus on Cath and tomorrow. But I can't do any of that until you tell me what Vander said."

I frowned down at her. I had hoped to gently ease her into the news, not jump straight in. Mari would always put Cath's happiness first, but this offer could come as a shock after months of preparation, and we didn't even know which direction Cath would go.

"I can see your wheels turning. Every second you don't tell me, the worse my thoughts," she said.

"No. No." I gripped her shoulders. "It's good news. Nothing to worry about."

Her gaze moved over my face; if I wasn't mistaken, her eyes were gleaming. She took a steadying breath in and out. "I know it's about The Burnouts tour. Just tell me." Her voice shook slightly.

I held her gaze a moment longer, my own confusion growing. "Vander asked Cath to tour with him and the band this summer," I said simply.

There. I put it out there.

"Oh," she said. Her breath whooshed out, a hand to her chest. "So you're not—wait." She shook her head. "Cath?"

Any momentary softening of her features was quickly overtaken by pinched disbelief. "Cath is barely eighteen. She's starting college. She can't—"

"Nothing is official yet," I said carefully.

She pulled away, a hand to her temple. I stepped forward, but she retreated. "I'm processing this."

I crossed my arms over my body, desperate to reach for her but giving her space.

"Why didn't you tell me this right away? All night, I've been assuming what I thought was the worst. I didn't even . . . I couldn't even fathom." She paced in a circle, her movement growing more agitated. "How could you not tell me?" she repeated.

"I only just found out," I said carefully. "You have to admit, the atmosphere at dinner wasn't conducive to that sort of news."

"But you could have told *me*."

Her implication was that we were a *we,* and I owed that to her. But this was where it got tricky being Cath's mentor and Mari's . . . whatever I was to her. She never clearly said. I knew that I loved her and had for some time, but did that mean I should have told her about this right away? Maybe she was right.

I pulled at my hair. "It's complicated. I haven't even talked to Cath. This is her decision. This is band stuff."

She flinched back. "Right. This has nothing to do with me. I'm just her teacher."

I stepped forward again only to receive a palm to stay me. "That's not what I'm saying at all. I'm sorry if I hurt you, but we don't even know how Cath feels."

"I knew she seemed off all day. I knew it. I tried to get her to talk." She spoke out loud, but it didn't feel directed at me.

I shrugged, feeling helpless. "I'm sorry. It wasn't my news to share."

"I thought you were leaving," she said, looking up at me suddenly.

Is that what had her so panicked? She thought I would leave her? After these last few weeks, I was here getting ready to ask her to move in with us, and she thought I was about to leave without another look back. The tension of

215

the day was starting to get to me too. I steadied myself before I spoke. "I told you that life wasn't for me."

She shook her head. "But on the call to Vander. You said you'd talk to me."

My eyes closed as I put the pieces together. "I said I'd talk to Cath. They leave tomorrow. They need her answer as soon as possible."

When I opened them again, Mari had paled. "This can't be happening." Mari shook her head. "How could this happen?"

"We don't know what she's planning to do."

"Join the rock band of her dreams or go to college? What would you do at her age?" She balled her fists.

"I know it is big news, but it's exciting. You helped a student who has two incredible choices."

Her arms went around her stomach. "I'm never gonna be allowed to teach after this. Pin Dick is gonna fire me for this somehow. I know it."

The comment came from nowhere. She was spiraling out. Her worries shooting in every direction like fireworks. I reached for her. "He can't do that because Cath joined a band." This time, she let me hold her.

"You don't understand." Her balled fists went to her eyes. "If he can, he will. All the money I raised, how hard I worked. It's all going to be for nothing."

"I have to go back there. I have to talk to her." She was already starting for her car.

I held on to her elbow. "And tell her to do what?" I asked gently. "This is between her and the band. I'm sorry."

She stared at me like she wasn't seeing me. "Am I already forgotten? Removed from the decision-making process?" She tossed out her arms. Hurt filled her eyes, and it felt like my chest was caving in on itself. "Everybody got what they wanted, and I'm no longer needed, right? Not pushy, Mari. Too needy, too loud. Let's not tell her because she'll just try to make us stay. That's why you didn't want to tell me, right? I'm just some ticking time bomb, so better to avoid me altogether."

"I waited to tell you because I know Cath. You do too. After everything, she isn't going to just skip town tomorrow. Have faith. She won't leave without saying goodbye."

Something about that made her go stock-still. She sucked in her lips but nodded. There was something on the tip of her tongue that she wasn't saying.

"Let's go in. Have some tea and just try to get some sleep before tomorrow," I suggested.

"I'm sorry." She stepped closer to her car. "I need to get to my place." Her voice was robotic, distant.

I didn't want to let her go. I wanted to get her to talk about whatever made her go so cold. But Mari was an immovable force. If she didn't want to stay, then she wouldn't. She needed time and space, and I could give her that. After tomorrow, it would all be okay.

* * *

Mari

My body felt numb as I sat in my car, waiting for Leo to go in. He was waiting for me to drive away first, watching me with this sad, pitiful face.

It was every hurt that I'd protected myself from unfolding in front of me. A long road of lonely nights and canceled plans.

This was just the beginning of the end. I never thought it would be different for us. I just wanted to deny the inevitable as long as possible. I should have ended things at Christmas. Let our relationship stay in that snow globe of perfection. That would have been the smart thing to do, but even thinking of Leo not tangled in every part of my life like we found our bodies tangled most mornings caused a sensation like a sharp hollowing out of my stomach.

I would always prefer the angry, quick breakup to the subtle fading away of love and of being forgotten.

I pulled out of Leo's driveway. I didn't make it far before Clara waved me down. I wasn't in the mood to talk, but maybe it would help. I still didn't get to bitch about Pin Dick, and maybe just having someone on my side to end this horrible day would help.

I couldn't bear the thought of being alone yet, even if it was my choice.

I glanced back to make sure Leo had gone inside. His house looked as dark and cold as our final words had been.

"Hey," I said to her after I'd gotten to the porch.

"Everything okay?" she asked.

"How much did you hear?"

"Not much. But the body language spoke volumes," she said.

Venting was exactly what I needed. I spent five straight minutes detailing the shit day, from the conversation about the bands to the revelation about Cath.

"Now Cath is going to go on tour. Pin Dick is going to cut band or worse. And Leo has no reason to be around me anymore." I slumped into her swing.

"That's a lot of terrible assumptions," she said.

"Are they assumptions if based on facts? Is it catastrophic thinking when so often I'm proved right?"

"Right about what?"

"People leave. People forget me," I said, unable to meet her eyes. Every breath caused a sharp pain in my chest.

"Man, your family sucks," she said.

"What?" I blinked at her.

"Not our branch of the tree. Obviously. But your parents? Your brothers? They suck."

"What does this have to do with anything?" I asked, looking for paralleled anger, not an analysis of my family dynamic.

"You don't think this is related? Come on. You make plans. They cancel. They make no effort. It's always you. That's shitty, and it hurts."

"They're just busy. They have real families." They were hard to coordinate with, but that didn't mean they were bad people. Even thinking that made me feel like a bad daughter and sister.

"That's bullshit, and you know it."

"I-I have nothing here to offer them."

"Mari, this isn't about you. You are a badass. You get shit done. They just suck. Look at my family. They come in all shapes and sizes but are there for me. They love me in spite of it all. But family isn't always blood. Sometimes the family you're born into just plain sucks. So you find the family that doesn't. You keep looking until you find people who fight as hard for you as you do for them."

A tight pain clenched my throat closed. If it wasn't about them being busy, then it just meant I wasn't worth the effort. I wasn't worth sticking around for, not even to my own blood. And if they wouldn't choose me, nobody would.

"What's wrong with me that I'm not worth the effort?" I asked, voice small and pathetic.

She squeezed my hands. "It's not you. Some people are just broken. Too in their own way or concerned about themselves."

"But—"

"No buts." She poked my arm. "Some family is made in an instant of meeting. You know they are meant to be a part of your life. Some family grows naturally."

I thought of Janice and Leo. Their relationship was beautiful, and their unconditional love never ceased to astound me. "I see your point."

"Do you? Because if family is people showing up for you time and time again, who is that in your life?"

"Leo. Time and time again."

"Exactly. You want to be chosen, but you never let yourself get picked. If you look at things in a different light, maybe one not so tinged by the hurts of your past, I think you'll see that Leo has made you his family. When have you chosen him?"

"I—" I flushed with shame. "I don't need to. I'm with him every day. I have completely opened every part of my life to him. I feel like I'm some cold, distant planet, unable to be explored."

"You aren't cold or distant, but sometimes you have to say things out loud. Have you flat-out told him how you feel about him? Have you told him how much your family has hurt you?"

"I don't like to talk about it. It's humiliating to admit that I can't keep anybody around. I don't want him to realize something is wrong with me." Saying it out loud made it seem so juvenile.

"Pretty sure Leo has seen all sides of you. Remember the Fall Festival? Or when he pulled you from a biker? It's not like you are only showing your most flattering angles."

I snorted.

"When you first started hooking up, did you not make it clear that you didn't want a relationship?" She was being lawyer-like, and I didn't appreciate when the defense was against me.

I winced. "No. But. He should have felt it."

"Maybe he did. But he might also need to hear it. Like you need to hear it. You often talk about having hard conversations, but here's one coming at you. I love you, obviously, but sometimes you are all talk. You say that you want honesty over everything else. You just wish that people would speak their mind, but what about the fact that you don't tell your family you wish you saw them more? What about Leo? You act like you aren't anything serious, but things couldn't be more serious. That man is deeply in love with you. He has turned his whole weird recluse life inside out for you. Yet you're so sure that if you told him your feelings, he would still leave."

Boom, mic drop.

The cold night sent a shiver through me. Not her incredibly chilling words.

"Mari, I'm not trying to be hurtful. I want you to be happy. I think you're pushing Leo away *because* you like him so much. I think he's the best thing that has ever happened to you, and you're freaking out a little. It's totally understandable. You fight for everyone, making you fearsome in the most kick-ass way. But it's time you fought for yourself too."

She was right. My feelings for Leo were unlike anything I'd ever felt. The fact that he continued to show up was terrifying because it felt too good. It's easier not to have the fear, but not necessarily better.

"And what about Cath's audition?" I asked after a minute of swirling thoughts.

"Give her the chance to talk to you. Regardless, I hate to say it, but Leo is right. She's an adult. It's her choice. You can't control this. Trust that she will show up. Don't push people away before they can even show up for you. You aren't forgettable. There is nothing wrong with you. You found your people. Let them help."

Truth washed over me in a painful wave, but in that pain was a sort of relief. What if I did trust that somebody could return the love I felt for them? What if I could be brave in this part of my life too?

I would go to the audition as planned tomorrow. I would trust in the people I loved.

And that was terrifying.

CHAPTER 32
LEO

With no news from Cath or Mari, I assumed the plan remained the same for the day.

I triple-checked the back of the van Ford Rutledge had dropped off at Devlin's place last night. Beatrice and the kids were loaded and ready. Unbeknownst to Cath, I would surprise her with the drums after the audition. Regardless of what she ended up doing, she deserved to have these. And there was a full circle beauty to think they might be on stage playing with The Burnouts again.

I had picked up my phone to call Mari a hundred times since she left last night but felt myself being too clingy and needy. I never knew where I stood with her. I was so sure of my deep feelings for her, but she kept parts of herself at bay. Every hour that ticked by, I felt her grow further away from me, but I would show up today. Just like every day and she would see.

I heard a sniffle behind me and spun on my heel.

"Cath?" I asked.

I stupidly moved to block the view of the drums, like she couldn't still see them. It made sense for me to be packing them up. One, they were my drums as far as Cath was concerned, and two, they weren't needed at the studio anymore. But I had been so surprised to see her, and it was so damn early, I hadn't been thinking.

It was barely sunrise, and we weren't planning to be at the college until nine, a solid two hours before her audition.

"What are you—how'd you get here?" I asked. Looking for a car I hadn't heard pull up.

She thumbed over to a bike leaning against a tree. I imagined her pedaling up to Devlin's house before the sun even started to rise. Winding, blind corners. No light. A fear gripped my chest. It was reckless, and thank God, she'd made it in one piece. Her arms wrapped tight around her middle, shoulders hunched, head facing the ground.

"What's wrong?" I asked.

I stepped forward, shaking palms facing her as I approached.

"I can't do this." Her voice was choked, and when her head lifted to me, her face was red and streaked with tears.

"What?"

"I don't know what to do." Her voice broke as she started sobbing silently into her hoodie sleeves.

I wrapped her up in a hug, and she shook in my arms. "It's okay. It's okay."

She looked up and sniffed in. "It's not," she said. "No matter what I choose, I'm going to upset people who have worked so hard for me."

"This is your life, Cath."

Her chin trembled as she nodded.

My phone rang loudly between us. She shrugged out of my hug as I pulled the phone out of my back pocket. Mari must have sensed a disturbance.

Cath saw the screen and scrubbed at her cheek. "Please don't get it."

"Okay. I won't." I nodded calmly, but I felt like I had negotiated a hostage situation. Mari was probably losing her mind, wondering where Cath was. "Do your parents know you're here, though?"

She nodded. "I told them everything this morning."

"Good," I said, eyebrows lifted in hope.

"Not good." Her voice broke.

And my eyebrows pinched. "Not good?"

"They said they support whatever I decide and they love me. *Ugh.*" She groaned loudly, dropping her face in her hands again.

"Can we sit? And talk?" I gestured to the back of the van.

She sucked in her lips, her face still wet, as she pulled herself onto the open bed. I handed her a stack of tissues from the front seat when I came to sit with her.

"Thanks," she said. After she blew her nose and wiped her face, she sat and took a deep breath in and out. "They're going to hate me."

"Who?" I asked.

"Everybody. Miss Mitchell. My parents. The school. My friends. Everybody."

"That's not true."

Her shoulders started to shake again. I looked around, confused at where I had misspoken. I wasn't great with kids, but I thought I had learned Cath pretty well.

"Hey, hey. What is it?" I asked her.

"I'm a terrible person."

"You are not. Why would you think that?"

She looked at me, her little chin trembling again. "When I got the offer . . . the first thing I felt was relief," she admitted.

"Because you want to tour? Nobody would blame you."

"No, it's not even that. I love the band and love playing with them, even if they are a bunch of old guys. No offense."

"Ouch."

"I thought at least now I had an excuse not to do this audition. I wouldn't disappoint anybody if I didn't go for a *real* reason."

"You don't want to go to Berklee?" I asked.

"I-I don't know." She tossed out her arms. "I just—I just feel like . . ." She squeezed her eyes tight.

"It's too much?"

"Yes." Her shoulders fell.

"I get that."

She made a sound like she didn't believe me.

"No. Trust me, I do. Listen." I waited until she looked at me, rubbing the last remnant of tear from her cheek. "I was fired from The Burnouts."

Cath glared. "But you were cool with Vander and the guys. You were friends. How could they do that?"

"Because I acted like a total shit."

Her eyebrows shot up. "I saw some videos, but I thought it was taken out of context," Cath admitted.

"Thank you for having faith in me. But no, it was me. Turned out, I didn't really like being in a band."

Her eyes widened. "What?"

"I loved the guys and playing, but I hated touring."

"Are you saying this so I don't go?" she asked. "Because you're dating Miss Mitchell?"

"No. No. Miss Mitchell and I . . . we don't have anything to do with this. Except in that we both care about you. I'm telling you because when I was

223

young, I played the drums because it made me happy. But then came all this pressure. I felt like it was either my happiness or everybody else's," I said honestly.

Her mouth slowly opened, and she nodded. "Yes. Exactly." She sat up straighter. "Between Miss Mitchell and the band and my parents, I feel like the drums have become this chore for me. I used to play them to escape and feel something bigger than myself. But now it feels like all I'm good for."

"I understand that. But you are many awesome things. Plus, you are a drummer." I mirrored the words Mari had said to me.

Cath sighed deeply.

"What is it that you want? If there were no people to disappoint or let down. Close your eyes and really think about it," I said.

She did and sat quietly for a minute before tentatively saying, "I just want to feel free when I play again and not this weight of expectations on my shoulders."

It was like she spoke the words I had thought a thousand times.

"People who really love and care about you are only disappointed when you aren't true to yourself," I said.

"I know. In theory." She glared at her fisted hands. "My whole life, I've been loved and supported. Miss Mitchell and my parents have done everything for me. My friends and the other staff. I'm like *weirdly* supported."

I snorted. "Damn loving community," I said.

She grinned but pushed her arms out. "I'm serious. My parents have worked so hard and sacrificed so much. There's no way I could ever pay them back."

"Pay them back for what?"

"Even if I go to college, how will they afford it? By working and sacrificing more. If I ever get a good job, nothing will be enough to pay them back. At least if I toured, I would be able to help them, but then I'd never see them. It's like . . . I'm *too* loved. I almost wish I was just a weird little freak so then I would only have myself to let down."

Cath's worries were wise beyond her years. Sometimes, loving someone felt like pressure to be who they needed you to be. Did I do that with Mari? Did I try to be exactly what she needed all the time so I wouldn't worry about her realizing that I was the burnout everybody thought I was? Just as I had for Vander and my mother? I felt this same pressure Cath did in my own way. My thoughts tumbled, but I stayed focused on Cath.

"I think," I ventured, "that they didn't do these things because they want to be repaid. I think they did it because all parents want is for their kids to have what they didn't."

"That makes it so much worse," she whined.

"But hey, hey." I squeezed her shoulders. "Whether or not you go today, they will still love you. If you buy them a big fancy house with your future royalties or only ever play for people on the streets as a busker. The ultimate goal is that you're happy playing."

She shook her head. "That's bull. Adults are always saying shit they don't mean."

I laughed. "I mean it."

"Is that how you feel?" she asked me, finally meeting my gaze and holding it.

More thoughts of Mari twisted in me. Why hadn't I pushed to clarify what our relationship was? Why did I feel like, at any second, she was going to look up and notice who I really was and decide to end things?

"This isn't about me," I said, voice tight.

"Convenient."

"I have something to tell you," I said, shifting gears.

"Okay?"

"I was going to give you Beatrice and the kids today. After your audition."

Her mouth fell open. She looked behind her and back at me. Her mouth snapped shut, and she shook her head, fists at her temples. "This isn't helping my feelings of pressure."

I gently nudged her with a laugh. "Just wait, there's a stipulation. I'll only give them to you if you promise to take some time and think about what you want. Because they need, nay, *deserve* to be played out of love. I've neglected them too long, and after all they've been through, they need you to save them. But if you force it, then you can't have them.

"Whether it's in a band or in class, I don't care. I don't care if it's only every once in a while as you work at Pizza Hut because you don't want to build your whole life around drumming. I get that too. No choice is good or bad; it's just what feels right at the moment. You can always change your mind. There isn't a choice you could make that would ever make the people who love you stop caring about you. Not the real ones. That real love is precious, and you have it in droves because of *you*, not your talent."

Her eyes filled again, but she nodded with determination.

She bit her lip. "You're seriously giving me these?" she asked with a growing smile as she turned to look in the van behind us.

"Dead serious. But you have to think about what makes you happiest. What makes you feel most in your body. And remember that feeling anytime in the future when you have to make a choice. Everybody here, except maybe Pin Dick, wants what's best for you and not for them. That's literally the whole point of all of this. Somewhere along the way, the pressure got to us all. But it's always about giving you the life that you want, Cath." I finished my speech and stood. "You talk to them. Take your time. I can wait for whatever you decide."

It took all my willpower to step away and wait patiently. I was desperate to tell Mari about the situation but still wasn't sure what the news would be. For several minutes, I thought about the advice I'd just given Cath and why it made the back of my neck burn with anxiety. Why had Mari shut down last night? Was she going to end things? Was this stuff with Cath really enough for us to break?

"Leo?" I spun on my heel.

Cath stood with her drumsticks in her hands. "I made my decision."

"Want a drumroll?" I asked. I already started drumming the pattern in the air, making the sound.

She rolled her eyes.

"No, that's an *eye* roll, silly goose," I said.

"Oh my *God*, just stop. You're an embarrassment to drummers everywhere."

CHAPTER 33
MARI

I arrived at the campus music hall alone. Many other nervous-looking students milled around with their equally stressed adults. The atmosphere was hushed and thick. Nails bitten. Legs shaking. This was the day so many of us had worked toward.

And here I was, alone and with no student. There was still time. Cath could still show up. Her parents could still show up. My gaze constantly looked for dark curly hair, a foot above the rest of the crowd, but found no familiar faces.

A woman with a clipboard and loudly clacking heels circled the room, checking students in before heading back behind an ominous door. Every time she came out and called a new name, a bolt of anxiety made my palms sweat.

I hadn't heard from anybody. I called Leo to see if he'd heard from Cath or Vander, but he didn't answer. I couldn't say I blamed him. I'd acted in anger last night and pushed him away.

Clara told me to trust that people would show up, but standing here alone, the darkness in my heart started seeping outward and into my body.

I was too loud and angry and needy. I pushed too hard. I needed too much. And all I had done was push everybody away. Clara was right. I was so scared to ever be the one left alone that I tried to control every situation. I bulldozed my way through life, bending people to my will so I could never be taken by surprise.

I sat on a low wall, feeling lower than I had in years. Since my brothers couldn't make my college graduation or the first time my parents' plans to visit fell through. How could it not be about me? I was the common denominator here. Wouldn't it be delusional to think that I was lovable when I kept ending up alone? I never gave them the choice. Even with Cath. I hadn't even considered that college wasn't what she wanted.

Nobody was coming. I wouldn't be chosen. Not by Leo. Not by Cath. Nobody wanted me. I was alone.

Because I'd made sure of it.

"Mari," Leo said.

I looked up to find him standing in front of me, looking down at me with his easy half-smile.

"You're here." I exhaled, jumping up to hug him without thinking.

Every part of my body felt lighter. I would be okay. Whatever happened next, I wasn't alone.

His light chuckle shook me. "Sorry, I'm late," he whispered.

"I'm so glad you're here." I squeezed him tighter, realizing my body was shaking.

"So is Cath," he said.

It was then I noticed her standing a few feet away with her parents. She glanced up and headed our way.

I broke the hug and stepped back but grabbed Leo's hand.

He was here. I hadn't messed this up. He showed up time and time again. And I wasn't going to let go. I was going to tell him how I felt and trust that I was enough to keep him around.

"Leo, I have so much I want to talk about." I needed him to understand how scared I'd been. How alone and terrified.

He cupped my chin. "I want to hear it all. But Cath wants to talk to you first."

"Okay. Yes," I said.

"After," he said and stepped back again.

"Can I talk to you?" Cath asked at my side, voice shaking.

"Anytime," I said to her.

We walked a few feet away. The woman with the clipboard had just left the closed door of doom, where students left either grinning or crying. She was headed this way.

Doesn't matter.

I gave Cath my full attention.

"Leo told you about The Burnouts wanting me to tour this summer?" she asked.

My heart hammered in my chest. "I'm so excited for you. That's such a great opportunity. Literally the coolest thing."

"I'm going to accept," she said simply. The choice hurt, but not how I thought it would, not because of the missed audition, but because Cath was leaving sooner, and I would miss her. I was so tired of missing people. "I didn't want you to think I don't appreciate you."

"Cath, I'm so sorry if I ever made you feel like your only value was this audition. I'm sorry I pushed you so hard."

"No. Don't apologize. It's weird. I don't like when adults feel bad." She held up her hands, and I laughed. "I just didn't want you to be upset with me," she admitted, and it was a top-five worst feeling of my life.

"I would never be mad at you. Not unless you were living for somebody else's expectations." I held her stare. "One of the most admirable and beautiful things about you, Cath, is that you have always lived to the beat of your own drum," I said, and she groaned.

"Such a Leo joke."

I laughed. "It's true, though. Don't start living for other people now. We all love you for you, not what you do for us. Berklee or The Burnouts. I support you and care about you."

She nodded, nostrils flaring, eyes trying so hard not to roll. Or maybe cry. "That's what Leo said."

"Well, he should listen to his own advice."

"That's what *I* said." She laughed.

"Do you feel better?" I asked her.

She nodded. "My parents basically said that too. I just needed to hear it, I guess."

I hugged her. "I understand," I said, genuinely meaning it.

She squeezed me tight back, a slight tremble to her body. She leaned back to break the hold. "But before I go, I'm going to absolutely crush this audition. Because I want to take a semester to see if I like college." She grinned.

I smiled back. "That's a great plan," I said. "And that can always change. You may meet some people your age and start your own band."

Her eyes widened. "Hell yes."

The woman with the clipboard called her name. We shared a look of *phew, that was close.*

Leo and I hooted for her as she walked back to the room. She glared at us in mortification.

Leo was at my side. He squeezed my hand. "Is it weird that I feel like a proud parent right now?" he asked.

"I think it would be weird if you didn't."

I pulled him to an alcove off the main room where we could talk. I wasn't sure how much time we had while Cath auditioned, but I couldn't wait any longer. My body was buoyant with hope and happiness. It had been so heavy and stiff only a few minutes ago, and now I barely felt my body, like I was floating.

"Are you okay?" he asked.

"Yes. Are you?"

"Weird morning." He scrubbed his hands through his hair, bags under his eyes. "I don't know that I did the right thing, but she seems better."

He probably didn't sleep great after last night, and the stress of the early morning couldn't have helped. Yet he was there for her. For me.

"You did great. You continue to blow my mind, Leo. That's what I want to talk to you about. I've been so guarded with you these past few months. I've grown closer to you than anybody I've ever known." His eyes watched me closely as I spoke, and he swallowed. "I was so sure that you would stop showing up. Eventually, get tired of all that I asked of you. Because . . ." My throat got so tight I had to stop to take a full breath in. He came closer to hold me. "That's all I've known. People leave, and I didn't want to tell you that because it made me feel shameful. Like something was wrong with me."

"Mari," he said and dropped his head to mine. "I'm so sorry."

"This time with you has shown me that you're my family. You and Janice." I shrugged. "And maybe even Vander, as like that one odd cousin who randomly comes to town sometimes." He grinned as I went on. "I don't feel so afraid. No. That's not true. I think I feel more afraid than ever. But I also feel happier than ever. I'm hopeful and excited. You've given me a place to call my own."

"You are everything to me," he said, and chills ran down my spine. Our hands clasped as our foreheads came together.

"I'm sorry I pushed you away last night. You told me to trust that people stay, and I couldn't. How all our lives folded together felt like it was too good to be true. Every minute, I waited for you to tire of my pushiness or bursts of anger. Last night, it was like I was trying to prove myself right. I felt how close you and Cath were. I felt Vander's return to your life, and I thought, 'I can't compete with that.' I mean, that's all Janice wanted when she reached out to me. And it was all working out. You were getting out more. You'd made up with friends. You were making a name around Green Valley. And I would serve no purpose anymore."

"What? What do you mean?" He leaned back to look at my face, head slightly tilted, like a puppy listening for food dropping.

"I thought that you wouldn't need me once your obligation to Cath was done," I said, cheeks burning red.

Saying it out loud felt so silly now. It was amazing how real thoughts felt until you gave them a voice. Then they just sounded like a lie.

"No." He smiled with a huff and a swallow. "Before that. All Janice wanted?"

"Oh. Yeah. Just that it was her idea for you to mentor Cath."

"Janice told you to ask me?"

"I-I told you that?" Dread filled me at his rapid shift in demeanor.

"You didn't. You said you wanted me. You fought for me with a marching band."

"That's true," I said slowly. "Devlin and Janice both suggested you, and Cath was a fan. It made sense."

"Janice told you that I needed help? That I needed to get out of the house?" he asked, voice rising.

He stepped even farther back, a hand running over his face. My heart was racing. This was all coming out wrong.

"When you say it like that, it sounds sad, but it wasn't anything shady."

"I knew you never wanted my help. I knew it never made any sense that you would ask me when you and the rest of this town thought I was another failure." He stepped in a circle, hands tugging through his hair, mostly talking to himself. I'd never seen him like this. Like this was some big reveal, and I'd set the trap.

"I did want you. I *do* want you. Did you hear the rest of what I said?" I asked.

"I'd been waiting for you to talk to me for months," he said. "Waiting for you to say these exact things, and now it's tainted. It was never about me. It was a debt to Janice. I was a charity case. Another person you had to help."

"That is not true. It was a good setup for everybody. Does it matter how it started if it brought us here?" I asked.

"It matters if this isn't real. If this is exactly why you kept yourself just a little out of reach from me. Because you never intended for any of this to happen."

"I didn't, but neither did you. Leo, I-I care about you deeply." I wanted him to hear that he was loved, but fear held my tongue. I'd told him that I wanted him, and he was fixating on a small detail.

"Don't say that just because you pity me."

"Pity you?" I flinched back in hurt. "I envy you."

"Come on." He scoffed. "I'm the town joke, right? The loser burnout."

231

"You are not. How many times do people have to say it until you believe it? Even if this town thought that, I don't. I'm telling you that I envy what you and Janice have. You are such a tight family unit. I felt like such an outsider."

"Don't talk to me about being an outsider. That's all I've ever been," he spat with rage he'd never shown before. It was like the version of Leo I'd seen on the internet.

This was Leo, full of fear and self-doubt. It wouldn't matter what I said now.

All my buoyant joy dissolved, leaving me unable to move with weighty disappointment.

"I'm gonna go." He stumbled backward. "After all, I'm not needed now, right? The plan worked. I got out of the house just like Janice wanted, and you got your tutor." He wouldn't look at me. Both of his cheeks were splotched with red. "Two birds."

I closed my eyes. "Leo. Please . . ." I wasn't sure what I was asking. *Don't go? Don't end it like this?*

"I'll talk to Cath later. Her parents have the drums," he mumbled as he walked away quickly, hands tugging at his hair.

"Please don't prove me right," I finished when he was too far away to hear.

CHAPTER 34
LEO

A shiver racked me as I walked into the house, numb and heartbroken. The kitchen was quiet. The only sound was the soft ticking of the wall clock.

Failure. Loser. Loner.

It was on repeat from the moment Mari had told me her feelings. I was desperate for relief from the negative, consuming thoughts. She had finally put into words the truths of what I felt about her for months, yet the revelation that this had all been some silly setup by my own mother filled me with shame. How long would I need other people to come to my defense? When would I be enough on my own?

I shouldn't have walked away from her, leaving her there with heartache written all over her face, but I was humiliated. I didn't want to be anybody's obligation.

I gripped the sink basin, my ears up to my shoulders as I looked down.

There was no comfort coming back here without Mari, no familiar safety of home. The house echoed loudly in silence and cold without her.

But then, knowing Janice was so embarrassed by me that she had to concoct a plan to get me out . . . I couldn't look at Mari, let alone talk about this.

My body physically winced. All the Bunco Broads, therefore the whole town, must know how sad I was.

This town never accepted me.

My mother needed space from me.

Mari had never wanted me. It was all a big joke.

I was a joke.

"Leo?" my mother said softly from behind me.

It didn't stop me from jumping and hitting my hip on the sink as I spun around. "Janice." I couldn't meet her gaze.

"Sit down, kiddo, we need to talk," she said in her no-nonsense voice.

"I want to be alone."

"Give me three minutes," she said, same as when I was a teen and never wanted to talk. Was I acting like a child now? The pain didn't feel adolescent. The pain felt aged and well-worn, an elderly man set in his ways. "I just got a call from Mari. She was worried that she'd messed up."

"She spilled the beans," I said icily. I slumped into the chair at the breakfast table.

"It wasn't a secret we were keeping," Janice said. I made a grunt of disbelief. She swallowed with a tilt of her head. "But I do regret asking Mari the way I did. I shouldn't have pushed her so hard."

"Oh good. Not only did she not want me. She actively fought against me. This is fun." I rubbed at the burning in my chest.

"She was reluctant, and I persuaded her. And I do regret it. I should have just talked to you. Like you should have told me that you were fired." She held my gaze meaningfully.

"How did you know?"

"Mother's instinct. Why didn't you ever tell me?" she asked as she reached for my hands. I stared at them, reluctantly grasping her, and formed my words. My defenses crumbled under Janice's gentle curiosity.

"I was embarrassed," I admitted, voice rough. "I had so much to prove, and I shot myself in the foot. After all your support and everything you did, I was a disappointment."

"That's not true. Why would you ever think that?" She squeezed me.

I explained to her about the panic attacks and the fights with Vander. How I thought I should be happy, but I always felt like a fraud.

"When I talked to him, he said he knew I would never quit, so he fired me," I said.

"Oh, sweetie."

"Coming back home was like admitting defeat. And to know that you—" My voice cut off. I squeezed my hands into my lap.

"I am so sorry, my son," Janice said. "I want you to know, first and foremost, that I never meant to hurt you. I had no idea you struggled with those things still. I should never have pushed so hard."

I sighed at the painful reminder that Mari had only ever done this as a favor.

"I thought you just needed some shaking up. And yes, I thought helping Cath would push you outside your comfort zone. I've always been a firm believer in helping other people as a way to get out of your own head. It's a perspective that feels good."

"I know. And I did love getting to know Cath and playing again. I understand that everything worked out peachy. It doesn't stop it from hurting."

"I'm so sorry. I just." My mom flushed. "I met Faye. And sometimes when you are in love, it makes you want that for everyone." My eyebrows shot up at her confession but she went on. "I had spent so much time with Mari, you know, over the years as she took over for me. She's such a lovely woman. She's sometimes misunderstood in her tenacity, but I knew you two would hit it off. You'd balance each other out." Janice picked at the table.

"I'm sorry, are you saying this was a setup all along?" I stared agog at her. Mari and I were a balance to each other. She helped me get out of my head, and I allowed her to be herself.

"I thought it was a situation that would help the most number of people." She patted her curls. "But I wished I'd known you were so caught up in these feelings of unworthiness." She brushed my cheek, and I closed my eyes tightly with pain. "You don't have anything to prove. Not to this town. Not to me. Nobody."

"Drumming was the only thing that I was ever good at."

"That's simply not true. But even if you were the loser you have so pictured in your head, you still don't need to do anything to earn love. I'm so thankful to have you as a son, so thankful I got to raise you. I'm sorry you had to deal with such cruelty when you were younger because I-I was your only parent, and we looked so different. It broke my heart, and I'm sure you only shared a fraction of it." Her eyes filled with tears, making my own burn.

"This is not your fault. Teens can sniff out insecurities like hound dogs and they abused my feelings of feeling different. Vander and you kept me mostly protected."

"You can't live your life hiding from the bullies. Why is it so easy for you to believe that you deserve the bad and not the good?" she asked.

"I think there's just something wrong with me," I admitted.

"That voice is a lie. You have to show it it's wrong. Time and time again, when it comes back, you show it that it's wrong. That voice is the biggest bully, and the call is coming from inside the house."

I huffed. "But being the weird kid with the regrettable fashion and a terrible sense of humor is so intertwined with my identity, I think it still messes with me. Saying it out loud feels so absurd."

"Somewhere along the way, you learned that your only value to people is what you can do for them or your rock star reputation. Even without the big house and being taken care of, I would still love you and still be proud of you because of who you are at your core. Not because of the band or the touring or what that success has meant for me. You are anything but a failure, Leo. You cannot be a failure when you love so fiercely. You just have to show up for it. You can't hide away the second things get hard."

I nodded at the table.

"The day they called and said you were born was the greatest day of my life. When I went to get you, it felt like you chose me. Your love has never, *ever* been a burden or something you need to earn. There isn't a single person who loves you for what you do for them." She stood, and I did too, towering over her. She hugged me, and I held on tight to her.

"Thanks, Mom," I said, throat tight.

"A mom always knows. Please don't let the bully in your mind let Mari go," she said. "Not if you love her."

"I do love her. I want to tell her. God, I messed up today."

"That girl has had a rough life. She's all alone and works too hard. I will never understand that family of hers. And those wounds are deep. Just like yours. She'll do whatever it takes to protect herself from hurt if she thinks you aren't going to stick around."

Shame made me nauseous. She'd been trying to open up to me today, and I couldn't hear it. I had been so stupid.

"What can I do?" I asked.

"Go big or go home. What's something you never thought you'd ever do for her?" Janice asked.

"Aside from use Roundup on my garden?"

She tutted and swatted my arm. "Bigger."

An idea percolated. Mari needed a big sign that I wasn't going anywhere. I believed that she loved me as much as I loved her. It was time I left the safety of my house. And for once, it didn't feel scary because nothing was scarier than the idea of Mari feeling alone and unloved.

"Oh, man. I have an idea, but I need your help. How do you feel about coming briefly out of retirement?" I asked.

"Lucky for you, I have consultant rates available."

"Do you think you could call up the Bunco Broads? I need the power of those women."

"Oh, they live for this sort of thing." My mother grinned and rubbed her hands together.

CHAPTER 35
MARI

Who would have thought I'd be back to sitting alone in the teachers' lounge eating a cold turkey sandwich? Well, I had. The autobiography of Mari Mitchell would be brief, depressing, and completely predictable.

It was the last day before spring break. I'd rushed through the day and had five minutes to eat before the final marching band rehearsal. The final rehearsal with Cath.

Pain threatened to swallow me whole.

No. I closed my eyes and took a deep breath. Giving up was not an option. Clara had been right. I always fight for what was right for my students. I wouldn't give up yet. No matter what, I would be okay.

I would go on as I always had. I would find a way to get funding next year. I would track down every school board member and make sure Pin Dick alone wouldn't have the power to cut the music program.

I may have put it all out there to Leo and gotten hurt, but I was still me.

I was ready to fight for my students. I would double my efforts next year. I would work harder and beg every person in Green Valley for donations, even if it meant going door-to-door.

I stood and looked around. I abandoned my pathetic food. I moved right, then froze and turned left. Then, I did it again. I was stuck with indecision, panic circling like a bird trapped in a house. Where to go first? What could I do?

I grabbed my bag and felt the weight of the gift for Leo in there. It was a small gesture, but it would convey all my gratitude for him. He may have thought how we came together cheapened it somehow, but he deserved to feel loved regardless of what happened with us.

Leo.

Had I really fought for him as I did for all other things? Or had I let his own hurt be the reason I shut down?

Cath knocked on the doorframe of the teachers' lounge.

"Hey, Cath," I said.

"This place was a lot cooler in my imagination," she said.

"Really? It looks exactly like every teachers' lounge."

"I guess I expected a dartboard with the faces of annoying students."

"Oh, we keep that in the closet," I teased.

She laughed with a roll of her eyes.

I was still standing in the middle of the room, thrumming with restless energy and not sure where to direct it.

"Ready?" she asked.

"Listen. I don't want to miss your last practice, but I have to go find Leo."

Cath's face fell. I didn't want to hurt her, but was this an instance of putting myself first? I wasn't sure. I worried my lip.

Her brow crinkled with mild disgust. "Am I in the middle of some sort of grand gesture?" she asked.

"No. Yes. Maybe. I don't know. I just feel like I need to try again. He's so sweet and sensitive, and I think I went about things all wrong. He has done so much, and I—"

The grossed-out look was no longer mild. She held up a hand to stop me. She stepped closer, and her features opened into wide eyes. "I wouldn't ask you if it wasn't really important. But I practiced something special that I want to show you. Can you just come to practice? I'm nervous about leaving and going on tour and everything." Her lip quivered.

I'd never seen this side of her before, so frank and emotional. We must have really made a connection.

"Oh, Cath."

"Please, Miss Mitchell, one last show before the road?" she asked me with brows contorted. I couldn't have said no if I tried.

"Of course." I shook my head. I would go to Leo after. A few more minutes wouldn't hurt. "Let's go." As we walked out of the school, I wasn't filled with the same chest-collapsing sadness I usually had as a long break spread ahead of me. There was a natural ebb and flow to life, people who come and go. It wasn't always a reflection of me. Then there were the ones that stayed for every season and every year. That was who I hoped Leo would be for me. I felt hopeful.

"Are you okay? Feeling good about things?" I asked her as we walked.

Cath squinted and looked ahead. "I'm a little nervous about the tour."

I bumped her shoulder. "It'll be great. But if it sucks, come home. They'll figure it out."

She nodded, chewing her lip.

"Just stay away from drugs and alcohol and try to eat and sleep well. Have fun, but don't get carried away with the glamour of it all."

She raised an eyebrow at me. "My parents already gave this speech."

"Okay, sorry. I can't help myself." As we got closer to the football field, we had to weave through the packed parking lot. "That's weird."

"What?" She flicked a look at me.

"There are a lot of cars here for a random afternoon practice."

"Huh," Cath said, unconcerned but picking up her pace. "I was thinking, I'm going to start college with major street cred. People aren't even going to believe that I toured with The Burnouts."

"Make sure to take lots of photos," I said distractedly as my head turned all around to watch a majority of Green Valley walk with us to the stadium. "Okay, seriously, is something going on? I swear, if Pin Dick booked something on our last practice, I'm going to burn this place down."

Cath's eyebrows shot up her forehead.

"Metaphorically," I added. "Also, pretend I didn't call him that."

"Eh. I'm basically graduated. I won't tell anyone. Also, we call him that anyway."

"Ha."

Cath fidgeted, and her steps sped up.

"What's going on?" The marching band was in their full regalia when I stopped before them.

"I told you, I wanted to show you something special," she said.

I stopped and studied her. All her reticence was replaced with restless giddiness.

"Wait, did you emotionally manipulate me? With all the 'please, it means so much' and the wanting me to be here?" I asked, outraged.

She shrugged. "You'll get over it." Cath looked out to the band and shouted, "Let's do this!"

"We should start charging for our services," a senior said to her.

"What?" I looked at Cath, but she was scurrying to get her quads on. I stepped out onto the field and was greeted with applause. Most of Green

Valley packed the stands. More than that, even the visitor side was overflowing. I spotted Clara and Nick, giving a thumbs-up. I shot her a confused look, and she just shrugged.

"Janice?" I went to take my spot, but she was already standing there. "What are you doing here?"

"Take a seat, I'm running this tonight," she explained. "I have some making up to do."

"Making up? What are you—" But a student pulled me away to a reserved spot in the stands. I was totally alone. Several people were looking at me, but I still had no clue what was happening. Good thing I was confident that I had value or all this not-being-needed thing might feel personal. I cleared my throat and sat up straighter, fighting a blush that was growing up my neck.

At Janice's side, Cath took a microphone. That was new . . .

"Thank you, Green Valley, for coming out to support the Black Bears Marching Band. We wanted to put on this surprise performance for Miss Mitchell as a thank you for all her hard work this year and for helping me get into the Berklee College of Music."

The crowd roared, and it shook the stands. I waved but felt even more singled out. This was amazing, but I wasn't used to so much attention as a behind-the-scenes person.

"The benefits of tonight's show will go to support the marching band and other art and music programs at GVHS from here on out."

"Benefits?" I said to myself. Nobody paid to see the marching band. I usually had to bribe people to come.

"Thank you, Miss Mitchell. I will always remember my senior year and all you have done to help me. I will never forget you." Okay, maybe I would be a little emotional, after all. This was all I had ever wanted. To help my students have the future of their dreams. "Sometimes music programs get pushed aside for other things, but Miss Mitchell has worked her ass off to make this program happen." I cringed when she swore and looked around to see if any parents were mad, but the crowd was buoyant. "After this, it would be crazy not to have a music program, right?" The stands roared and clapped.

I glanced at where Cath had been pointedly talking. Pin Dick sat with his legs spread and arms crossed. His face was beet red with barely suppressed rage. *Good luck trying to cancel the music program now that all of Green Valley knows.* Ah, so that was what this was all about. The marching band sparkled their fingers in my direction, yelling out affirmations of love. My heart felt so full. I sometimes doubted that my work was making a difference, and I hadn't been sure anybody noticed. I could fly out of this seat.

As the band started up, they played a song I recognized but not from our rehearsals. They somehow managed to work a whole repertoire under my nose. How had they even found the time?

The song was one that Leo and I had hotly debated on one of our many car rides. He thought it was a silly pop song. I thought it rocked and would be a fun cover for the marching band.

I was clearly right.

They played on, and the crowd was up and dancing and clapping. My chest ached, wishing he was here so we could share a look of understanding, so he could hold my hand and celebrate this with me.

I searched the stands for Leo. Knowing that coming out here, in front of the whole town, was the definition of a nightmare for him, especially in light of the most recent news, but hoping, nonetheless. But with every note they played, it became clear that he wasn't here.

Then I had an idea. I turned and bent to see through the cracks in the bleachers, heart hammering with hope. I angled my head awkwardly, sure that whoever saw me thought I was having some sort of breakdown.

No, no, I wasn't trying to crawl into the stadium to hide. I was just looking for the great love of my life. Normal stuff.

If I angled my head just right, I could find the little cove for the ne'er-do-wells.

But Leo wasn't there. Nobody was. I was disappointed but not giving up. If anything, this amazing display by Cath and the marching band fueled my motivation to seek him out.

With my face still pressed to the cracks, booty facing the whole of Green Valley, I heard the set come to an end.

If I thought the crowd had gone wild before, nothing could have prepared me for this. The stadium shook so hard with raucous screams. My hand went to my racing heart as I looked to see what had caused the change. A guitar strummed through the air, followed shortly by the quick taps of a snare.

I stood and turned to face the center of the field. The marching band was parting to reveal a stage where students I recognized from theater were quickly scrambling to set up a band I knew well. And Leo sat at the raised drum kit. The Burnouts were set up and ready to play right here at Green Valley High School.

"No freaking way," I said.

The crowd continued to scream as the band started to play their biggest hit.

Leo was too far away to spot me, but the instant joy at seeing him loosened the knots in my body. He was here. This was . . . this was insane. Leo was focused solely on his drumming. I could see his nerves in the tightness of his shoulders and the line of his mouth, but only because I could compare it to how relaxed he'd been in the studio when he played for Cath or me.

Then Vander turned to him, bobbing his head with the tempo, looking all the rock star, as he strolled up to Leo. They shared one of those smiles that made the Burnnies go wild. Vander yelled something to him, and Leo grinned to pop one dimple, then his head shot up, and his eyes immediately met mine.

This beautiful, kind, wonderful man. Here, once again for me. How could I ever think that he didn't care when he had shown up time and time again?

He nodded to me as his hands were occupied, but it was like a straight shot of adrenaline to my heart. The teenager inside me wanted to jump up and down and squeal, "Did you see that? That's for me!"

God, he looked so incredible. The money this raised for the band . . . It was one thing to have the marching band perform, but The Burnouts playing would be . . . I couldn't imagine. How had I missed all of this? Maybe in the weeks of moping, I might have missed something. It didn't matter. Nothing else mattered. Just Leo. I would show him every appreciation possible.

The song ended after an incredible drum solo that made the crowd lose their minds.

"Thank you, Green Valley. It's great to be back." Vander wooed the crowd. "Thank you to Green Valley High School, my alma mater, for hosting us." Cheers went up. "We look forward to a long future for the marching band. Proceeds from this show and a portion of our album releasing this summer will continue to support the programs. Thanks for coming out tonight. We've got a great show. But first, uh, wait, sorry. Hang on—"

I had burst forth from my seat, rushing the band at full speed. I ran up to Leo, and he barely had time to realize I was heading for him before I tackled him off his stool.

Somewhere behind us, Vander was laughing.

CHAPTER 36
LEO

"Mari," I gasped out her name as we both fell back into the grass. "You're always tackling me."

"Thank you. Thank you. This was too much. Thank you." She straddled me in the middle of the field, her happy gaze moving over me.

"You're welcome," I said through her peppered kisses. The whole of Green Valley and much of the surrounding counties filled this stadium. I was vaguely aware of hoots and hollers from her students and the fans.

"I'm so sorry I didn't tell you about Janice. I didn't even think," she said and kissed me.

"Mari," I broke the kiss to say.

"I won't ever do it again."

"I know but—"

"I'm sorry I kept myself so locked up. I was just afraid you wouldn't choose me."

"You don't have to worry."

"Sorry for not sharing about my family when you've been so open."

"Mari, I—"

"And sorry for tackling you. I couldn't wait. I just couldn't take another moment of you thinking I didn't feel the same. I guess it was assumptive to think you did all this for me and not the band. Oh God. I just realized this could have only been for the school." Her eyes grew wide as she spoke. "You're so thoughtful and sweet and do things for everybody even when you grumble about it, but if this wasn't for me—"

I tugged her back to kiss her again. "It's all for you, Mari. It always has been. Since the moment you showed up on my lawn." I looked up at her. "I love you, Mari Mitchell. I will always be here. With you."

"I love you, Leo." Her eyes sparkled as she swallowed.

The crowd went absolutely wild.

"But just so you know, we have a few more songs to play. These people paid good money to see a whole set," I said. "Though, really, how important is a drummer?"

She bit her lip, a flush spreading up her neck. "Okay. I guess I should maybe not be doing this in front of the students. I will never hear the end of this."

"For years and years. It will be lore passed down to every new student. The time Miss Mitchell attacked the drummer."

"I can only hope." She had so much love in her eyes, and it was all I could ever want.

"I'm not done with you yet. Wait for me?" I asked.

She started to move off me. "Always."

We finished the show, and it was the most fun I'd had in a while. I might not love touring, but I did love playing with this band. Vander and I made plans to meet up any time they passed through town, and I told Devlin I was available for drumming tracks anytime a band needed help. But more than anything, I just wanted to be in my garden with Mari and think about the rest of our lives.

I found Mari waiting for me at my car, leaning against it with a huge smile on her face.

"I just realized," she said as I stepped closer, "you stole my move."

I reached for her hands and laced our fingers. "Oh yeah? What's that?"

"Using the marching band to make a point."

"It's a good move," I said.

"They're going to demand money."

"Maybe they'll unionize, and Pin Dick will really have an issue."

"I really hate that man," she grumbled.

"Who doesn't? Are you worried about him?" I wondered if she would want to get revenge, maybe TP his house or something much worse.

"I'm not happy, but I don't care about him. I'm more focused on us." She nuzzled herself closer to me. "If nothing else, he'll be in the dunk tank at the Spring Carnival, and I've been working on my aim."

"There she is," I said. She laughed. "Us," I repeated her word. "I like the sound of that."

It was dark now. Everybody had gone home except Mari and me standing in the light of a street lamp in the parking lot. I kissed her again. I didn't think I'd stop touching her. I probably never would.

"I got this for you. It's nothing compared to a rock show, but I'm serious about us." She handed me a wrapped package from her bag. Inside was a snow globe with a picture of us that I took at Christmas.

"I want to start a new life with you," she said. "I want to make new memories, good and bad and everything in between." She swallowed with difficulty, and I felt my heart beating through my whole body. "I want a life with you. I choose you as you've chosen me time and time again. I'm sorry it took me so long to see it. You are my family."

"I'm sorry I didn't feel worthy enough to hear it to begin with," I said.

I held the snow globe tight between us.

"Want to get out of here?" I asked. "I don't want you to go back to your place. I want you to come live with me. I know it's fast and maybe weird because of Janice —"

"Okay. I want that too. And maybe it's weird for other people, but not for us. I never feel as at home as I do at your house. I love being there. I love you wherever you are. I don't care about having my apartment. It was never my home."

We kissed again.

"Thank you for choosing me," she said. "Thank you for reminding me that some people stay."

"From the moment you blew into my life, I've not stopped thinking about you. And that's not anything you have to fight for. I'll be here when you're too tired to fight. I'll be here when you want to break shit. I'll be here when you want to cry and laugh. You are so many things, but you will never be forgettable, and I will never leave you. I don't know where I'm going next or what I'm meant to do, but I'm more than okay figuring it out right here with you."

She nodded with tears in her eyes. "I'd like that."

"Not once have you ever been forgettable. You've given me something to feel excited about. A future to look forward to. You make me laugh in new and surprising ways all the time. I'm obsessed with your body and mind. I'm a modern man."

"Good album name." She sniffled. "You are the most wonderful man I've ever met, Leo. I like your dad jokes. I like your cooking and your music. I like all parts of you, not just that you can play the drums pretty well." I raised an eyebrow. "Really well. But those are all just little parts. I love all of you."

"I thought I was a failure. I thought getting kicked out of the band was the worst thing that could've happened to me. But none of it can be a regret when it led me to this time and place with you."

She smiled a watery smile. "Let's go home."

CHAPTER 37
MARI

eo was bent plucking a weed as I made my way out to the porch. He stood and looked around our garden with pride. It had grown even bigger and better this summer. I'd helped him propagate flowers from Clara's yard, and together, we spent many long spring days making the garden into a masterpiece. When I said *we*, I really meant I would sit on the porch and watch him work. Still, we made a good team.

I stubbed my toe on the corner as I made my way to him and swore some unladylike things.

"Everything okay?" he asked with a worried look.

"No. I hit my foot." I frowned.

"Oh no. Come here." He collected me into his arms. I let loose a long breath and felt some tension melt away.

He rubbed my back. "Better?"

"Yes." I straightened, and my eyes widened. "Oh wow, look at the phlox. I've never seen it bloom so much."

Leo rubbed my shoulders. "It's so hot when you talk gardening to me," he said, his darkened eyes focused on me.

"I haven't even mentioned the new compost I want to try." I narrowed my eyes seductively.

His head tossed back with a groan. I couldn't help what those neck muscles did to me. I stepped up on tiptoes and kissed his neck.

Our joking melted into a real kiss.

"We are deeply weird," I said with a laugh when we finally broke apart.

"I wouldn't change a thing. Speaking of . . ." He grabbed my hand to twirl me in display. "You look beautiful."

It was nothing special, just jeans and a nice top. I'd kept my hair down and styled, but I suspected what he saw was all my joy glowing out. I had a home and family, and even though it was small, it grew in increments. Faye and her grown children. Cath and her parents. My students, both old and new. Vander and The Burnouts. I wasn't alone. Not even a little.

And then there was tonight.

"It's not too much?" I wiped my sweaty palms on my jeans. "I'm more nervous than I should be."

"No. You're the right amount of nervous. They are scary," he said.

I moaned, a wave of nerves making my stomach twist.

"Hey. You know this town. You are a beast who gets what she wants," he said, trying to pump me up.

I felt my defenses rise but took a breath. It was a compliment. "And that's a good thing?" I confirmed.

"It's a great thing. You're an inspiration. If anybody can make tonight happen, it's you. Look at all you've done for Cath. For this town. For your students."

Leo and I were flying up to Chicago in a few weeks to see The Burnouts play with Cath. It worked out well because I had another former student who'd moved up there I wanted to visit. He was an incredibly talented singer-song-writer whose career was taking off.

Leo had extended an open invitation to my family to come visit any time since I'd moved in with him. They hadn't taken us up on the offer yet. It hurt sometimes still, but I was talking to somebody about it. And most nights, I was too busy being surrounded by the people I chose, and who chose me in return, to worry about it.

The rest of the time, there was always the Rage Room.

"Ready?" he asked me, squeezing my hand.

"Nope. Let's go."

"That's my girl."

As we walked up the road, he cleared his throat. "I was thinking. What if I went back to school to get a teaching degree? I've loved tutoring a student here and there, but I'd like to help with the bands at Green Valley High." His voice shook. "Would that be something I could do?"

My heart swelled with excitement, picturing us teaching side by side. The little ways we could lovingly taunt each other. We would have the Janice Cooper Band Room donated by The Burnouts—a separate rehearsal space that no sports club could take over. I grinned up at him, tugging an arm around his waist as we walked. "Of course. That would be amazing. So long as you're doing it for you. I can handle the class loads."

"I know you can." He smiled. "I enjoyed helping Cath. I have enough knowledge about music that I could maybe make a difference. At least help with some of the classes or maybe jazz band. Or whatever else."

"You would be great."

We came to a stop all too soon and looked up at Faye's house.

"We got this," Leo said. "I'll go first. They love me in there. I will make the case, and you will close the deal."

"We are an unstoppable duo." I nodded with determination.

Leo rang the doorbell, rocking his head side to side to crack his neck.

The door opened.

But not the screen door.

Faye stood smiling, Janice right behind her. "Hey, kids," Faye said.

"We're here for bunco night," Leo said and reached for the door.

The two women didn't move.

"No," Janice said.

Leo's face fell. Janice glanced at Faye, who nodded. Janice had slowly started moving into Faye's house three months ago, but we all pretended not to notice. When I brought it up to Leo, he just smiled and said she'd tell him when she was ready.

Several more women from the Bunco Broads stood behind them.

"You aren't welcome here!" Maxine yelled.

"No offense," Julianne added gently.

"We are at capacity. Get out of here," Maxine said.

"What she's trying to say is that we have all the people we need tonight. Why don't you two go out and dance," Faye said.

"While you still can," Belle added ominously.

I wasn't sure if that was a threat or a warning against aging. Either way, it was clear my attempts to join bunco night were a no-go. Part of me was relieved. As much as I wanted to participate in Leo's interests, the idea of a competitive dice game where a dozen women grilled me for gossip didn't sound relaxing.

"Mom?" Leo asked pitifully.

I put my arm through his.

"Sorry, love," Janice said, meeting his gaze.

Leo lifted his chin. "Fine. Make me go spend the night alone with my beautiful girlfriend. Whatever will I do?" he asked sarcastically. "I don't even understand the game. I was pretending."

"We knew, doll," Becky Lee said.

Leo made a faux indignant huff, and we left.

I turned around and smiled back at Janice. She gave me a little wave. After the performance at school a few months ago, Janice had apologized for putting me in a rough spot. She told me I was always welcome and that my coming into her life was more than she'd ever hoped for. I folded so easily into their lives, it was like I'd always been a part of them. Janice and I were closer than ever, and I loved her like a mother. She made it easy.

Leo and I decided to head to Genie's. Clara and Nick, and a few other teachers, were there celebrating a long summer ahead. Leo laughed and joked easily with everybody and seemed genuinely happy. When I sensed his social battery starting to go low, I brought him to the small dance area.

We rocked slowly to the bluegrass band playing, my head resting against Leo's chest. Warmth suffused me as I thought of how much my life had changed in the past year.

"Until it stops working," he mumbled. "That might be a while," he added when I looked up at him.

"I think we can do better than that," I said.

"Yeah?"

"When it stops working. Even when things get hard, and our worst insecurities come out, even then."

"Especially then." He swallowed tightly. It was hard to imagine a time when Leo and I wouldn't be desperate for each other or obsessed with each other's company. I doubted there would ever be a morning when I woke up and didn't instantly think about him or devise ways to make him smile. But just in case, it was good to have a plan.

I kissed him.

"This is it for me. I will work every day to make you feel seen," he said.

"I will spend every day making you feel loved."

I dropped my head back to him as we rocked slowly to the acoustic guitar.

"Sounds like a better plan," he said.

"I do love a plan."

ABOUT THE AUTHOR

Piper Sheldon writes Contemporary Romance and Paranormal Romance. Her books are a little funny, a lotta romantic, and with just a little twist of something more. She lives with her husband, toddler, and two needy dogs at home in the desert Southwest. She finds writing bios in the third person an extreme sport of awkwardness.

<u>Sign Up for Piper's Newsletter!</u>

Find Piper Sheldon online:
Facebook: http://bit.ly/2lAvr8A
Twitter: http://bit.ly/2kxkioK
Amazon: https://amzn.to/2kx2RVn
Instagram: http://bit.ly/2lxxV7H
Website: http://bit.ly/2kitH3H

Find Smartypants Romance online:
Website: www.smartypantsromance.com
Facebook: www.facebook.com/smartypantsromance/
Goodreads: www.goodreads.com/smartypantsromance
Twitter: @smartypantsrom
Instagram: @smartypantsromance

ALSO BY PIPER SHELDON

THE SCORNED WOMEN'S SOCIETY

My Bare Lady Book 1

The Treble With Men Book 2

The One That I Want Book 3

Hopelessly Devoted Book 3.5 - A novella

It Takes a Woman Book 4

UNLUCKY IN LOVE SERIES

Stranger Than Fan Fiction Book 1

Better Date Than Never Book 2

Down For the Word Count - Book 3

THE UNSEEN SERIES

The Unseen Book 1

The Untouched Book 2

The Unspoken Book 3 - Coming Spring 2024

You can find all of Piper's books at pipersheldon.com

ALSO BY SMARTYPANTS ROMANCE

Small Town Silver Fox Series

Love in Due Time by L.B. Dunbar (#1)

Love in Deed by L.B. Dunbar (#2)

Love in a Pickle by L.B. Dunbar (#3)

The Green Valley Library Series

Prose Before Bros by Cathy Yardley (#1)

Shelf Awareness by Katie Ashley (#2)

Dewey Belong Together by Ann Whynot (#3)

Checking You Out by Ann Whynot (#4)

Scorned Women's Society Series

My Bare Lady by Piper Sheldon (#1)

The Treble with Men by Piper Sheldon (#2)

The One That I Want by Piper Sheldon (#3)

Hopelessly Devoted by Piper Sheldon (#3.5)

It Takes a Woman by Piper Sheldon (#4)

Park Ranger Series

Happy Trail by Daisy Prescott (#1)

Stranger Ranger by Daisy Prescott (#2)

The Leffersbee Series

Been There Done That by Hope Ellis (#1)

Before and After You by Hope Ellis (#2)

The Higher Learning Series

Upsy Daisy by Chelsie Edwards (#1)

Out of this World

Made in United States
Orlando, FL
07 May 2024

46621522R10162